It's Only Lipstick, Right?

It's Only Lipstick, Right?

Dear Barb,
Thank-you for always supporting me!
♡,
Dianne

Dianne Dearmon

ISBN: 0999171593
ISBN 13: 9780999171592

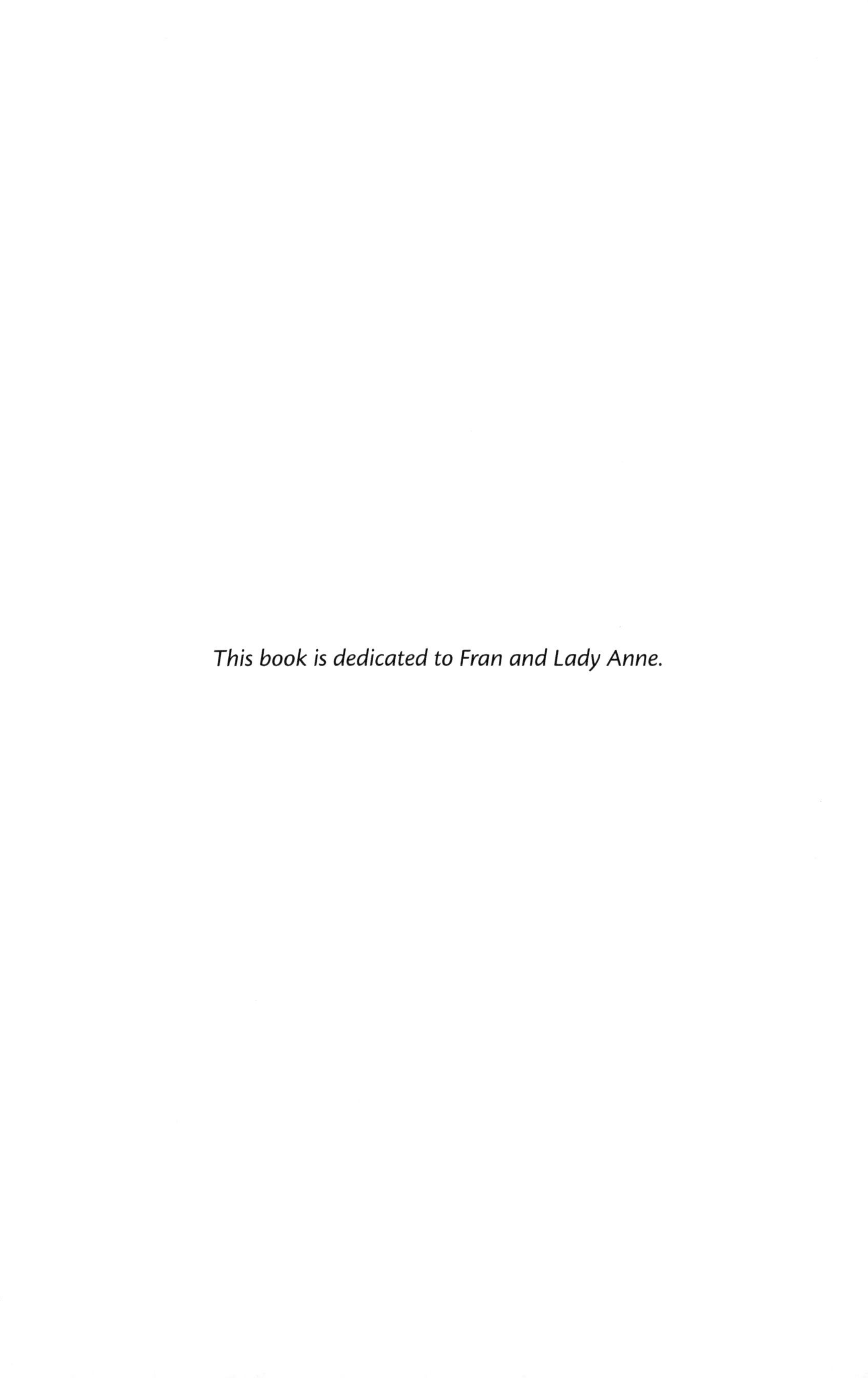

This book is dedicated to Fran and Lady Anne.

Acknowledgements

I wish to thank: my mother, Aimee Lindsay Dearmon, a gifted writer and editor who has always been my rock; Inas Warren, the talented, creative force behind this sexy, beautiful book cover; Cliff Carle, my editor, who is as brilliant as he is patient. He never stopped pushing me to take my work to the next level; Susan Schwartzman for taking an interest in my story and who indirectly, led me to Cliff; and my siblings, Valerie and Carl, for always believing in me.

Chapter 1

At first glance, most people would probably think I was just another pretty girl at a makeup counter. But, I don't think of myself that way and after you read my story, I doubt you will, either. Only five weeks ago, every day was business as usual at my cosmetics counter, Cesonne (pronounced Sess-own). It's located in an upscale department store, which shall remain nameless, on the Magnificent Mile in Chicago (however, for the purpose of this story, let's call it Norniesakmans). I know everyone's felt this way once or twice in their lives, but it really amazes me how much things can change so dramatically in a matter of weeks. However, this is the cosmetics industry and anything is possible here. And, I do mean anything.

My name is Toy. I'm thirty years old. When I was a little girl, my younger sister couldn't pronounce Tory, so she called me Toy. It stuck. I have long blonde hair, which I usually wear in a messy side braid. People say it's a sexy look for me. I say it's simple. I have a very light complexion that I never tan. I'd never risk premature wrinkles to look like a former cast member of *Jersey Shore*. My eyes have been called both blue and green, usually depending on what I am wearing. I call them turquoise.

I'd first like to say that yes, I did finish high school *and* four years of college. That's crazy, right? A girl at a cosmetics counter who can actually multiply as well as apply eyeliner! I make that joke because almost every day I have at least one customer who is shocked when he or she finds out I have an education. I'm going to let you in on a little secret. I work here because I make more money than most of my friends who I went to college with, and my job is anything but boring.

I'm the business manager for the Cesonne cosmetics and fragrance counter. Norniesakmans has at least 300 employees. The cosmetics department alone has forty makeup counters and employs about seventy people of all ethnicities and eccentricities. For some reason, the beauty industry attracts some highly unusual people. Anytime you walk into a cosmetics department, you can be sure of a few things: There's scheming going on amongst associates as well as sexual liaisons (perhaps even in the stockroom at the very moment you're trying on that fabulous new lip color at your favorite makeup counter), and someone is in the department manager's office crying or screaming that someone else has stolen her client.

Still, dealing with my crazy team of associates was nothing compared to the ongoing battle I fought against senior management. I know how to make my business successful and I don't need the input of people who rarely step into the cosmetics department, let alone have never managed one. I'd proven my ability to run my counter time and time again, by reaching goals that no other cosmetics counter in Norniesakmans could touch, yet they still felt the need to micromanage. Particularly Diabolical Debbie, but more about her later.

I'd worked in cosmetics long enough to know that if you were successful, you attracted both good and bad attention. The good was you could get away with more than other associates, but the bad was most of your supervisors felt threatened and made it their life's mission to make you look stupid. If I implemented half the ideas they came up with in Fantasy Land, also known as the corporate office, my counter would've already been yanked out of the store. If a brand pulls their counter from a department store, you know the business was mismanaged.

For all of you who walked by that intimidating-but-beautiful cosmetics department when you were little, for all of you who didn't want to become a doctor or a lawyer, but rather one of those gorgeous, impeccably dressed women with stunning, red lipstick on, this book is for you.

So, grab a skinny latte (or a full fat mocha), get comfy, and enjoy the adventure that's about to unfold.

A little over five weeks ago, everything in my life started to get complicated. That particular November morning the weather was quite windy and cold. I'd just walked into work and greeted Clyde, the same security officer I'd said hello to for the past three years. I scanned my employee ID and went into the locker room. I took off my ankle-length, black Valentino winter coat, hat and gloves to a reveal a form-fitting black dress with a lace, cap sleeve jacket. The Chanel dress slimmed my thighs and accentuated my small waist, which made my okay bottom look great. It also pushed my 34-C breasts up to expose just the right amount of cleavage. Cesonne's look was sexy and chic, and what I wore emphasized my 5'5" frame to a T. All that was missing was my signature #11 red lipstick. I applied it, did a once-over in the mirror and was on my way.

I was stressed that morning because I had a meeting with my regional account director, Debbie, and my department manager, Sharee. Anytime Debbie called a meeting with me, I knew it was going to be painfully long and obnoxious.

While walking out of the locker room toward the main floor, I heard someone come up behind me. I knew without looking that it had to be Jean-Luc, my dear friend, and the counter's resident fragrance expert. His cologne gave him away.

I slowed to let him catch up. "Mmm... you smell great," I said. "Intoxicated by Kilian, right?" I asked with a raised eyebrow.

"Of course not!" He declared. "Why would you accuse me of such a thing?"

"Yeah, right," I said. Every time I confronted him about wearing one of our top competitor's fragrances he denied it.

Jean-Luc was French and no one could ever deny that he had style. Lucky for me, we clicked the first day we'd met. I found his sarcastic humor hilarious, but not everyone shared my opinion. He was quite the character, and if he didn't like you, then you'd better watch out.

He was thirty-four, attractive, 6'3, with sandy blond hair and big blue eyes. He was very thin and worked out constantly to stay fit. I joked with him that he needed a few more pounds for ballast, but he scoffed at the idea. Jean-Luc was not only a close friend, he was also my strongest salesperson, which didn't help him win any popularity points with his co-workers in the cosmetics department. Even after three years of working with him, I still couldn't figure out if he was straight or gay, though he swore he was "straight as an arrow" anytime the subject came up. I caught him checking out other men a number of times, the same way I'd look at a man, but then I'd think maybe he was just comparing himself to the guy, you know? Clothes, build... those kinds of things. I was determined to find out one way or another.

"Tell me, beautiful," he flirted with his charming French accent, "how is my Blonde Ambition doing today?" He darted ahead of me, and then whirled around to kiss me on both cheeks.

I remembered our initial meeting like it was yesterday. He hadn't even said hello. He'd cut right to the chase, engaging me in a battle of wits over the notes of a fragrance.

"*You* are the manager? You probably don't have the slightest clue what it takes to sell this kind of luxury, honey," he'd said snidely, holding up an expensive perfume.

Smiling, I'd snatched the bottle from his hand, sprayed the perfume on my wrist and inhaled deeply.

"Hmm. The top notes smell like lemon and ginger," I'd said, and then waved my arm to let them evaporate to reveal the middle notes. "The middle is rose and jasmine, and if you'll excuse me, I'm almost late for lunch," I'd said, and tossed the bottle of fragrance back to him.

He caught it — barely.

"When I get back I'll tell you what the bottom notes are. That should give it enough time to dry down."

Then, I'd headed to our store bistro without looking back. When I'd returned thirty minutes later, his attitude had completely changed. He'd been amused by my witty remarks and realized that I was more than just a pretty blonde.

Since then, I'd not only won his friendship, but I'd also acquired my new pet name: "Blonde Ambition." I didn't like it. He said it suited me.

I put my hands on my hips in a mock authoritative manner. "Jean-Luc, the question is, what're you doing here this early? You aren't scheduled for another three hours."

"Honey, I am going to do some cleaning and go have a coffee. What? You do not want me here? You would rather your superstar, Tommy, be here instead dressed in his faux Armani suit?"

I sighed, "And where in the hell would one purchase a faux Armani suit?"

"If you do not know, then it would be cruel and unusual to explain it to you," he said, his nose held high.

I suppressed a laugh. Jean-Luc didn't like Tommy because he didn't think Tommy was the right image for our counter and that he made no effort to improve himself. I found Jean-Luc's perspective of Tommy amusing, but I couldn't let him know that. There was no doubt in my mind that he meant every word he said. He always looked disgusted when he talked about the guy. In truth, Tommy was Jean-Luc's only rival. Both were good-looking, both were excellent salespeople, and both were extremely self-absorbed. I bet Jean-Luc would spontaneously combust if he knew just how similar they were.

"Stop being so dramatic." I shook my head. "You know what I mean. And why is Tommy even being brought into this conversation?"

He turned to me, stopping right in the middle of the main aisle, incredulous. "Because he is a moron and I do not know why you allow him to even continue as part of this counter. He is an embarrassment to this company and to everyone around him. Did you not see the white socks he had on yesterday? White socks! With black pants and black shoes!"

"Well, we have bigger issues to deal with than the way Tommy dresses, Jean-Luc," I said, mirroring his theatrics. "So, as much as I appreciate your passion and would love to continue this conversation with you, I have to go. I have to be in a meeting in less than five minutes."

With that, I blew him a kiss and headed for Sharee's office. I hoped to make it there without someone else stopping me over something completely ridiculous. In cosmetics, that was always a risk.

On the way to Sharee's office, I passed by my counter only to see that I had new stock that needed to be unpacked and put away before the store opened. It'd just have to wait even though there was no telling how long this meeting would last.

I knocked on Sharee's door while gently pushing it open. She was seated at her desk and barely looked up from her computer.

"Hi, Toy. Debbie should be here any minute. Have a seat. I'll be right with you. I just need to finish submitting these annual reviews."

Sharee was known throughout the company for being a very tough boss. Personally, I thought she was one of the best managers I'd ever worked for. Unlike my previous boss, she never asked you to do anything she wouldn't do herself. And let's face it, she managed a group of seventy catty cosmetics divas and queens and she had to answer to Debbie. Now that I really thought about it, she might actually be the next Mother Teresa.

"No problem."

I sat down in the chair across from her and looked at the clock. It was 8:00 AM. Debbie was always late and she was the one who'd called this meeting so early.

Ten minutes later, Debbie barged into the office without knocking. "Hi, you two!" she called.

Debbie had shoulder-length dark, blonde hair with four-inch roots, a pink Hermes scarf wrapped around her head like a headband, and wore an off the shoulder Rag and Bone T-shirt with leggings that were about two sizes too small. She was slightly overweight, but that didn't stop her from stuffing herself into clothes that didn't fit. She looked to be in her mid-40s, yet dressed like a character out of *Sixteen Candles*. No one in Cesonne, none of the employees anyway, could understand how she'd been promoted from the cosmetics department manager to the regional cosmetics director so quickly. She wasn't polished at all. She was loud, obnoxious and the most disorganized person I'd ever met. If it hadn't been for Sharee I don't think I could have stayed in my position this long.

"Hi Debs. How are you?" Sharee stood up to grab a file, and as she did, I compared the two women. Sharee was thirty-seven, had a short and chic curly bob with side swept bangs and huge, golden-brown eyes. She was tall and beautiful with the most flawless chocolate skin I'd ever seen. She could've been a fashion model. Her outfit consisted of a perfectly pleated pencil skirt with a fitted white blouse, a simple Prada statement necklace, and a pair of black Louboutins. Again, how Debbie could be in a higher position than Sharee was a mystery to all of us.

"I'm doing well," said Debbie. "Let's not let squander any more time. Let me tell you two exactly what's going on. This is extremely confidential, so I don't want to hear that anyone knows but the three of us, got it? I'm going to make the formal announcement tomorrow."

I found it kind of ironic that she was the one who's late to the meeting, yet she's telling us we're wasting time. The fact that she'd probably disclose this "extremely confidential" secret to at least twenty other people before noon today, made me want to laugh out loud.

"I was on FaceTime with corporate last night and our Cesonne counter has been chosen for a personal appearance from Frances herself! She'll be doing a signing of her new artistry book here."

Frances was the founder of Cesonne and never made personal appearances. This was huge!

"Oh, my God, Debbie! That's fantastic!" Sharee jumped up and hugged me. "Toy! This is such a great opportunity for the team."

"Of course, I had to pull a lot of strings to make this happen," Debbie added, fishing for the praise she thought she deserved.

"Of course, you did," Sharee smiled, sweetly, "and we appreciate you so much."

Sharee and I made eye contact. Pacifying Debbie was seriously, like appeasing a three-year-old child.

"Toy, you realize this means you've got to have a counter meeting with your team. This event needs to be the biggest any cosmetics counter has ever had," warned Debbie.

"Just let me know when you'd like me to have it," I said.

We were at the point where she'd apply the pressure. I already knew it was coming. I was only waiting for the number she was about to give me. *The number.* The number that would be repeated countless times over the next few weeks. The number that would cause me extreme anxiety until the event was finally over. *Ugh!*

"As soon as I make the announcement, you can schedule the counter meeting. I'll call and let you know when to go ahead with it. Frances really believes that we should be able to achieve $150,000 in one day due to the fact that she'll be here signing her book and debuting her new lipstick," Debbie said, nonchalantly. "I think that's totally realistic."

Debbie continued to blab, but all I could hear over and over in my head was *$150,000!*

Sharee beamed. "I have all the faith in the world in Toy and her team. If anyone can make it happen, they can. I believe this will definitely get Toy the national makeup artist position she's been waiting for."

Debbie turned to me, "That's what I was going to tell you, Toy. If you make this event happen, Frances said that she'd personally make you her national makeup artist for the brand. You'll have all of your team to help you, and of course, you have Sharee and my support anytime you need it."

I put on a fake smile to conceal the fear I felt growing. Not only was this goal outrageous, but now my promotion, which I'd been working my ass off for since I was told I was a candidate, was on the line.

This isn't fair.

Even though I knew Sharee would try her hardest to support me, I also knew she had a lot on her plate managing a department as big as ours. The biggest help Debbie could give would be to leave me alone so I could focus on this damned event. Anytime she tried to help out at the counter it ended in disaster. She'd move the testers from one part of our semicircle, glass display rack, shuffle them around, and then expect everyone to applaud her creativity. And, of course, we did. We needed our jobs, even though we knew that her *innovative* arrangements never failed to end up making more work for us. It usually took us an entire day to get our counter back to the way it was before she came to help. She had no idea how product displays were supposed to be set up. Our tester displays are always located above the product in a cabinet, or below the product on a shelf for efficiency and convenience. Whether the display testers were tilted a little off center or arranged in order of their size, she never seemed to comprehend that our skincare products were supposed to be placed underneath the fragrance bottles and the lipsticks above the eyeliners.

"Okay, Toy. You can go. I'm going to talk to Sharee about a few other things. Thanks for coming in so early," said Debbie, as she shooed me away with her hand.

I looked at Sharee and felt sorry for her. I knew she didn't like Debbie any more than I did, but she never said anything negative about anyone.

Thank God Debbie isn't my immediate supervisor, I thought.

I walked out of the office, disgusted with Debbie. I wanted so badly to find out how the hell she'd gotten the position she was in. I needed to do some serious digging. However, right now I had a much bigger challenge at hand — a $150,000 challenge. For any other counter, $50,000 in one day would be an outrageous goal. But hey, how could I miss with Debbie's support?

What a joke!

I walked back to the cosmetics sales floor, remembering how one of the worst arguments I'd ever had with my ex-boyfriend, Ben, had started. He was a first-year resident straight out of med school and couldn't imagine anyone's stress being greater than his.

I was a nervous wreck over a huge trunk show my counter had been chosen to participate in. Each year, a select group of cosmetics counters were invited to be a part of a runway show sponsored by The Peninsula Hotel to present the latest in beauty trends, and this year it was our turn.

A trunk show was a great event for customers. There was wine and hors d'oeuvres, a fashion show and complimentary hair and makeup services, not to mention the free gifts. To us, it meant a hellacious seventy-hour workweek, calling preferred clients, scheduling facials, ordering supplies, and arranging stock. Add to all this every big shot who happens to be in the area and I'm in charge of it all!

The day before our big argument, I'd worked seventeen hours straight without a single break. We'd made the goal, but I hadn't even received a thank you from Debbie. Instead, she'd already started talking about the next event we'd be participating in. I'd felt belittled by her lack of gratitude and exhausted at the same time. After sobbing and pouring out my heart to him, Ben wrapped his arms around me, kissed my forehead and said, "Babe, it can't be as hard as you're making it out to be. It's only lipstick, right?"

Chapter 2

Today was my new makeup artist's first day on the job. Biljana was a twenty-four-year- old from Europe with a lot of talent. She was petite with long brown hair and brown eyes. I wouldn't describe her as a knockout, but she was definitely attractive. When I first met her, I was afraid she was too nice to work with my team of sharks, but after I saw the job she did with the makeup and how well she handled the client I'd chosen for her interview, I knew I wanted to hire her.

She showed up ten minutes before noon, ready for her first day. The counter had been unusually busy that day, which was a good thing. Busy at Cesonne meant no time for drama.

"Hi, Biljana," I said, hoping my smile would put her at ease. I knew how nerve-wracking starting a new job could be.

"Hi, Toy. I hope you do not mind that I am a little early," she said. Her Slavic accent added to her appeal.

"Not at all. I admire someone who's prompt!"

"And, what about me, love?"

I turned around and saw one of my favorite people in the world. Chance was Chinese and remarkably beautiful; porcelain skin, thick black hair that he kept short with side bangs, and a tiny figure that he loved to sashay about. With just a little mascara and some shiny nude lip-gloss, he was the prettiest guy in the cosmetics department, and he knew it.

He and I had met on the first day of high school. A lot had changed since then, including his name. Back then he'd gone by Chang. I still laughed when I'd recalled our first interaction.

We'd been in PE class and I was sitting in the bleachers, distraught, filing my nails. Over the summer, my very best girlfriend, Lizzie, had been scouted by a modeling agency. We'd always been inseparable and now she was off traveling the world while I was here alone. It was beyond depressing.

"Hey, do you think I could use your nail file when you're done?"

I looked up and saw a petite figure with one hand on his hip, chomping on some chewing gum.

"Um, sure," I said, handing him the file.

"I said when you're done, girl! I don't need it this very second," he rolled his eyes and plopped down next to me on the bleachers. "Don't you just hate PE? Like, why are we being sentenced to an hour of smelling dirty socks when we could be doing something fun?"

"Oh my God!" I exclaimed. "I hate the smell in here, too! I tried to get out of this class but they said PE is mandatory."

"Me, too!" he said, finally cracking a smile.

"I'm Toy," I smiled back, and handed him the file.

"Toy?" he asked, raising his eyebrows. "Okay, but you better thank God you're pretty enough to pull off a name like that. I'm Chang."

"It's nice to meet you, Chang."

"Likewise. So, what foundation are you wearing? It looks great," he said, not very secretly studying my skin.

I smiled, knowing I'd just found my new best friend. From that moment on we were always together.

"Um, Earth to Toy," Chance said, snapping me back to the present.

"I absolutely love your promptness," I acknowledged, and then turned back to the new girl. "Biljana, this is Chance. He's our lead makeup artist, so he'll be doing a lot of your hands-on training today."

"O-M-G! We're going to have so much fun today," gushed Chance. He took Biljana by the hand and led her over to his artistry chair where the two began to chat.

I watched her for a while and saw the skillful job she was doing. She certainly appeared to be getting along with Chance. My initial apprehension disappeared. She was a fit.

The rest of team was busy with clients and the late shift wasn't set to start for another hour, so I decided to take advantage of the calm. I grabbed my phone and wallet.

"Guys, I'm going to take my ten. If you need me just call my cell," I said, and headed for the men's department to buy my dad some cologne for his upcoming birthday. This wouldn't take long. My father had been wearing the same Hugo Boss for as long as I could remember.

I walked into men's and looked around to see if I could find Oscar, the men's fragrance manager. Oscar was an older African-American man who had been on the job probably longer than I'd been alive. He had a huge clientele and if anyone deserved it, it was him. He was extremely knowledgeable and just a nice guy in general.

"Do you work here?" asked a masculine voice with a Slavic accent.

I turned to face a pair of gorgeous caramel-colored eyes gazing back at me. His hair was light brown and cut short to reveal a strong forehead. His razor-stubbled jawline was squared under a rather prominent, but not overly large nose. He had to be at least 6'4" and had just the right size build. *And God, those lips...*

"Do you work here?" he repeated, but this time he had a smirk on his face. I could feel my cheeks heat up. It was obvious he was aware of the effect he was having on me.

"Yes I do, but not in this department." I struggled to regain my composure. I was used to meeting hot guys. Every guy I'd ever dated would be considered good-looking, but none of them held a candle to this one. He wasn't just attractive. He was probably the sexiest man I had ever seen — ever!

"You look like a woman who knows what men like. Even if you do not work in this area, I am sure you could still help me," he said, flashing an incredible smile.

In an instant, I was over my shock. *Who is this guy? And who does he think he is talking to me this way?*

"As a matter of fact, I do know a lot about men's fragrances," I replied, irritated. "Pour Homme, 1 Million, Un Jardin sur le Nil, Green Irish Tweed... *Que dire de plus*?" I'd taken a little French in High School.

He hesitated for a second.

Gotcha.

He was gorgeous, I gave him that, but making a veiled sexual reference within the first two minutes of meeting me wasn't a good sign. I should've walked away right then. So, why didn't I? *Who* is *this guy*?

He picked up a bottle and smelled it, then casually, "So, tell me, beautiful, what is your name?"

"Toy. And yours?"

"I am Nikola. Hmm, Toy, what an unusual name. I love toys. I like to play with them."

I felt the blood rush to my face, and immediately shot back, "Like I haven't heard that line before."

What a chauvinist. I turned my back on him and looked at the colognes. Inexplicably, I hoped he wouldn't give up, although I knew it would be best.

I felt hot all over. Between his looks and his accent, I had an image of him ripping my clothes off right in the middle of the store and doing whatever he wanted to me. Instead of playing out my fantasy, I turned to face him. "You know what?" I pointed to Oscar, "There's the sales manager of this department. His name is Oscar."

Nikola opened his mouth to respond, but I didn't give him a chance.

"Wait here. I'll go grab him for you." I crossed the aisle. "Excuse me, Oscar, but there's a man over there who *definitely* needs help." I'd have to get my dad's bottle of cologne later.

I raised an eyebrow at the exquisitely handsome Nikola, turned my head and walked away. I couldn't help but take one last glance over my shoulder. He was staring right back at me. He flashed that searing smile of his.

I refused to return it. Instead, I went straight into the elevator to get back to my counter.

I'd never met a man who'd gotten me so hot and bothered so quickly. *Nikola.* What a sexy name. It suited him.

Rule number one in my book: Never date anyone you work with. Rule number two: Never date a customer. So far, I'd managed never to break either of them, but after seeing this guy, with his beautiful eyes, sexy accent and those lips — those luscious lips, I hoped I could continue to stick to my second rule.

The next day I was scheduled to start at noon. All morning, I'd been working on my counter meeting agenda, which I had to have done as soon as possible. I was headed toward the counter when Ed came rushing up. *Oh boy,* I thought. *What's he up to today?*

At first impression, Ed seemed like a really nice guy. He was in his late 30s, tall, thin and blond. He wore Tom Ford glasses that he thought made him look more intelligent. They didn't. He smiled a lot and seemed very polite, even friendly. But, Ed was a snake. He detested nearly everyone; employees with decent positions or natural talent, men with more money, better bodies, or more charisma than he had. He wasn't just a gossip queen, he was a queen in general. His eyebrows were arched and filled in so dramatically that if anyone ever wondered about his sexuality their curiosity was immediately put to rest.

The worst thing about Ed was that he had a direct link to the HR manager's ear and had no problem going to her with anything that might put whomever was on his hit list on her shit list.

Nearly bursting with glee, he yelled, "Oh my God, Toy! You aren't going to believe this! Tatyana is being attacked at the counter!"

"Attacked?" I gasped. "Did you call security?"

He grabbed my hand and headed for the counter.

As we approached, I could see there was quite a little scene going on. Clients and employees alike, mobbed the counter to watch.

There was an elegantly dressed woman, in her mid to late 40s, obviously engaged in an argument with Tatyana. It was a loud confrontation, but a far cry from the catfight Ed had implied. I pried his hand off my arm and shot him a look. I thought about calling security, but I decided to try to diffuse the situation myself. I was a little shocked Sharee wasn't out here already.

I made my way to Tatyana and positioned myself in front of her.

In my most professional tone of voice, I said to the woman, "Excuse me. My name is Toy and I'm the manager of this counter. Is there something I can help you with?"

"I doubt it, unless you can convince this whore to leave my husband alone!" she yelled. She smoothed her jet black hair with a perfectly manicured hand, sporting an at least, 6-carat diamond on her finger. I assumed she and her husband were very wealthy.

Tatyana laughed, "Who are you calling a whore?"

I spread my arms as wide as I could and over my shoulder said, "Tatyana, please go take a break. I'll meet you in the conference room in a few minutes."

"Fine by me." She grabbed her phone and bottle of water before storming off the sales floor.

I came around the counter and softened my tone with the enraged woman. "Would you like me to bring you a coffee or tea?"

"I don't need your coffee or tea. I need this Ukrainian slut to leave my husband alone. She's destroying my family and she doesn't even care!"

I made a palms down gesture. "I'm asking you to please lower your voice. I don't want security to get involved. I feel terrible for what you're dealing with, but I really don't think that this very public area is the right place to handle this."

"I don't care. If the only satisfaction I get is that everyone that little tramp works with knows what a slut she is, that's good enough for me." With that, she grabbed her Birkin bag, which confirmed my assumption of her financial status, and sailed out the door to Michigan Avenue.

"Honey, did you see that bag? That rock? She was exquisite," said Jean-Luc, watching the woman leave the building.

I stared at Jean-Luc in disbelief.

He turned back to me. "What?" He cried, defensively. "I appreciate a woman who has style, baby, and she definitely has it. Did you see her Manolos? I will bet you anything she has a personal stylist."

I closed my eyes, shook my head and headed to the conference room where I expected Tatyana to be waiting for me. I took a few steps, then turned and looked back at the counter. Everyone was still in a huddle, chattering madly. Biljana stood alone in the corner looking like she'd been the one involved in an altercation.

I clapped my hands. "Hey! Guys! Can we all get back to work? This isn't going to set the tone for the rest of our day. Ed, I want you to start working with Biljana on how to gather a call list of clients, you know, how to clientele. I believe she's had enough training with Chance."

I glared at Chance, who as usual, was right in the center of the gossip circle. I caught his eye. When he saw the look on my face, he turned and began to rearrange some skin care products on a shelf.

Ed narrowed his eyes at me. "Fine, but you know the clientele book isn't my strong suit."

"Well, see if you can make it your strong suit," I snapped.

I knew Ed must be furious that he couldn't run around the department for the next twenty minutes telling everyone what happened. *Who cares what Ed's feeling?* I thought. *I need to take care of the Tatyana situation. Damn. I still haven't even announced the counter meeting!*

I opened the big black door to the conference room in the back of the cosmetics department and found Tatyana talking on her cell phone as if nothing had happened. I slammed the door behind me. She hung up the phone.

I took a seat across from her.

Tatyana had moved to the United States two years ago and had no problem admitting that she'd come to find a wealthy man. She loved to drink and from what I'd heard, alcohol wasn't the only substance she was fond of. At 5'9 she was tall and curvy. She wore her fiery red hair short and board straight. She had a homely face, but I supposed her huge, surgically enhanced breasts, toned body and European accent more than made up for it. She was able to seduce some very wealthy men. As my lead esthetician, she generated most of my skincare sales or I wouldn't have tolerated her this long.

"So?" I said. "Would you like to explain what that was out there?"

"Toy, it is not my problem when these rich bitches cannot satisfy their husbands," she said, matter-of-factly.

"Really? Well it is, in fact, your problem when your personal life starts to interfere with my business. Why don't we talk about that?"

Her nonchalant attitude pissed me off. I never really liked Tatyana. She was a gold digger with a shitty attitude. Now, to see firsthand how far she'd go to get what she wanted, disgusted me.

"While you were dealing with her on the floor, I was on the phone with Michael," she said, tossing her head.

"And, let me guess. Michael is that woman's husband."

"*Da*." She shot me a look, and then casually picked up her cell and started texting. "And, he said it will never happen again, so there. Happy now?"

"Put down the phone, Tatyana. No, I'm not happy. I'm not happy that our counter is going to be the talk of the department for who knows how long and that our clients had to witness something like that. And, I'm damn sure not happy that I had to apologize to a wife whose husband you, one of my associates, are sleeping with!"

She set down the phone and looked me in the eye. "Toy, you think you are so perfect? Well, give it time. You have never been in my shoes, so do not be so quick to judge."

"You're right, Tatyana. I'm not perfect. I never said I was, but one thing I can tell you is I'm *nothing* like you. I work for everything I have. And I'd never destroy another woman to get what I want. You have no empathy for anyone. You're heartless."

Out of nowhere, my foul-mouthed makeup artist, Yvonne, swung the door open. I spun around in my chair.

"Hey, Captain!"

She called me captain because she, quite rightly, equated our department with a war zone.

"You comin' back out on the floor, or what? I really need to go get a coffee. This fuckin' caffeine pill I took ain't doin' shit," she said, smacking her gum.

Yvonne was Latina, in her early 50s with long brown hair, big brown eyes, and breasts so large they'd make Dolly Parton jealous, but years of hard partying were beginning to take their toll.

"Yvonne, language! And don't you ever knock? We're in the middle of a conversation. I'll be out in a few minutes."

"Geez, sorry," she said, and traipsed back out the door.

I turned the chair and my attention back to Tatyana.

"May I go, boss?" she asked. She knew I hated being called boss.

"Sure, but I don't want one word spoken about this on the floor. Not one word. And let me know if anyone asks you about it. I won't tolerate gossip."

She rose, sidestepped the table and opened the door behind me.

With my back to her, I said, "Tatyana?"

"*Da*?"

"One last thing." I slowly swiveled the chair around. "If you ever speak to me like that again, I don't care how much business you generate for this counter, I'll make sure you're gone. In case no one ever told you, everyone is replaceable, even you."

Without a response, she left.

A minute later, I walked out of the conference room and just as I was about to turn the corner, I heard two familiar voices. I peeked around it and sure enough, there was Ed, sitting down at a competitor's empty counter yakking with Yvonne. Unmanned counters really frustrated me. It was usually the result of associates taking breaks and lunches together. Still, it never ceased to amaze me how Yvonne and Ed thought it was okay to go over to another counter in the department, plop down in two chairs, and act as if it was afternoon teatime.

"So, I wonder where the Christmas party will be this year," Ed pondered, filing his fingernails.

"I don't know, but who gives a fuck? Those parties are painful to get through, man." Yvonne grimaced. "All the bosses, laughing and talking about bullshit I don't give a rat's ass about. And, they only serve free drinks, no shots."

"I hope it's not at that dive they had it in last year. It was a three-star restaurant. Why can't they do it at like, The Langham, some place classy like that?" Ed was clearly paying zero attention to what Yvonne had to say.

"Yeah, yeah. I wish they'd just cancel it," grumbled Yvonne.

"Do you think there'll be any co-worker hookups at this year's party?" He paused and stared thoughtfully.

"I don't know. I wonder who I'd have to talk to about getting some fuckin' shots served," she snorted.

I was just about to break up their important conversation, when Ed brought up our boss.

"Every year I wait to see if anything can compete with the juiciness of the Christmas party a few years ago, when Debbie was first hired. So far, nothing has," he said, now buffing his nails.

"Was I there?" Yvonne asked with a blank look.

"No, but that has *absolutely nothing* to do with what I'm about to tell you. Do you want to hear it or not?" he snapped.

"Fine, what is it?"

"Okay, but you can't say a word to anyone. Not anyone," he said, dropping the file on the counter.

"You've got my word." Yvonne made an X across her lips.

I had to stifle a chuckle. Between the two of them, I wouldn't have been surprised to see Debbie doing a rebuttal on *CNN* tonight.

"Well, I'd arrived a little late to the party. Everyone was already trashed. I never drink at social gatherings for work. It's a recipe for disaster, honey. Anyway, I ordered a club soda on the rocks and before I'd taken a sip, guess who I saw all over each other?"

"Debbie and who?" Yvonne perked up.

"Mr. Bissette."

"Get the fuck outta here! No way!"

My mouth fell open. Mr. Bissette was the vice president of all Norniesakmans full-line stores in North America. He was also incredibly professional. I couldn't imagine such an elegant man having anything to do with the likes of Debbie! Ed had to be making it up.

"Sure was, baby girl. They were sitting at a table alone and practically sharing the same chair. That's not even the exciting part. He supposedly went to help her hail a cab," Ed said, smugly.

"Okay, what's so juicy about that? They sat at a table together and he may or may not have gotten her a cab."

"Damn it, Yvonne, patience! I'm getting there."

He took off his eyeglasses and leaned closer to her, lowering his voice so that I had to strain to hear him.

"I was interested in what was going on, so I followed them. I mean, the curiosity was killing me. I stopped short of the door and watched them through the glass. They were in a full-fledged make-out session, and then left in the same cab!"

I was dumbfounded. If this was true, it would explain why anytime Mr. Bissette came into the store and Debbie was there, he practically ran in the opposite direction. It would also explain why she held such a prestigious position. If memory served me right, Mr. Bissette was married. I'm sure Debbie would've used that to her advantage. So many things made sense now.

"You're full-a shit, man," laughed Yvonne.

"I had a feeling you might say that. I just so happen to have a picture. Here, take a look" He tapped the screen a few times then handed over his iPhone.

I'd have given my eyeteeth to see what he had.

"Holy fuckin' shit," she said, sliding her thumbs over the screen.

"Give that to me," he said, snatching the phone from her. "Don't you know how to do anything?"

"I was trying to zoom in on the picture," she protested.

"Well, duh-uh," he said.

"You're a prick, Ed. Fuck off." Yvonne got up and stormed away.

"Dick or not, keep your pie hole shut!" he called after her.

Ed was such a bastard, but a bastard who'd just given me the kind of information that started — or ended — people's careers.

Chapter 3

The following day, I was at the counter and had just hung up with Debbie. She'd made the announcement to everyone about the event, which gave me the green light to get to work on my meeting.

Scheduling nine people in retail, especially for meetings, is a tough job when you need coverage all day, but I made it work. I went ahead and called the meeting for 8:00 AM the next morning. I decided to hold it on a Saturday because everyone worked weekends, so no one had to come in on their day off.

Tommy had just arrived, so I took the opportunity to go to lunch. I'd tried to wait for Chance to join me, but he was still working on a makeover and I was starving.

Normally, I wouldn't ask Tommy to let the team know I was leaving because he always asked me to buy him lunch, but with everyone busy with clients, I had no choice.

"Tommy, I think I'm going to run down to Friends Sushi. Will you let everyone know I'll be back in like, thirty?"

"Sure. Um... you mind bringing me back a salmon roll? I had to work last night and woke up late. Didn't get a chance to eat."

Never fails.

"Sure."

"Thanks, Toy."

Absolutely no shame. Tommy never noticed that footing the bill for a grown man annoyed me, but for some reason, I always did it.

Tommy was the opposite of someone you'd expect to be working at a cosmetics counter. He was a typical American white guy, very handsome with curly black hair and green eyes. He was tall at 6'3 and had a lean, muscular build. If he hadn't been such a man-child, I may have been attracted to him. Tatyana introduced him to me and said he'd make a great salesman. That was before I knew he was a bouncer at the club she frequented. I had some sincere reservations about anyone she might refer, but after interviewing him, my doubts faded. I thought it might be a good idea to have a bona fide straight guy selling women's fragrances at the counter.

As bad as I hated to admit it, especially after finding out just how shallow she was, Tatyana was excellent at her job and it seemed she also had promising talent as a headhunter. Tommy wasn't as well put together as Jean-Luc would like him to be, and he did come into work hung-over most of the time, but so far, he was pretty good at what he was doing and the women, including the employees on the floor, loved him.

A blast of bitter-cold air hit me when I walked out the employee door. I pulled my Burberry coat tighter. Thank goodness Friends was only a block away.

The hostess greeted me with a warm smile before leading me to a table for two in the back of the restaurant. I sat down, ordered, then scrolled through the new selection of boots by Gucci and Chanel on my iPad. I'd just gotten my Philly roll and was about to take a bite, when I glanced up into a pair of familiar, caramel colored eyes that were riveted on me.

"Toy?" asked Nikola, in that sexy accent that made me melt.

Careful to keep my voice level, I said, "Yes. Nikola, right?" I hoped he couldn't tell how nervous I was.

"May I join you?"

"Um, sure. Have a seat." Still a bit startled, I put my iPad away. "Do you work around here or something?"

"Yes. I work down the street. I would ask where you work, but I already know." He looked directly at me as he spoke, causing a flutter in my stomach.

"That's right, you do know where I work," I laughed, nervously. "I'm sorry I left so abruptly the other day. I have a lot going on at the moment and I feel like if I'm away from my counter for more than ten minutes, all hell will break loose."

Well at least part of what I'd just said was true. *Should I also tell him that since meeting him I haven't stopped imagining him on top of me, behind me, or in any other position for that matter, as long as he's inside of me?*

The waiter approached. Nikola ordered Salmon Nigiri and a side of miso soup, and then returned his attention to me. "You know, you are a very beautiful woman, Toy. I have been thinking a lot about you since we met." He picked up a piece of my sushi with his fingers and popped it into his mouth.

"Oh really? And what exactly, have you been thinking about?" I said, doing my best to seem relaxed.

"How I needed to see you again," he replied, oh-so-nonchalantly. "And how nice it would be to kiss those lips of yours."

I threw my head back and laughed. "Oh, my God! You're really good at this, aren't you?"

His face held no trace of humor. "Not at all. I just know what I like. If I did not run into you here, I would have come back to your work and found you. I want to know you."

For once in my life, I was at a loss for words. I stopped eating. All I could do was stare at his incredibly handsome face.

The waiter arrived with Nikola's miso soup, breaking the unbearable tension.

"You seem like a girl who never takes chances. You have a daily routine you never break away from, if you can help it. You have not dated much and have always been in a relationship. I am right, no?" he said, coolly.

"Who are you?" was all I could manage.

"I am Nikola."

"Well, I know that," I smiled.

He laughed. "Okay, I am Macedonian. I came here to work with my uncle. You probably do not know where Macedonia is even located, right?"

I smirked at how arrogant he was. "As a matter of fact, I do. It was part of Yugoslavia before it broke up and it's located above Greece."

He nodded his head in approval. "I am very impressed. I have noticed most Americans do not know geography. It is nice to see you are educated."

I didn't bother to defend the entire American population because he obviously thought he was paying me a compliment. "Thank you. But, I have to know. How do you know so much about me? You only met me for like, five minutes."

"I read people very well."

He could 'read people'. *Yeah, right.* If I wasn't convinced he was a player before, I was now. How could he not be? I didn't even know this guy and he made me want to strip down in the middle of a sushi restaurant and serve myself to him. That's at least some kind of proof, isn't it? And isn't that what players are best at? Making women swoon over well-rehearsed lines? Or, was it basic animal attraction? Either way, these feelings weren't comfortable to me, not at all. If I were smart I'd run right now and never look back, but his comment about my not taking chances bothered me. I knew it was only a strategy to get me into bed, but God help me, it was working.

"Oh you can, can you?" I leaned in toward him. "Well, what am I thinking right this second?"

"You are thinking you want me to kiss you, just like this..." He bowed his head a little and kissed me with what seemed like the softest lips I'd ever felt. His tongue played with mine and for an instant it felt as if only he and I existed.

I pulled away and looked around, thankful we were in a corner where no one could see us. I didn't want any of my associates to catch me kissing some stranger in a public venue.

"Stop worrying about what other people think. That is your problem. You cannot enjoy the moment."

Damn! He did it again!

"I'm sorry, but I do work practically next door. And I like to keep my private life just that, private."

The waiter brought Nikola's entrée, and just as he was about to leave, I remembered Tommy's request!

"Excuse me, could you please add a salmon roll to my bill? And make it to-go?"

"No problem, miss. Would you like me to bring it out now? Or do you want a little more time to finish your meal?" he said, shooting a glance at Nikola.

"As soon as the order's ready you can bring it with the check, thank you. I'm in kind of a rush."

"Of course." He spun on his heel and made a beeline for one of the sushi chefs.

I almost hated to see him go. Nikola made me so nervous.

"In a hurry to escape my company?" teased Nikola.

"No, it's just, I don't know, well, I need to get back to work," I stammered. *God, could I possibly sound any dumber?*

"Well, Toy," he said, melting me with his gaze, "would you like to join me for a glass of wine tomorrow night? I know this quiet little wine bar right up the street."

Would it be reckless to go out with a guy I'd just met? Should I invite him out with a few of my friends the first time we hang out instead?

"Come on," he said when I hesitated, "what are you afraid of? Live a little. It is just a drink."

He's right. It's only a drink. I'm a grown woman and I can handle it.

"I'm not afraid," I said with false confidence. "Text me the address, and I'll meet you there. How about nine?"

"Nine it is."

Did I really just make a date with this stranger?

We finished our meal, rather, he finished his meal, with small talk, until finally it was time for me to go. He picked up both of our bills, including Tommy's, and we stood up to leave. I couldn't help but notice how he towered over me. I loved it.

We exchanged numbers and to my surprise, he only gave me a friendly kiss on the cheek. I floated all the way back to work on a high I'd never felt before. Ever. Not even with Ben.

It felt so good, but at the same time, it scared me. Based on past experience, the most exhilarating feelings could also turn out to be the most painful. Some say life's all about taking risks. Well, I was about to find out!

Later that day, I had a makeup appointment with one of my regular clients, Sharon, a wealthy widow who loved to share her dating experiences with me. She'd just started telling me one of her many stories when Biljana, who was off the clock, eased over and waited for a break in our conversation.

After a few seconds, Biljana's text alert went off. After reading it, she held up her phone and said, "My boyfriend just arrived to pick me up. I would very much like for him to meet you."

I turned to Sharon, who said, "Go ahead Toy, I'm not going anywhere."

"Thanks. I'll be right back, I promise."

I followed Biljana through the store. We walked out the side entrance door, where a black S550 Mercedes was parked at the curb. Biljana rushed up to the car just as the driver got out to greet her. I moved closer until our eyes met. Then, I froze.

What — the — hell?

Biljana adoringly put her arm through his. "Niko, this is Toy, my boss. I wanted you to meet her."

My stomach lurched. I didn't know what to do or say, whether to slap Nikola or burst into tears.

"Hello, Toy. It is nice to make your acquaintance," Nikola said, extending a hand. His face was blank, unreadable.

With great effort, I said, "Nice to meet you, too. You have a hard working girlfriend and I'm glad to have her on my team." As I spoke, Biljana gazed up at him lovingly and squeezed his arm.

"I'm sorry to have to rush off, but I have a client waiting on me," I blurted, spun around, and rushed back to finish up with Sharon.

I felt like I had a clump of lead in my stomach throughout the rest of the day, forcing laughs and feigning interest. Like a zombie, I cleaned up my beauty station, cleaned my brushes, and said goodnight to the team. I walked to my locker, woodenly going through the same motions I went through every day. Then, it crashed over me like a waterfall. My life was nothing but one long, boring routine — I'd give Nikola that. But then, just when things were starting to get exciting, it turns out I'd been played.

I didn't even know this guy, but seeing him with someone else made me feel like… like I was nothing. He'd made me feel alive, and now he'd made me feel like a fool. Why didn't I go with my first instinct and avoid this jerk?

Later, I was waiting outside of work for a cab in the freezing cold, when my text message alert sounded on my phone. I retrieved it from my coat pocket.

The text read: *Hi. It is Nikola. I am sorry.*

Me: *Don't text me. You're an asshole, not to mention a liar.*

Him: *Please. It is not what you think.*

Me: *Oh? You don't have a GIRLFRIEND who works for me?*

Him: *LET ME EXPLAIN. Please meet me tomorrow. Like we planned. Nothing has to happen.*

I hesitated for a moment.

Me: *No. This has already started out badly. Can't possibly get better.*
Him: *I am not a liar. I can prove it. Hear me out.*
Damn him! Now he had me wondering.
Me: *One drink. You explain. Then, I'm outta there.*
Him: *Thank you. I will text you the address tomorrow.*

I stared at the blank screen for about a minute. All of a sudden a thought came to me. I was no better than Tatyana. After giving her a lecture on morality, I'd just accepted a date with another girl's boyfriend, another girl who happened to be my employee.

What the hell am I doing?

Chapter 4

I'd just gotten home from work when I heard my phone ringing.

"What now?" I grumbled, digging through my bag to find the blaring chunk of metal.

I glanced at the screen. Cesonne. I hadn't been gone fifteen minutes and already they were bothering me. I was tempted to ignore it, but I knew Yvonne and Chance were the only two left at the counter.

"Hello," I said, sharply.

"Toy, we have a crisis!" Chance blurted out.

I sighed into the phone. "Seriously?"

"This customer wants to return a jar of moisturizer with barely a smidgeon left in the bottom and a fragrance that's completely empty. That's more than a thousand-dollar return, Toy. It's going to put us in a deficit for the day!"

Something suddenly occurred to me. "Chance, are you saying all of this in front of the client?"

"Um, yeah, duh," he said, oblivious to my rising ire.

"Damn it, Chance," I said through clenched teeth, "I'm on my way back right now. Just ask the client if she'd like a bottle of Evian water and tell her your boss is on her way to take care of the matter."

"She's trying to return empty products. You really want me to give her an Evian?" he said, incredulously.

Before I could respond, I heard Yvonne in the background, "Lady, no friggin' way on God's green earth are we taking back empty containers!"

"Chance, listen to me. Get Yvonne away from the client. Act like a professional and get the lady an Evian. I'll be there in a few minutes. Whatever you do, don't let Yvonne say another word to her."

I shoved the phone into my bag and slung it back over my shoulder. I slipped my cold feet back into my still wet snow boots and prepared myself for the trek up Michigan Avenue.

About ten minutes later I walked up to the counter to find Yvonne leaning up against it, brushing her hair, and Chance standing with his arms crossed, defiantly tapping his foot.

Then, I saw the client. *Oh, God! Not Mrs. Shue.*

"Toy, I kept asking for you," she said, pitifully.

I should have known. I refocused on her to keep my eyes from rolling and plastered a smile on my face. This woman had some nerve!

Mrs. Shue was notorious among retailers in downtown Chicago. She bought and returned more merchandise in a month than most people do in a lifetime; and always with what she thought was a clever excuse: "They gave me the wrong product" or "I'd never buy this for myself. It was a gift." She'd been banned from almost every boutique on Oak Street and most major retailers on the Avenue. I was shocked she was still allowed to shop here.

"I'll tell you, Toy. I'm not so good," she frowned. "That woman over there is just vulgar. I'm surprised a professional such as yourself, would allow someone like her to work your counter." She shot Yvonne a scathing glare.

Yvonne slammed the hairbrush on the counter and squared her shoulders, preparing for battle. I warned her with a glare. She glared back, but after three seconds, gave in and stalked away.

"I'm so sorry, Mrs. Shue. I'll make sure to address this with her. But for now, what can I do for you?"

"She wants to return two empty products," Chance piped up.

"Chance, will you please go to the stockroom and find some more bags for the counter?" I said, desperately trying to sound cheerful.

He let out a huff and stomped off.

I turned my attention back to Mrs. Shue, who seemed pleased with Yvonne's and Chance's dismissal.

"Okay. Now, what may I help you with?"

"Toy, I paid a fortune for this supposed miracle cream and all it did was give me an allergic reaction. It did absolutely nothing for my skin. Oh, and this fancy, brand name perfume that Jean — whatever the heck his name is — sold me, leaked all over my bathroom counter. Very cheap packaging!" She pulled the two empty, un-boxed products out of a Target bag.

Hmm. If I had a nickel for each time a client came in with an empty jar and said it had given them an allergic reaction after they'd used the entire product, I'd be living on a luxury yacht off the coast of Fiji.

Nothing would give me more pleasure than to simply call security and have Mrs. Shue escorted from our store. But, then I'd have been the next to get the boot, thanks to Norniesakmans' intractable return policy, which states, and I quote: *No receipt? No problem! We promise to always take back any product you aren't 100% satisfied with, anytime!* So, I was required to play nice.

"I'm so sorry for the inconvenience. May I exchange these products for you? Perhaps we can find something a little gentler for your delicate skin," I offered, wishing I could place a large bet on what she was going to say next.

"No, I think I'd rather have cash back."

Bingo!

"My dermatologist says I should use something plain from the drug store until my skin is balanced again."

"Fine. No problem. Do you have your receipt?"

"Uh, no. Can't you look it up in the system?" she asked, taking a whiff of a new fragrance we'd just put on display.

"Sure, I can. Do you know when you purchased these items?"

"I don't know. Maybe three months ago?" she said, clearly annoyed by the question.

Three months. Amazing, but if Norniesakmans insisted on adhering to their ridiculous return policy, far be it from me to balk. I scrolled through her customer profile and located the purchase. Jean-Luc hadn't even been the salesperson. It'd been someone from the shoe department! She'd probably had a sales shark from footwear ring them up along with her other items. "One thousand, seventy-two dollars and sixty-two cents," I said, counting the cash into her hand.

"Thank you so much, Toy. I'll be sure to only buy from you from now on."

"Thank you, Mrs. Shue, and again, I apologize for any inconvenience you may've experienced." I gave her the same plastic smile I'd greeted her with. I thought my face would break if I had to keep this farce up much longer.

"It's not your fault customer service isn't what it used to be." She shrugged, tossed the cash into a knockoff Coach bag, and walked away.

The minute she was out of sight, I went to find Yvonne and Chance. I didn't have to go far. They were both seated at another counter just a few feet away.

"Chance, Yvonne, get over here!"

Without any sense of urgency, they made their way toward me.

"I can't believe you allowed that witch to return those products," Chance pouted.

Yvonne chimed in, "Yeah, Captain. I'm kinda blown away, too. Why the hell did you do that?"

"Okay. First of all, I'm the manager, not you two. I get paid to put out fires before they burn their way to upper management. So, even though I know it sucks, you have to remember our return policy," I explained, finding the words difficult to say with any conviction.

Neither Chance nor Yvonne had any comment. Instead, Chance drifted over to the register with Yvonne not far behind.

"Will you look at this? Oh my God!" said Chance.

"What?" I was becoming annoyed.

"Yeah, what is it, Princess?" said Yvonne.

"This woman's bought and returned everything she's ever purchased here!" griped Chance, making room for Yvonne to look at the screen.

"Chance," I said, "we aren't the cosmetics police. Let it go."

"I don't care. It's bullshit the store makes us take back used garbage and it gets counted against us for our monthly goal. It's not fair!"

"Trust me, I know. I've had plenty of battles with management about this issue and lost. I'll talk to Sharee tomorrow and see if she can speak with someone in corporate we haven't already reached out to. Now let it go."

"Fine," he mumbled. He sashayed over to a stool, plopped down on it and began to apply some foundation.

I looked around and realized the store was about to close. The counter looked like a hurricane had blown through. Used mascara wands, dirty tissues and mirrors, some with entire handprints on them, cluttered the counter space. Tester products for customers to try on were missing from their designated spots and cookie crumbs were all over the floor.

"Um... are you two planning on cleaning tonight?" I shot them an icy stare.

"Clean what?" Chance's eyes never left his reflection in the mirror.

"Yeah, Captain. I already cleaned up once," said Yvonne.

I threw up my arms. "Are you two blind? Am I the only one who knows how to clean around here? If the health department came in we'd be closed down. This is disgusting."

"You okay? You seem a little tense tonight." Chance tossed aside the makeup sponge and poked through a pile of brushes with a finger.

"Tense? No. I just don't like my counter to be confused with a booth at the flea market."

"Okay, fine. We'll freshen it up a little bit," Chance offered.

I almost laughed. Almost. "Freshen it up?" I took a deep breath. "I'm going home now. If another crisis erupts in the next five minutes, and I realize this is difficult for you two," I said, pointedly, "try and keep it professional, alright?"

"I'm *always* professional," said Chance, blotting his lipstick on a tissue.

"Yeah, Captain." Yvonne gave me a half-ass salute. "When it comes to professional, you've got yourself a real kick-ass team here," she added.

I stared at them for a minute, surprised my jaw hadn't hit the floor. Were they really this deluded?

My question was answered the moment I watched them slap a high five.

I spent all night tossing and turning, thinking about Nikola and that kiss. Never in my life had a kiss so brief seemed like such a blissful eternity. It was *so* intense, but unfortunately, he was *so* taken. I knew I shouldn't listen to his explanation, but there was something so fascinating about him. The thought of not meeting him stirred more sadness in me than his having a girlfriend. I knew I was in over my head.

I got up early Saturday morning to arrive at the conference room for our counter meeting before my associates did. I opened the door and there was Chance, leaning up against a wall, anxiously tapping his foot and playing with his cell phone. This was unusual for him. Chance was never the first one to a meeting and generally preferred to be the last to enter the room, making a grand entrance to snatch as much attention as possible. He didn't care what kind it was.

The minute I saw his face, I knew something was wrong. "Awe, what's up, babe?"

I put my hand on his shoulder and was again, struck by how tiny he was. Tears filled his eyes and he started to cry.

I grabbed a few tissues from a box on the table and handed them to him. "Oh my God, Chance. What's wrong?"

"You touched me."

I drew my hand back. "What? Did I hurt you?" Yes, he was pint-size, but this was ridiculous.

His sobs became hysterical. "You shouldn't have touched me. You know how when you're on the edge? I mean, you're just about to lose it and then somebody touches you?" He sniffled. "Well, that's how I feel. I can't hold it back anymore!"

If I wasn't so concerned, his melodramatic weeping might've been comical. He pushed his tear-streaked face into my shoulder.

"You're going to think badly of me, I know it," he whimpered.

"Look, the team is going to be here in less than half an hour. I need you to tell me what's going on so I can help you pull yourself together. We can't let them know anything. You're my top artist and I need you for what I'm going to tell all of you today."

He dabbed at his nose and looked at me with red-rimmed eyes. "What's up?"

Even in his desperation he was nosey. "You'll just have to wait like the rest of the team. Now, come on. What's going on?"

"Okay, I'll tell you, but please don't lecture me," he pleaded. He sat down, crossed his legs, and patted each eye lightly with the tissue. Snow White had nothing on Chance.

"After work last night, a few of us went to Boystown to have a few drinks."

Boystown was a popular Chicago neighborhood on the Near North Side, and one of the largest gay communities in the country. I'd had some really good times there with Chance.

"Ed went, too. I don't know who invited that bitch, but it sure wasn't me! I'd never have gone if I knew he was going. You know how jealous he is of me."

I nodded sympathetically. I was quite skilled at theatrics myself.

"So anyway, I was dancing on the bar to *Billie Jean* and everyone loved it. I mean, *all eyes were on me,* Toy. When the song finished, I jumped off the bar and into the arms of this hot-ass Colombian guy, and we started making out. Ed must've been green with envy, 'cause all of a sudden he yelled out my name. I was super pissed at him for interrupting me with the hottie, but I still looked up to see what he wanted."

In an Academy Award-worthy move, Chance put a hand to his forehead, and cried, "He was holding up his iPad, Toy! Playing a video of me!"

Now, he had my attention. "What kind of video?"

"You *know* what kind. Now, everyone in the department is going to know. How am I going to work here with everyone looking at me and whispering?"

"Let's get back on track," I said, firmly.

Chance let out a miserable sigh. "Okay, it's like this: One night last summer I was really drunk at Sidetrack. I was sitting at the bar talking to this rich, older man, David. He invited me back to his penthouse. He'd been buying me drinks all night, had his own chauffer service, and lived in like the most beautiful condo you could ever imagine..."

He seemed to forget he'd been completely devastated only three seconds ago.

"When we got back to his place, two guys, who I assumed were his boyfriends, greeted us at the door. One was this really hot black guy with a body to die for, and the other was just an average looking white guy, but he had the biggest—"

"Okay, okay, Chance," I waved him on. "Get to the point."

"Well, David said he'd pay me $1000 cash, right then and there, to play with the two other boys while he filmed it."

I put my hands on my head. "Oh, Chance! How could you?"

"I know, Toy, I know! It was stupid." He was blushing Dragon Girl red. "It didn't seem like a big deal at the time. The guys led me to the bedroom and both of them started kissing me. Before I knew it, I was giving the one guy head and the other was, well, you know exactly what the other one was doing. I was so wasted, I wasn't thinking clearly."

I cringed. When would Chance ever get it? This was exactly the kind of careless behavior that kept him knocking on HIV's door.

"I hope I don't already know the answer to this, but were they wearing protection?"

He looked down at the floor and mumbled, "I honestly don't know. I was too drunk to remember."

"Chance! How many scares do you need?"

"I know! This is why I didn't tell you last summer. I knew you'd lecture me." He grew quiet for a second, then irritated, and then snapped, "Well, do you want to hear the rest?"

"Yes. Please, finish." He had some nerve putting on attitude with me when I'd been the one going with him to all of his doctor's visits and lending him a shoulder to cry on.

"Turns out, David owns a bunch of gay Internet sex sites that I'm guessing horndog Ed regularly trolls. He obviously recognized me in *that* one, and gleefully paid the download fee. So, like I said, Ed, bitch that he is, played the video last night in front of everyone. I was mortified! The only thing I was grateful for is I looked really good in it." He put his hand on his chin, eyes narrowed, "Actually, now that I think of it, the Colombian guy did still ask for my number."

"Um, I'm a bit confused," I waved my hands to get his attention, "Why exactly, are you so, how did you put it? *Mortified*?"

He looked at me like I was daft. "I already told you. Now that Ed knows, so will the entire cosmetics department. Who knows how this will affect my career or any future relationship I may have? What do I do now? My life is over!" Again, his tears flowed with passion.

"I think you're being overly dramatic. Your life isn't over. If Ed brings this up at work, I'll handle it. I'm not going to deny that having a porno out on the web is scary, but we all have to live with the decisions we make, good or bad."

His face registered disbelief. "How would you know, Toy? You're Miss Perfect. Have you ever even had a one-night stand? Have you ever even made out with a complete stranger? God knows you'd never make a video, but I'm gonna let you in on something, honey. Shit happens when you least expect it."

I lost it. "You know what, Chance? You're right, but I don't think having one-night stands has made you very happy. In fact, your carefree lifestyle may have finally caught up with you."

I regretted having said it the second I saw his face. He rose to leave.

"Chance…"

"It's okay, Toy. Don't worry about me. I'm going to have a smoke. I'll be back in time for the meeting."

That hadn't gone well. I shouldn't have been so insensitive. And, Ed. It seemed he was becoming quite the little photojournalist. Or should I say paparazzi?

It was a little past 9:00 AM and I'd told the team we'd been the only Cesonne counter chosen by Frances herself to hold this event. The feedback had been exactly what I'd expected. Jean-Luc was on cloud nine. A $150,000 goal didn't faze him. He was ecstatic about meeting Frances. Ed complained, and the rest of the team didn't care one way or another. Chance, who'd been glaring at Ed throughout the entire meeting, hadn't made a peep.

My assistant counter manager, Fiona, a notorious brown noser, played the role of cheerleader as she always did. I glanced at her and did a double take. Her naturally brown hair had recently been dyed jet-black and she'd either gained four inches of hair length overnight, or she'd gotten extensions. I'd bet heavily on the latter. She caused the least inter-department drama, but also rivaled Dr. Jekyll/Mr. Hyde when it came to being two-faced.

Until about a year ago, we'd been friends for five years. We'd met in college. I got her the job with Cesonne. I'd even tried to hook her up with a few of Ben's friends. Each of them in turn, dumped her. Their complaint? She was too high-maintenance.

Fiona could be bossy at times and was the type of person who, even when proven wrong, could never admit it. I knew her flaws and did my best to see the good in her.

Nine months ago, when Ben took the job in Massachusetts, which led to our final split, I'd been devastated. I then made the mistake of looking to Fiona for consolation. I couldn't believe it. She'd been cold as ice and told me she didn't blame Ben for leaving. She said I always acted too needy around him, and never gave him room to breathe.

Until that moment, I hadn't realized how calculating Fiona was. It dawned on me she'd secretly wanted Ben all along, but I'd been too blind to see it. So, I lost my boyfriend and someone I thought was my friend all in one fell swoop. Reeling from the double whammy, I'd wanted to scream at her, rip her hair out, and make her hurt as badly as I did. Instead, I turned around and walked away with what was left of my dignity.

A few days later, I'd bumped into Sharee in the copy room.

"Hi, Toy, what's up?" Sharee said, fishing.

"Not much. Just making copies of next week's schedule for the team."

"I can see you're making copies, silly. What's going on with you and Fiona? I've noticed some tension between you two."

I swallowed the lump that was forming in my throat. "Without going into a long, drawn-out story, I found out Fiona has been after Ben for some time now. Needless to say, we're not friends anymore."

"I'm really sorry, Toy." She paused thoughtfully. "Have you ever seen the movie *All About Eve?*"

"No."

"You should watch it. It's a totally different scenario than the one you're in, but I think you may find some similarities between Eve and Fiona." She gave me a wink before leaving the room.

Later that night, I decided to give Bridget a break and watched *All About Eve,* instead. I'd assumed Sharee had recommended it because of Fiona's disloyalty. After watching the classic about ambition and betrayal, it dawned on me that Fiona was after my job, too.

Ed, being roommates with the HR manager, had come in handy on this occasion. He'd told Yvonne, who I later overhead telling Tatyana, that Fiona had been asking Sharee about her own "growth potential" at my counter for months. When that hadn't been successful, she tried to throw me under the bus in a meeting with HR. She'd accused me of sexual discrimination by allowing Yvonne to call Chance "Princess". So far, none of her half-assed attempts at sabotage worked.

Despite all I'd learned about "Eve", I'd have to somehow manage to work with Fiona. I had no choice but to remain professional, because she had Debbie in her pocket.

Counter meetings were always dreaded in cosmetics. They always ended up being longer than they needed to be. This was because like most meetings, everyone got off topic and brought up issues that should have been one-on-one conversations, not group. I only had them with my counter associates when we had an upcoming event or a major issue that needed to be addressed as a group. To my surprise, this one was moving along rather quickly.

Everyone was confirming their presale and appointment goals, when Debbie walked in unexpectedly.

Spoke too soon.

"Hi guys!" she called brightly, and slung her overflowing Louis bag on the table in front of me.

Mumbles of less than enthusiastic, "Hi's" and "Hey's," rippled through the crowd — except from Fiona, of course.

"Hi Debbie! So happy to see you made it in! We were all wondering where you were," fawned Fiona, "although with your hectic schedule it's a miracle you can keep up with anything. How do you do it?"

I forced my eyes to stay put while others involuntarily rolled or widened theirs.

I watched brownnoser Fiona in action, and it was as if I was seeing her for the first time. I'd always thought she was attractive and had even defended her when the other associates said she looked plastic and wore too much makeup. Like I'd been given a new pair of glasses, I could now see they were right: huge implants on a stick-thin frame, way too tanned skin, overly-injected collagen-filled lips, and her squarish head topped with a recently added layer of hair extensions. She looked artificial, like a brunette Barbie doll, but not nearly as attractive. And, now I knew she was just as fake on the inside.

"Discipline and excellent time management skills, Fiona," Debbie announced.

I thought I was going to vomit.

Debbie dug through her messy bag until finally, she pulled out a clipboard.

"I'd like for each of you to list three ideas you think we could implement to make this event more exciting. I don't want generic ideas like "more gifts for clients". Think outside the box."

Of course, she wanted our ideas so she could pass them off as her own when she talked to corporate.

"Jot them down and turn them in to me before you leave the room," she commanded, then turned her back to us and conferred with Fiona.

A loud, collective sigh went up right behind Debbie. She spun around to silence the room with a glare, but instead, nearly fell. She didn't know how to walk in heels. The only thing that kept us from laughing was the thought of the unemployment line.

Forty tedious minutes later, after hearing at least ten times how Debbie went out of her way to make this event happen, we grudgingly filled out our "idea sheets" and were excused. She wouldn't have let us go then, but the store was set to open in fifteen minutes. Saturday morning at Cesonne required all hands on deck.

The team poured out the door ahead of me. I was pushing through it myself when Debbie called my name.

So much for a clean getaway.

I forced a much-practiced smile. "Yes?"

"You know how important this event is, don't you?" she said menacingly.

"Yes, Debbie. I'm well aware of how important it is. My team is up for the challenge," I assured her.

"I hope so, because I've been hearing some rumors that your team isn't as well put together as you try to make it appear."

Fiona! That little snake!

I looked her straight in the eye. "I have no idea what you're talking about, but I can assure you whatever you heard isn't true. My team is as tight and ready to go as ever."

"I hope so, Toy. I know I told you your promotion depends on this event. I wouldn't want you to miss out on it or jeopardize your position altogether." She grabbed her heavy bag and heaved it over her shoulder.

Was she threatening me? Her smeared black mascara and choice of lipstick, nude, made her look more like a corpse than a department head. If I weren't so angry, I'd have laughed. This cartoon of a beauty director had ironically become the representative of one of the biggest and most prestigious cosmetics companies in the country. I guess people really *could* sleep their way to the top, however, one thing was obvious. She didn't have enough sense to know that the numbers my team achieved were one of the few things that made her look good.

"Don't worry. I know how important meeting this goal is. I'll make it happen."

"For your sake, let's hope you do. Have a good day, Toy. Email me how much your counter did at the end of the day."

With that, she strode past me and through the door.

I hated Debbie. She was a horrible person. She treated everyone around her terribly, and still managed to have a fantastic job and a great salary. It wasn't fair.

I shook my head and walked out of the room.

"Toy?"

It was Biljana. She was waiting for me a little ways outside the door.

"Hi, Biljana," I said, doing my best not to appear startled. "What's up?

"I am a little nervous about this event," she said with a cute little shudder.

I lowered my voice to an intimate tone. "Don't be. I purposely made your personal goal a bit smaller because I know you're new."

"I know this event means a lot to you and I appreciate the chance you took hiring me. I know I did not have a lot of experience and you could have hired someone else. I owe you a lot and I do not want to let you down," she said, sweetly.

I looked at her and felt such intense guilt I could barely meet her eyes.

"You don't owe me anything. Just do your best and if you make your goal, that'll be icing on the cake."

She looked at me, blankly.

"Icing on the cake. That means more than I could ask for."

"Oh," she laughed. "Yes. I will do a very good job. I am very grateful. Thank you so much."

She hurried off to the counter. Instead of following her, I took a detour over to Starbucks, which had a center aisle kiosk in the mall. I sat down, took out my phone and pulled up Nikola's name from my contacts.

I typed in: *I can't do this* and hit Send.

"Goodbye, Nikola," I said out loud and turned off my phone.

Chapter 5

I returned to the counter to see a young woman in a black DVF dress with a chic, jet-black bob engaged in conversation with Tommy.

"I believe this fragrance was created just for you." He flashed a shy, Tommy-boy grin and spritzed the perfume on a sample card.

She blushed and batted her lashes, drinking in his flattery, when suddenly Jean-Luc swooped in like an eagle.

"Honey, I hate to interrupt you, but I am astonished that a woman of your pedigree would even consider this, this… putrid tap water. Allow me to show you our newest fragrance, one that truly symbolizes a woman of your caliber." He placed a firm hand on her elbow and escorted her over to another display.

I looked on as Tommy's face turned a deep crimson. I was worried he might explode. He stamped toward me with his hands balled into fists.

"You need to rein in Tinkerbell, because one day I'm going to lose my patience," he growled, struggling for control.

While there was no policy in place regarding whose client was whose, there was a tacit agreement between associates to rotate and not jump in on other people's sales. Jean-Luc sometimes chose to pretend this understanding didn't exist.

"You're right. I'll have a talk with him once the customer leaves. She's already been interrupted once. I don't want to lose the sale," I said, moving over to the register and pretending to work. I wanted to listen in on the rest of Jean-Luc's pitch.

It looked like the client was already under Jean-Luc's spell. Now, the $200 bottle Tommy had been trying to sell her was being upgraded to a $1200 fragrance Jean-Luc held out to her like a vintage bottle of wine.

"This is the last limited-edition bottle in the company, Cherie. Would you like me to wrap it for you?" Jean-Luc practically salivating over the imminent sale.

"Yes, but I'm running late for lunch with my mother." She checked her iPhone. "Can you put it on hold for me?"

Jean-Luc's demeanor changed in less than a second. "Sweetie, this is the last bottle in the company, *the entire company.* I cannot promise you it will be here in five minutes, much less when you finish your *little luncheon,*" he snorted, turning his back on her to adjust a few fragrance bottles on the display case.

I watched the client's face, waiting to see if she was going to tell Jean-Luc to go fuck himself, or if his snooty sales technique was going to work. She looked at the bottle longingly, then at Jean-Luc, and I knew he had her.

"What if I gave you my credit card information to hold it?"

Jean-Luc pirouetted, folded his arms on the counter and dazzled her with a smile.

"I just don't want to let my mother see what I purchased. She and my father think I spend too much," she divulged.

Yeah, I bet they did. She couldn't be a day over twenty-one and was sporting a $6,000 BVLGARI *handbag.*

"Of course, my darling," Jean-Luc agreed, conspiratorially. He shot me a quick, barely perceptible smirk.

A few minutes later, he had all of her personal information and was giving her a kiss on each cheek.

"Adieu, ma belle." He waved as if they'd been friends for years.

"Good-bye, Jean-Luc," trilled his latest victim, smiling ear to ear.

He finished entering her information in the computer, then spun around. "Excuse me, can everyone please come over here for one moment?" he called, beckoning Yvonne, Tatyana and Biljana.

I was glad Tommy had stormed off in time to miss whatever Jean-Luc had in store for us.

"What is it?" barked Yvonne, annoyed at being pulled away from reapplying her makeup,

"Just come," demanded Jean-Luc.

"Peckerhead," muttered Yvonne.

I shot her a look, "What was that?"

"Nothing, Captain," she said, smiling widely, her pearly whites smudged with bright, red lipstick.

I didn't even bother to tell her. What was the point?

"I want everyone to know that I, *Jean-Luc*, just sold the last *limited edition* Cesonne fragrance in the *entire* company," he beamed, hands swinging as if he were directing a symphony.

"Big freakin' whoop," said Yvonne, and beelined back to her mirror.

"Oh, so you did your job?" Tatyana deadpanned, and returned to her client.

I had to admit it. Sometimes Tatyana cracked me up. She was the only person who could even come close to putting Jean-Luc in his place.

"Jealously is not attractive, Tatyana," Jean-Luc called after her.

"Yeah, it takes a strong salesperson to steal someone else's client right out from under him," Tommy jeered, appearing out of nowhere.

I shivered involuntarily. *How long has he been standing behind us?*

"And a weak excuse of a salesman to allow it to happen," Jean-Luc fired back.

"You know," Tommy snarled, inching closer, "you're lucky we're at work right now or I'd take your head and —"

"Okay, enough!" Like a referee, I pointed my palms at each fighter to keep them apart. Tommy, go take a break."

Tommy snapped off one last scowl at Jean-Luc, then turned and headed for the mall.

"Jean-Luc," I squared off with him and said, "I saw what you did and it wasn't cool at all."

"Not cool? You are telling me, the person who just added more than a thousand dollars to your counter goal, I am not cool?" Jean-Luc said, incredulous.

Again, the language barrier was a problem, although sometimes I suspected he played it up a little. "You're misunderstanding me. I'm not saying *you* aren't cool. I'm saying stealing sales from your co-workers makes for a poor team environment."

"I cannot believe this! Even *you*, my Blonde Ambition, are turning against me? Why must success come with such a burden?" he cried, spinning around and fleeing the counter.

I wasn't about to run after him. Sometimes his theatrics were funny, but this outburst was unacceptable, top salesperson or not. It was time to put a cap on Jean-Luc's ever-ballooning ego.

A few hours later, Jean-Luc's client returned to pick up her fragrance. By then, he'd returned to the counter.

"Honey, how was your lunch?" he asked, and reached into the drawer that held our on-hold merchandise.

"It was wonderful. We went to —"

"Where is my hold?" Jean-Luc cut her off, stooped down and started ransacking the drawer.

I stepped over and squatted down next to him. "What do you mean? I saw you put it in there."

His voice rose, "It is gone!"

"Shh! There are clients here," I whispered.

He leapt up and inspected every inch of the counter, toppling a fragrance display.

"So," he cried, setting his hands squarely on his hips, "someone is playing a little game, no?"

By this time, the customer was visibly upset.

"No one's playing a game with you," said Tommy, reaching for the hold drawer.

"Do not play innocent with me!" Jean-Luc threw himself in front of it. "Where is the bottle?"

Tommy looked stunned. "What?"

"Jean-Luc, calm down!" I pushed my way between the two of them.

"Excuse me, I'm late. I'll get the fragrance some other time," said the client, and scurried away.

Jean-Luc leveled a finger at Tommy. "This is what you wanted, right?"

"Man, you need to back off," Tommy replied, leaning in toward Jean-Luc.

"You two, come with me now!" I yelled.

That did the trick. I rarely raised my voice, but the argument was way too heated, and to be honest, it scared me. I led the way and they followed.

Once we were off the floor and in the conference room, I slammed the door behind us.

"What the hell's going on with you, Jean-Luc?" I demanded.

"*Me*? What is going on with *me*?" he gasped.

"Yes, *you*! First you intercept Tommy's sale, and then, in front of the client, accuse him of stealing the fragrance!"

"Yeah, what the hell?" Tommy blustered.

I twisted my head toward him. "Tommy, let me take care of this. I wasn't really impressed with your behavior, either."

"Sweetie, our counter just lost a client, someone sabotaged me, and you are okay with this?" cried Jean-Luc.

My head snapped back to Jean-Luc. "Oh, stop playing victim. No one on our team would sabotage you," I said, not quite sure I believed my own words.

"Someone did, and I have no doubt it was this peasant standing in front of me." Jean-Luc took a wide stance with his hands on his hips, and glared at Tommy.

Tommy laughed, sardonically. "Can I go, Toy? I can't take another minute of this childish shit."

"Yes, go," I said, suddenly worn out.

"I will not stop until I find out what you did with my fragrance," Jean-Luc threatened, intensely.

"Yeah? Let me know if you get any leads on the investigation." Tommy winked at Jean-Luc on the way out the door, slamming it closed behind him.

My eyes threw flames at Jean-Luc.

"Hon-ney..." he said, emphasizing the syllables.

"Don't you dare honey me. I don't want to hear any more of this. You've got to control your aggressive behavior. I can't allow you to keep acting out at the counter. It's not fair to the team or me."

"Someone stole my bottle, Toy. I am not crazy. It did not vanish into thin air," he said with a flip of his hand.

"No one stole anything! I don't want to hear another word about it. It was misplaced and that's that. Please don't make me write you up, Jean-Luc. I don't want to, but if you keep acting like this, I'll have no choice. I can't show favor to one employee over the others."

"I cannot believe this!"

"You know I care about you, which is exactly why I have to be careful how I treat you. Accusing Tommy of sabotaging a sale is a serious allegation."

"Fine," he pouted. "May I return to the floor now?"

"Jean-Luc, don't act like this."

"May I return to the floor?" he repeated, staring straight past me.

"Yes, go."

He walked out of the room and I dropped into a nearby chair. Dealing with Jean-Luc was becoming a full-time job.

Two days later, I was opening the counter when Yvonne walked up, late as usual. I often asked myself why I still had Yvonne on my team. I'd been at the breaking point with her numerous times. Then, out of nowhere, a client of hers would come raving to me about what an incredible artist she was and I'd give her another chance.

"Sorry. That fuckin' traffic, man," she said, and reached for her personal drawer.

"Language, Yvonne," I reminded her for the umpteenth time, or was it the millionth?

I was spraying the counter with alcohol to remove the dirt and grime from the night before, then polishing it with a paper towel. *I guess Chance still doesn't understand the concept of clean...*

"My cocksu— my darn drawer's stuck," she corrected herself, and jerked the drawer up and down. "I need my client cards. I gotta make some phone calls."

I set down the alcohol and paper towels and went over to assist before she broke the handle off. "Here, let me help."

I pushed it in firmly, then back out. It wouldn't budge. "It's stuck on something."

"Don't worry about it, Captain. I'll get it." Yvonne tried to shove her way in between the drawer and me.

"No, let me. I think I've almost got it."

"No, really. I'll get it," she said, practically shoving me aside.

"Yvonne, stop. Look, I've got —"

The drawer popped open and I saw what had been blocking it — the fragrance bottle Jean-Luc had accused Tommy of stealing!

I snatched the fragrance from the drawer and held it up to her.

"I can explain," Yvonne blurted, before I could say a word.

"It better be good, because you almost caused a fist fight between Jean-Luc and Tommy the other day. Not to mention, you cost us a twelve-hundred-dollar sale," I said, sternly.

"Jean-Luc's a conceited son-of-a-bitch. He needed someone to put him in his place," she declared.

I stared at her in silence, waiting for the rest of her explanation. It never came.

"So that's it?"

"Yeah. It's the truth. What were you expecting?"

"I don't know, maybe an apology?" After a moment, I sighed, "Never mind, I can't deal with this right now, Yvonne, but you're not off the hook. You stirred up a lot of trouble."

"But, he deserved it," Yvonne whined.

"I don't want to hear it! I'm going to put *this* in Sharee's office until I can figure out what to do about it. For now, don't tell a soul what you did, or you'll be in even more trouble. Got it?"

"Got it, Captain," she said. "Can I go get some coffee?"

I dropped my head and waved her on, then sagged against the counter, exhausted, watching my little corporal march toward the main aisle. I wondered if she had any idea how much chaos she could stir up in a day.

My eyes popped open. I looked at the clock on the nightstand: 11:00 AM! I jumped out of bed in a dead panic. I ran to the closet and had ripped a dress off a hanger before I realized it was Tuesday and I was off.

I heaved a huge sigh of relief and flopped down on the side of the bed. I glanced at my pillow and considered laying my head back down on it, but finally decided sleeping the day away wouldn't be very productive. Not that I had much to do, but I had so little time to myself these days. I wanted to enjoy it. I tossed my dress on the bed and headed for the bathroom.

I brushed my teeth and thought about the night before. Jenny from designer handbags had asked me to go out with her, but I decided to go home to a nice bottle of Tesco Prosecco instead. My head ached a little and my stomach felt queasy. I'd probably overindulged, but the tension between Tommy, Jean-Luc and Yvonne's little stunt, combined with the guilt and sadness over the Nikola situation, made the day feel like it had dragged on forever. I'd needed something to take the edge off.

I washed my face and was going to leave it at that, but then, I felt like a hypocrite. I tell everyone, clients, friends and family, that they need a morning skincare routine, yet I could skip it? I let out a groan and began the regimen that only took a few minutes, but this morning, felt like an hour. After patting on toner, serum, moisturizer, sunscreen, and eye cream, I could move on to my hair. I brushed through my naturally straight, long blonde hair, which I kept braided so often it seemed permanently kinked, then worked the strands into another long, side plait. I wrapped my new Hermes scarf around my neck, and then checked myself in the mirror. I thought about putting on a little makeup, but for what? I was only going half a block to get some coffee.

Le Cafe. The name wasn't very exciting, but I loved this place. For the five years I lived downtown, I never missed an opportunity to spend time there. I'd gotten to know the owners who opened the place more than thirty years ago. The older woman, Mattie, ran it herself now. Her husband had passed away just a few months ago from heart failure, a sad event for her and for all the regulars. For the longest, whenever I crossed the threshold, I half-expected him to pinch my cheek and repeat his mantra, "What kind of a name is Toy?"

There was another benefit to getting my coffee at Le Café. I always brought a novel to read while I enjoyed my coffee and I didn't like being interrupted. With a Starbucks on nearly every corner, I didn't have to worry about bumping into anyone I knew.

I walked in, wiped my feet on the mat and unbuttoned my coat. Mattie, as always, greeted me.

"Good morning, Toy. The usual?"

"Yes, please. How are you, Mattie? You look fabulous."

"Oh Toy, go on," she blushed. "How fabulous can a 68-year-old broad look? I'm just grateful to be alive," she laughed, steaming the milk.

"I'm glad you are, too. Where else in the world would I find anyone who makes a mocha like you?" I kidded.

"Awe, you'd figure something out," she said, and handed me the coffee drink and six crisp singles in exchange for my ten-dollar bill. I put two of them in the tip jar, headed for my favorite chair in front of the fireplace, threw my Prada coat over the back of it and pulled a book out of my bag.

I was only three chapters into Anne Rice's *Taltos*, when I sensed someone standing near me. I turned my head to the left and looked into a familiar pair of caramel colored eyes staring back at me.

I slapped the book shut. "Nikola! What are you doing here?"

"I live a few blocks south of here. I was walking by and saw you through the window," he said, his gaze so penetrating that I drew my scarf a little tighter.

"Well," I said, and shoved the book into my bag, "I was just leaving." I stood up and grabbed my coat.

He put a gentle hand on my arm. "Please, stay."

Although his eyes seemed sincere, I didn't trust him, but I couldn't help but wonder what he could possibly have to say to me. And, oh, did I mention he was looking even more gorgeous than before?

"Please, sit down."

Against my better judgment, I did as he asked.

"You are so beautiful. More so without all the makeup you usually have on," he said, just barely brushing my cheek with his fingers.

I shrank from his touch. "Is that all you have to say?" I shook my head, and then stood up and shoved my right arm into my coat sleeve.

"No, no. Please. Hear me out."

"Then get to the point!" My cheek was still on fire from his touch.

"Okay. Sit down, please."

I did, but on the edge of the seat.

"I want to spend time with you."

"Excuse me?"

"I said I want —"

"Yeah, I heard you. But you have a *girlfriend,* or did you forget?" I stood up, beginning to feel like a jumping jack. "I really don't have time for this nonsense."

Nikola attempted to help me into my coat but I brushed him away. "Wait a minute. You did not even let me explain my situation. You think I am like this with every girl I meet? I have had plenty of opportunities to have sex with women if that is what I wanted."

I struggled to shove my left arm into the sleeve and nearly ran straight into Mattie as I headed for the door.

"Coffee to go, Toy?"

"Oh, uh, no thanks, Mattie. I think I've had enough caffeine for the day," I stammered, slipping the coat up over my shoulders. Her eyes slid from me to Nikola, and then back to me.

"Okay, you kids have fun," Mattie said, winking.

I somehow managed a smile. "Yeah, well Mattie, see you soon. You take care, okay?" and pushed through the door.

Nikola followed.

After a few steps, I spun around. "Will you stop? This isn't going to happen. It can't. You have a girlfriend." I turned back around and kept walking.

"Will you please stop running away?" he pleaded.

I grudgingly stopped and turned around to face him.

"What do you want?" I asked, crossing my arms.

"Your friendship and a chance to explain to you about Biljana. That is all."

"Why should I believe anything you have to say?"

Nikola shrugged. "You have no reason to believe me, but if you give me a chance to sit down with you and talk, I promise not to cross the line. You have my word." His eyes were burned into mine.

Maybe I should just have the word sucker tattooed on my forehead.

"Okay. We can meet in the library of my building."

Nikola considered my suggestion for a second, then said, "That is silly. It is childish. We are both adults. We meet at your apartment. If at any point you want me to leave, you only say it once."

"I don't know..." I said, fidgeting with my scarf.

He slowly spelled it out for me again, "If I make you uncomfortable, you say go. I will leave. I promise!"

I laughed. "Okay, you can come to my place, but I'm holding you to your word. I'll text you my address when I get home and leave your name with the doorman."

"Great," he said, and lit up like a kid at Christmas.

Tiny snowflakes had started to fall and we both looked up at the sky, and then at each other.

"The first snow," he grinned. "Now, every year, I will think of you when the first snow falls."

My heart leaped. *How does he do that to me? And more importantly, why is it so damn hard to say no to this guy?*

Chapter 6

It was a little past 8:00 PM and I was so nervous I had to down a glass of Relax Riesling to finish getting ready. Before I'd even gotten a chance to text Nikola my address, he'd texted me asking for it.

Last summer, I'd leased an apartment on the twenty-second floor of an opulent high rise located in Chicago's Gold Coast neighborhood, just a few blocks away from "The Mile". The new apartment was perfect, everything I'd ever dreamed of when, as a teenager, I imagined myself out on my own. A classic, yet elegant fireplace was the centerpiece of my living room. It added the touch of warmth the otherwise rather stark room needed. It was November, a record-breaking cold November, that allowed me to experience the luxury of bundling up in a blanket in front of a roaring fire that wasn't my parent's.

And, I was obsessed with my bathroom! It had just been remodeled when I moved in. The walk-in steam shower lined with a marble bench and the round, Japanese soaking tub, still took my breath away.

After college, instead of getting a crappy little place of my own, I'd moved back home to save money. My friends thought I was insane for paying the rent I did each month, but I always thought, if you worked hard for what you want, you should get some kind of reward. Mine was a high rise in Chicago with a view of Lake Michigan.

Under normal circumstances, I wouldn't spend a lot of time deciding on what to wear for a night in, but tonight, choosing the right outfit was an undertaking. I didn't want to come off as trying too hard, so I decided on a pair of my favorite Paige jeans, with a white, not-too-tight Vince T-shirt that didn't reveal just a hint of cleavage.

I took one last look in the mirror, right down to my recently French manicured nails and toes. There was nothing left to do but wait. Seconds felt like hours and my nerves had me on edge. Patience was not one of my virtues.

When the doorbell finally rang, I took my time to open it. There stood Nikola, holding a bottle of Shafer Cabernet Sauvignon. Handsome didn't begin to describe him. He had on a dark brown leather coat that was opened to reveal a tight, white V-neck T-shirt, dark jeans, and soft, brown Gucci moccasins. And oh my God, he smelled good.

"Come in," I said. I stepped aside to let him pass and closed the door behind him. "Can I take your coat?"

"Yes, thanks," he said. He handed it to me, and then leaned in to kiss my cheek.

My heart began to race as I opened the closet in the hallway and hung up his coat.

He held out the wine bottle. "This is for you."

"Thank you," I said, and went to the kitchen to set the bottle down on the island.

Without me saying anything, he took off his shoes, placed them by the door, and joined me in kitchen.

"You look very nice," he said, looking me directly in the eyes.

"Thank you." In spite of myself, I felt my face color. "You look nice, too," I said, sounding just a tad awkward. I felt so self-conscious around this guy. I didn't understand it. *I've never been timid.*

"I hope you like the wine. I was not sure what to get."

That was the first time I'd ever seen him show the slightest lack of confidence.

"I like wine in general, so I'm sure it'll be fine."

"Should we try it?" he asked, moving a little closer to me to grab the bottle. "Do you have a corkscrew?"

I pray to God he can't tell how nervous he makes me!

"Sure." I pulled two wine glasses down from the wine rack directly above the island and drew the corkscrew from its holder. I set it all down on the counter. He opened the bottle and poured the wine. I lifted mine by its stem and watched him as he scanned my apartment.

"Amazing place. The art is incredible," he said with genuine admiration. "Did you decorate it by yourself?"

"I wish I could create something that looked like this," I said between sips of wine. "My client, Jason, owns an interior design company, DecArte. He did this."

"He is very talented," he nodded.

"Incredibly. So, would you like to sit down?" I motioned toward the living room.

"Yes, please." He went over to the sofa and made himself comfortable. When he noticed I hadn't budged, he patted the cushion next to him.

God, I wanted him to stay, but I knew I had to put his word to the test so I could be sure. And, it would require some acting on my part, although my nervousness wasn't an act. I took a couple of steps toward him, then froze, made a face, which I'm sure was racked with indecision, and shook my head.

"Nikola, I can't do this. I thought I could, but I just don't feel comfortable having you in my apartment, drinking wine…"

He was already standing up. "Okay, if that is how you feel. I will respect your wishes." He walked past me into the kitchen. I watched him put his wine glass down and head down the hall. He slipped his feet into his moccasins, slung his coat over his shoulder, and closed the closet door.

"Nikola?" I said, softly.

He turned around and I could see the disappointment on his face. "It is okay. Do not worry, I understand. Goodbye, Toy."

"Wait! I'm sorry. Please don't be mad, but I had to see if you were serious the other day, about leaving when I wanted you to."

"Of course, I was serious," he said with a gaze I could easily get lost in. "And if you really feel uncomfortable with me, I will leave."

"No, no. I feel fine. Would you please come back and sit down?"

"Yes, I would like that," he said, gently pushing the door shut. After removing his shoes and coat again, he returned to the living room and sat back down.

I went to the kitchen, grabbed our wine glasses, handed him his and placed mine on the coffee table. Then, I took a seat on the opposite end of the couch.

We made small talk for a few minutes. I asked him if our weather here in the US was different from his homeland. He asked me if I enjoyed the cold. Finally, I moved on to the subject he was here to discuss.

"So, you were going to tell me about you and Biljana," I said, looking at him over my wine glass.

"Yes. Biljana and I grew up together. Our families have known each other for many years and we come from the same city in Macedonia. Her family lived very close to mine. We were practically neighbors. We have been friends since we were children. Like I told you, I am here to work for my uncle who owns a trucking company. A few months ago I received a call from my parents telling me Biljana was coming here to America."

"So let me get this straight. You two are good friends and she, out of nowhere, decided to move to America?" I asked, dubiously.

"Yes, that is exactly what I am saying. We have something called the lottery in our country. She won."

"We have the lottery, too," I said. Then, confused, I added, "Wait, she *won* the lottery? So why is she working as a makeup artist?"

He laughed. "No, not like your lottery in the US. With our lottery you win a United States visa. Every year, 50,000 permanent resident visas are made available to randomly selected applicants from countries with low immigration to the US."

"Oh wow. No, I didn't realize that even existed."

"Yes. Well anyhow, she won. Her parents asked me to look after her. They worry about her being a single woman in a strange country. Given the relationship our two families have, I could not refuse. So that is how we know each other."

"Okay, but that still doesn't explain why she calls you her boyfriend."

"She does not like for people to know that I am watching over her, so she calls me her boyfriend. She has had a crush on me since we were kids, but I do not see her that way."

"Why would you let her say you're her boyfriend if you know she likes you more than a friend? Isn't that leading her on?" I asked, taking a sip of the wine I hadn't touched since he began his story.

I don't buy they've been "buddies" all this time and nothing's ever happened!

"To be totally honest with you, I tried dating her before I moved here," he said, as if reading my mind. "We went out a few times and even had sex, but I do not feel for her like that. I made it clear we were never going to be anything more than just friends, even if we did continue to, as you Americans say, 'hook up'. I keep hoping she will meet someone who is right for her, but so far no luck. So, how is that leading her on?"

"I don't know. I guess I wouldn't want to be the girl in love with a guy who would hook up with me but not seriously date me," I said with resignation.

"Look, I have always been very clear with Biljana. I really care for her but my heart is not there. And I realize it even more since meeting you," he said, and stood up.

"Where are you going?" I asked, surprised by how quickly I reacted.

"To the kitchen," he smiled. "Do you want more wine?"

"Sure." I could feel my face flush.

He brought the bottle over and refilled our glasses. He set the bottle on the coffee table and sat back down.

"Now," Nikola said, turning to face me, "I have a problem. For the first time in my life I feel something more than sexual attraction for someone. You, Toy, and I do not know what to do."

I looked in his eyes, then at his mouth and wanted him in the worst way. I leaned in to press my lips against his, and he stiffened.

"What's wrong? I thought you wanted this?" I pulled back from him, feeling both embarrassed and confused.

"I am a man of my word and I promised I would not cross the line."

I watched his sensuous lips as he spoke those words and I couldn't help myself any longer.

"I know you promised — but *I* didn't." I leaned in once again to kiss him, and this time he responded.

I took his hand and led him over to the fireplace. I eased down in front of the hearty fire I had going, pulling him down next to me. His animated, light brown eyes drew me to him. I brushed his cheek with the back of my hand.

He took me in his arms and in the same second, his mouth covered mine, and I knew there would be no turning back.

"I want to see all of you," Nikola said, tracing my lips with the tip of his tongue.

I deliberately pulled off my shirt, revealing my toned belly. He reached around and unhooked my bra, freeing my breasts. He moved his head down and tugged at each of my nipples with his lips until I uttered a soft moan. He was on his knees now. I pushed my leg between his and could feel him grow against it. He pulled off my jeans and threw them aside.

"Touch yourself," he whispered, unbuttoning his shirt. I did as I was told, pulling my panties to the side and slowly massaging, amazed at my total lack of restraint. He tore off his shirt, revealing his gorgeous body to me, inch by luscious inch, as his clothing hit the floor. He rose to unzip and remove his pants.

God, he's sexy.

"You are so beautiful," he said. His eyes never left me as he pulled off his boxer briefs. Naked now, he kneeled down onto the rug, put my legs over his shoulders, and started kissing one thigh, and then the other. He took his time, taking care to tease me and make me want more. When he felt me start to tremble, he moved his lips up my body, running his tongue over my belly, my breasts, my neck, finally planting his lips firmly on my mouth. He pulled off my panties, and slipped two fingers inside me. As his fingers went in and out, I knew it was finally going to happen.

"Relax. I will go slow," he said gently while kissing my neck. I reached down to feel his erection and instantly became even more turned on when I felt how large and hard it was.

He entered me, slowly as promised. It hurt just a little, intensifying my pleasure. I rocked my hips back and forth pulling him deeper inside of me. Our rhythm was in perfect sync, our bodies a perfect match.

"Oh Nikola! Yes, right there," I cried out as he lifted my legs higher on his shoulders, touching a spot I didn't know existed.

"I want to feel you come," he said, thrusting faster and harder.

I started to quiver as my body reached its climax. "I'm coming, Nikola, oh my God!" I screamed, as I dug my nails into his flesh.

"Me too, baby. Me too." His face hovered inches from mine. I watched his eyes lose focus as we came in unison.

We were laying there, exhausted, catching our breath for a while when he whispered, "*Neverojaten*," I didn't understand what he'd said, but I didn't speak. He was soon asleep. I stood up quietly, grabbed a blanket from the couch, and laid back down next to him, covering us both. I watched his handsome face and his broad chest rise and fall. It was a moment I wished would last forever.

I was awakened a little later to Nikola drawing circles around my nipples with his tongue. I pulled his head up and kissed him, alternately darting my tongue into his mouth and taking his into mine. He flipped me over on top of him. I rubbed my body against his as I made my way down to take him inside of my mouth. When I knew he was about to explode I stopped, stood up, and eased myself down on him. This time it went in easier. I felt no pain, only pleasure. I moved back and forth on top of him, pinning his arms up over his head.

"Ride me baby, yes, yes, just like that," he urged, then pushed his arms down and grasped my hips firmly.

Our bodies moved as one, and I felt him hit the same spot he'd helped me discover earlier. The passion was building like a volcano inside of me.

"Nikola, I'm going to come," I said, breathlessly.

In response, he started moving my body up and down on him, faster and deeper.

"Oh, yes!" I screamed, as my body fell into orgasm. I realized after I felt him go weak, that he'd come too. I rolled off next to him. He threw an arm around me and we lay in a comfortable silence for the next few minutes.

He flipped onto his side to face me. "You make me come so hard. You are incredible." He traced a finger lightly from my nose to my navel.

"Thank you," I murmured.

"Your skin is so soft. One day I want to spend an entire day and night kissing every inch." He gave me a long, slow kiss, then pulled away. "When I told you I wanted to know you, I did not mean just physically, although I do very much enjoy your body." He flashed a sexy smile.

"What do you want to know?"

"Where you are from? What kind of childhood you had. How you got to where you are right now. Everything."

"Hmm. Where should I start?" I said, running my fingers through his hair.

"Wherever you want."

"Okay. I was raised in the suburbs in a town called Downers Grove. I had a good childhood. After high school, I went to college in New York, but came back because I missed all of my friends and family. I have one sister who's younger than me and away at college right now.

"My dad's an attorney and my mom's a teacher. They divorced when I was twenty. That's a story all its own. I was in a long-term relationship that ended almost a year ago and... I recently met a tall, dark stranger who is making me do things I never thought I'd do," I teased.

"Oh really? Making you?" he laughed, then told me about his country and what he missed most about it. I listened, loving the way he pronounced each word.

After talking for what seemed like a blissful forever, my eyes started to flutter until they closed. The last thing I remember before falling into a deep sleep was him whispering, "*Sudbina*," and the feel of his soft lips on my forehead.

I woke up to find Nikola gone. I glanced at the clock on the wall. It was a little past 4:00 AM. I looked down and noticed he'd covered me with the blanket.

I sat up slowly, a little painfully, and stared into the dying fire. I was flooded with emotion. Had I had been reckless by sleeping with him so soon? I should've had him wear a condom, even though, thank God, I was on birth control; not that he'd asked. I was upset that he left without even saying goodbye, which made me wonder if he'd used me.

I stood up, wrapped myself in the blanket, and stepped into my bedroom. I walked into the bathroom to shower and brushed my teeth. When I finished, I put on my favorite Victoria's Secret nightshirt and fresh panties, flipped off the lights and crawled into bed.

As I curled up in my comforter, a crazy, unknown fear assailed me.

Okay, he'd convincingly said Biljana wasn't his girlfriend, but what if that wasn't the whole truth? Maybe there was more to their lifelong "friendship" than he hadn't let on. It was indeed a possibility he was lying to get me in bed, so how in the world could I let myself become this emotionally and physically involved with him in such a short time? I wanted to cry.

All at once, I missed Ben. Granted, we never had the kind of physical chemistry Nikola and I had, but we had trust. I knew after Ben and I made love he would be there when I woke up. For all I knew, Nikola could be in bed with Biljana right this very minute. The sad part was her bed — or *their* bed — was probably where he belonged, not mine.

How could I have done this to her? She was so nice and I betrayed her. *What kind of person am I becoming?* I wondered miserably.

After tossing and turning for what seemed like hours, I finally flipped on the TV and hit the button on the DVR. I had *Bridget Jones's Diary* recorded and I fell asleep around the part where Bridget sits at home, eats ice cream, and lip syncs to Celine Dion's *All By Myself.*

Talk about life imitating art.

The next morning, I thought I was dreaming, but finally realized my phone was ringing over and over. Still groggy, I grabbed it. *Jean-Luc! Damn it! Only 9:00 AM. This better be good.*

"Hello," I mumbled, my tongue sticking to the top of my mouth.

"Honey, I know it is early, but we need to speak immediately. It is an emergency. I'm in the lobby at the front desk. I have coffee."

I jolted upright in the bed. "Wait, you're here?" *What the hell is he doing just showing up like this?*

"Yes, you are on speakerphone. Your doorman knows who I am, but he still will not let me up. Baby, tell him it is okay."

Mike? This guy is unbelievable!

"Even though Jean-Luc didn't let me know he was dropping by, *Mike,* by all means, send him up," I said with as much sarcasm as I could muster.

"Okay, he is letting me come to you. How do you deal with these morons, honey?" he said, clearly unfazed by my tone of voice.

"Deal? Maybe he's just doing his job. I hope there are extra shots in my coffee." I ended the call. *Ugh. Why couldn't I have slept all day?* When you sleep you don't feel the depression, which in my case happened to be named Nikola.

I jumped out of bed and threw on my robe just in time for the doorbell to ring. As soon as I opened it, Jean-Luc kissed me on the cheek, held up two coffees, and blew right past me without even bothering to take off his coat or shoes.

"Well, come on in," I muttered after him, and slammed the door shut. The first time I had two days off in a row in three months and I was up by nine.

"Honey, I think I was drugged last night," he said so seriously, I had to clasp my hand over my mouth to keep from bursting out laughing.

"Glad to see you think it is so funny," he said, glaring at me.

I struggled to control my amusement. "No, no. It's not funny at all. Just shocking. Go ahead."

"Last night, as I was leaving work, Chance asked me to have a drink with him. He said he was very upset about something and needed to talk. I wanted to go home, but agreed to have one drink to listen to his story." He paused to sip his coffee.

Uh-oh. Any story that involved Chance, someone thinking they were drugged, and alcohol, drew my full attention. Just as he was about to continue, my phone rang. It was Chance.

Now I knew something was going on.

"Who is it?" asked Jean-Luc.

"My mom. Let me take this. I'll be right back," I got up and stepped into the bedroom.

"Hey girl, what are you doing up?" Chance asked, unusually cheerful considering how devastated he was a few days ago.

"Why are you calling if you didn't think I'd be up?"

He ignored my question and gushed, "I think I've had the man of my dreams right under my nose and didn't even know it."

Oh, no, I thought. My stomach grew queasy. "Okay..."

"I've got to be at work in like fifteen, so to make a long story short, I think I'm in love."

"With?" *Please don't say Jean-Luc.*

"Jean-Luc."

Shit! "Chance, you can't —"

"I'll call you with the glorious details on my smoke break, but I will tell you two things. He is definitely not straight, and he is hung, girlfriend. Like, I don't know if I can sit today," he laughed.

"Ewe! T-M-I! I did *not* need to hear that, especially about Jean-Luc!"

"Ha-ha, I knew you'd love that part."

"Jerk."

"I can't help it. You're so easy to get a rise out of. Okay. I'm here and I see that bitch, Ed, is already walking in. He'd love it if I was late. Talk to you later, boo."

"Wait! Hey, hold on!"

"What's up?"

"Don't tell *anyone* at work," I said as an order — not a request. "I can't deal with anymore drama at the counter, okay?"

"Okay, I got it."

"Promise?"

"Fine! I hate when you make me promise. You take all the fun out of everything! Okay, I promise."

"Thank you," I ended the call and tossed the phone on my bed.

I walked back to the kitchen, feeling awkward. Chance and Jean-Luc were both close friends of mine. I was used to Chance telling me about a new sexual conquest weekly, sometimes daily, but I never expected it to include Jean-Luc!

Jean-Luc flirted with our female clients. Sometimes even got their numbers. He'd mentioned women he'd dated in the past, but I'd never seen him with anyone. The many times I'd hinted at his sexuality, he'd gotten defensive and insisted he was straight, so I'd drop the subject.

"Sorry, she was upset about something that happened at work," I said. "I told her I'd call her back."

I felt bad lying, but this wasn't a situation I was used to being in the middle of.

"It is okay. So I think I left off at having a drink with Chance," he said, pulling a cigarette out of his pack.

"Not in here," I said.

"*Ma belle*, but why must you be so American?" he complained and put the cigarette away.

"Can we please finish the story?" I was interested to hear how he felt after what happened last night. Apparently, his feelings were not the same as those that Chance had for him, since he claimed he'd been drugged.

"After the drink and listening to his latest sob story, I told him I needed to get home. I felt bad about how upset he was, but I did not know what to tell him. As I got up to leave, he asked me to have just one more drink. I felt guilty leaving so soon, and I agreed to have one more." He put his head in his hands. "Mon dieu," he moaned. "Please, may I smoke?"

"Okay, c'mon."

I snatched the throw from the couch and we stepped out onto the balcony. "Now, go ahead."

"You know I do not drink much, Toy, so after the second drink I was feeling a little drunk. This is when I think I may have been drugged." He shivered and had a hard time lighting his Gauloises, clearly distressed.

I wondered if he'd ever get to the part where he'd had sex with Chance.

"Okay," I said. "So what exactly makes you think you were roofied?"

"This is so hard for me to tell you, but I am just going to say it. I woke up in my bed this morning, naked."

"Okaaay," I said. "Is there anything else you'd like to tell me?"

"I was naked Toy, with Chance!" he cried, "That is bad enough, no?"

I sucked in my breath, feigning shock.

"I know. I just froze when I saw him sleeping next to me, but the worst was when he woke up, grabbed me, and asked me if I wanted to do it *again*!"

"Oh, my God! What did you say to him?"

"I wanted to tell him to get out, but I did not want to hurt his feelings, especially after how upset he had been last night. Instead, I told him I had an appointment I was running late for and needed to jump in the shower. He seemed disappointed, but got dressed and kissed me on the cheek. He thanked me for an unforgettable night, and left." Jean-Luc's face pinched. "Can you imagine? *An unforgettable night*?"

"Oh, good God," I said, shaking my head.

"I know, right? I don't remember anything from last night past that second drink. This is why I think I was drugged!" He tamped the cigarette butt out on the railing and flicked it into the wind. "Oh, *merde*," he groaned, miserably.

He followed me back into the apartment and took a seat at the island, crossed his arms on it and dropped his head on them.

"I don't know if you were drugged," I said, reaching into the freezer. I grabbed a bagel, pulled it apart and popped it into the toaster. "I think you probably had a blackout."

"Blackout? What is this?" he shuddered.

"It's when you drink so much that you can't remember what happened."

"Oh, my God. Oh, my God!" He leaped up, put a hand to his forehead and paced back and forth. "Toy, what have I done? I think something probably did happen with Chance last night."

"Well, Jean-Luc, maybe so, but you can't beat yourself up about it, especially if you don't remember," I said, wondering if he really had the memory lapse he was claiming to have, or if he was pretending to save face.

"Yes, I can! I am not gay! Do you not get that?" he practically screamed.

"I know you're upset, but lower your voice a little."

"I am sorry. I have got to go. I need another cigarette and must talk to Chance. This cannot get out to anyone. Please pray I did nothing with him, Toy. Please." He kissed me on both cheeks then rushed to the door and bolted down the hallway.

I went to the still open door. "I will, but please try to calm down. And, text me later," I called after him..

I now felt it was a safe bet that Jean-Luc was 100% gay, although I thought he was in denial. Maybe this incident with Chance would yank him out of the closet. I sure hoped so.

I walked back to my bedroom and checked my phone for any new messages. Nothing from Nikola. Now I was pretty much convinced he'd used me. I was just another piece of ass to him, and the thought hurt like hell.

Chapter 7

Right after Jean-Luc left, I'd gone back to bed, restarted *Bridget Jones's Diary*, and cried myself to sleep. When I woke up the next morning, a little after 7:00 AM, I couldn't believe I'd only gotten out of bed twice since the previous day, and then only to get water and use the bathroom. I was still emotionally drained from the night before last, so maybe sleep was what I'd needed. I picked up my phone, which I'd set on silent about twenty-four hours ago. Thirteen messages and ten missed calls! My heart sank when none of the texts or calls were from Nikola. A little part of me had left my phone on silent in hopes of being surprised by an apologetic text or voicemail when I finally checked it.

Instead, I had Chance and Jean-Luc blowing me up, a voicemail from my mom, a 911 text from Ed (who knew what that could mean), and to my surprise, a voicemail from *Ben*, telling me he'd be in town this coming weekend and would like to see me.

I listened to the voicemail from Ben three times to make sure I'd heard it right. Since he'd moved to Massachusetts there hadn't been a peep from him. His voice stirred mixed emotions in me. I felt angry that he hadn't cared enough to inquire how I'd been for almost a year, but also curious to know how he was.

I gave it a little while to debate whether or not to text him. Then...

Me: *Hello stranger.*
Him: *Stranger?:)*
Me: *It's been almost a year...*
Him: *It could be 10 yrs and we wouldn't be strangers.*

I ignored his sentimental comment.

Me: *Why are you coming to Chi?*
Him: *Med Conference. I'll be staying at The Peninsula.*

I could almost hear his voice as I read his messages. It made me realize that I really missed him. We met a little over five years ago. I'd just broken up with a guy I'd been dating for about six months and it hadn't been easy. I'd really wanted to stay home that particular Saturday night, but my girlfriends, Ashley and Megan, dragged me to this dance club, Enclave, anyway. Who knew? I was actually having a great time. I stopped dancing with the girls long enough to get another drink at the bar, and there he was, standing amongst a few of his friends. We had brief eye contact and while I waited for my drink, he approached me.

"Why aren't you dancing?" he asked.

"Clearly because I'm getting a drink," I said, not bothering to look at him. I wasn't in the mood to deal with guys on the hunt that night.

He laughed. "Quite the little smartie-pants."

I turned around and smiled, "I sure am."

As a short silence ensued, he stared at me.

He was quite tall, had a medium build, and wavy, brown hair. He looked like your All-American guy. My immediate thought was cute, but not my type.

"You're cute."

"Excuse me?"

"I said, you're cute. Just making an observation," he replied, with a straight face.

"Nice observation," I shot back.

"I'm Ben."

"Nice to meet you, Ben." I grabbed my Ketel and pineapple and brushed past him.

"You do realize you are breaking every rule in the Midwest etiquette guidelines book I read before I moved here," he said, raising his voice above the music.

I turned around and laughed. "I bet you spent all day coming up with that line! It's a good one, though. At least one I haven't heard."

"No, it just comes naturally."

I smiled in spite of myself. *He does have pretty green eyes...*

"Okay, I suppose I overcompensate for being socially awkward by being charming and witty," he smirked.

I glanced at the dance floor where my friends were now grinding with three of the club's promoters. Let me define the typical male promoter for you: Unattractive, over thirty-five and can't get a girlfriend. Instead, he gets young girls to fawn all over him in exchange for free admission passes and free drinks. I wasn't one of those girls. Of course, that meant I had to buy my own drinks and wouldn't be out there dancing with my friends anymore that night.

"Charming and witty, huh? Where are you from?" I ventured, turning back to Ben and sipping my drink.

"Oh no, you have to tell me your name before I agree to go forward with the interrogation process." He acted serious but his eyes twinkled.

"My name is Toy."

"Toy. Interesting."

Hmm, no smartass comment about my name? All of a sudden, his stock was rising.

"Well, Toy, it looks like you've almost finished your drink. Shall I buy you another?" He lifted his hand to signal the bartender.

I glanced down at my drink. I'd barely touched it. Before I knew it, I had two drinks in my hands.

After chatting for over an hour at Enclave, we ended up saying goodbye to our respective friends, and went to Tempo Café, a few blocks away. We talked over blueberry pancakes for hours. He impressed me. Not only was he funny, he was intelligent and indeed witty.

He offered to walk me to my building. I said, "Sure." and when we got there, I took off my five-inch heels.

"You know," he said, "I didn't even want to go out tonight. The only reason I did was because it was my buddy's birthday."

I grinned in surprise. "I wasn't going out tonight either, but my friends are very persuasive when they want to be."

"Well, I guess it must have been kismet for us to meet," he shrugged. Without my shoes on he towered over me.

"Are you glad you came out?" I said, ignoring the obvious.

"Are you kidding? Absolutely. If I hadn't I wouldn't have had the best pancakes in town," he teased. Then, he took my face in his hands and very sweetly, kissed my forehead.

The sound of my phone vibrating interrupted my reverie. Ben had texted me:

Him: *Toy? You there?*

Should I tell him? Oh, why not.

Me: *Yeah... just thinking about the night we met :)*

Him: *Still one of the best nights of my life.*

Me: *Really?*

Him: *Really. What happened between us didn't erase all the good times.*

Me: That's just it! I don't know what happened between us.

Tears were spilling down my face. All the emotions I'd been trying not to feel for the past nine months had erupted.

> Him: *I know you don't owe me anything, but I'd like to see you when I'm in town.*
> Me: *I'm just scared.*
> Him: *Of what? Me? Come on, Toy. When you're offered a moment to be with someone you have a good time with, to get your mind off the everyday bullshit, you should take advantage, because it rarely happens.*
> Me: *I don't know. You appear out of nowhere and expect me to just drop everything for you. It's kind of shitty.*
> Him: *I didn't think you'd meet me without givin' me a fight, LOL. MEET ME! If only to slap me and tell me how horrible I am. Meet me! ;)*
> Me: *Okay text warrior, you win THIS battle :) Drinks at The Bar at the Peninsula this Friday? 9 PM?*
> Him: *Perfecto!*
> Me: *See you then. Have to get ready for work...and don't be surprised if I take you up on your offer when I see you ;)*
> Him: *He-he, deal!*

I put down the phone and stared into space. I couldn't understand how Ben could just pop out of nowhere and act like he hadn't disappeared from my life for almost a year. Sure, him breaking up with me and then begging me back had become the norm the last two years we were together. Still, those "breaks" never lasted more than a couple of weeks at a time. I hoped I'd find out what had been going through his head these past nine months on Friday. But, for now, the only head I needed to figure out was my own. I still had my huge event coming up at work. No one was worth messing up this opportunity to advance my career. *No one.*

While walking to work, I called Jean-Luc only to get his voicemail. Next, I called Chance.

"Thank God! I was about to call the police!" he shouted into the phone.

I laughed. "I'm sorry. Had my phone on silent. I didn't think I'd sleep as long as I did."

"Well you've certainly missed out on plenty of work drama."

"When is there *not* work drama?" I said with such sarcasm, if he'd listened close enough, he could've heard my eyes roll. "Hey, more importantly, did we make our goal yesterday? And is everyone on track with pre-sell and appointments?"

"Um, yeah, I think. I know I am. You'll have to ask Fiona. She was riding all of our asses about it. Anyway, Tatyana was sent home yesterday by Sharee. Apparently, when I was on my lunch break, the wife of the guy she's having an affair with came in again."

"Seriously?"

"Yep, and this time with her two small children!"

"Oh, my God."

"I heard she made quite the scene and Tatyana was, well, Tatyana."

"Those poor little kids. Tatyana has no shame when it comes to gold-digging."

"Ed said the children started crying and Sharee had to intervene."

"Damn, will we ever have just one week where there isn't some kind of incident at the counter?" I said, shaking my head.

At least Fiona had done something right. I'm sure the ulterior motive was to get me promoted so she could manage my counter, but still, I was glad someone was focused on work and not all the petty bullshit.

"Well..."

"What, Chance? Don't tell me there's more!"

"It's nothing serious. I'm just really upset about Jean-Luc. He told me he didn't remember what happened. I think that's total bullshit, but when I tried to tell him he wouldn't even listen."

I was trying to be sympathetic, I really was. It just wasn't working. I had Nikola and Ben on my mind, not to mention the stress of the event coming up while my counter was in total disarray. I didn't want to hear any more.

"Babe, why don't we have lunch today and talk about it? I'm running behind and I've got to open this morning."

"Fine," he said, "but lunch! Don't back out and say you're too busy."

"Okay. See you soon," I said, then tossed the phone in my Prada bag. I was dreading the talk with Sharee that I knew was coming.

I was only about a block away from work when tiny snowflakes started to fall.

"The second snow. Definitely, not as good as the first," I whispered to myself and swallowed the oh-so-familiar lump that had just formed in my throat.

That morning, Fiona and I opened the counter. Usually, I dreaded the awkward silence between us, but today I welcomed it. I needed quiet. I needed to think, which was hard to do when I was immersed in chaos every second of the day. I considered letting her know that Ben and I were having drinks Friday just to screw with her a little, but why create unnecessary problems? I had enough going on.

Yvonne walked in a little before eleven, hungover as usual. She last night's makeup on and her hair was a mess.

"What's going on, Captain?" she said, smiling with a trace of lipstick on her teeth.

"Not much," I sighed.

"Well, I was glad you weren't here yesterday to experience this goddamn shit storm, it was outta fuckin' control."

I put a finger to my lips, although I couldn't quite wipe the smile off my face. Thank goodness for Yvonne. I needed some comic relief.

"Oops, sorry," she whispered.

"Toy, can I see you in my office in ten minutes?"

I twisted my head to see Sharee standing a few feet behind me. She didn't look too happy.

"Sure," I said in the peppiest voice I could muster. Her expression and tone clued me in: this wasn't going to be just a fun conversation.

After Sharee left, Tatyana, looking as if nothing were out of the ordinary, walked straight past me without any acknowledgment.

"Well, hello to you too, Tatyana." I said, a little louder than necessary. She turned around and I closed the distance between us. "I heard your little misconduct drew quite a few spectators yesterday. Now, I have to go clean up the mess with Sharee."

"I cannot be blamed for crazy bitch exploding at the counter," she said, her words coated by her thick, Slavic accent.

"You're right. You can't control other people's actions. But this entire mess is the result of *your* actions."

Her eyes went up and she let out a heavy sigh. "Toy, I had to listen to this from Sharee for over one hour yesterday, and then I am sent home. I missed two appointments I had booked, which would have each been over $1200 in pre-sale. Can I please try to work and get through today without more problems?"

I'd never heard her sound so exhausted. She was clearly upset. Maybe she wasn't as cold-hearted as I'd thought? I'd let the subject rest, at least until after I talked with Sharee. Besides, I felt like a hypocrite in light of the Nikola situation.

Chapter 8

I walked into Sharee's office hoping this wouldn't take too long. I just wanted to come to work, do my clients' makeup, sell, and go home. Instead, I felt like I was a character in an unending soap opera.

"Hi, Toy. Have a seat," said Sharee, turning her chair to face me. "I'm sure you've already been filled in on yesterday's *event*. Tell me, how should we proceed to handle this?"

Oh, I hated it when she started a conversation off with a question. This meant she was coaching me instead of telling me how to handle it. Usually, I was up for the challenge, but today, I just wanted to be told what to do.

"Well, I spoke with Tatyana briefly a few minutes ago. She did seem genuinely upset, which is unusual for her. She normally blows things off like they're no big deal. I'm in a tough place. On the one hand, I think she should be written up and told to get this situation under control no matter what she has to do, or there will be more serious consequences. On the other, she's one of the strongest people on my team, and I don't need her losing morale before the biggest event this counter has ever held. I'm torn, Sharee."

She looked at me for a minute without saying anything. Then, "What's going on with you, Toy? Is it Debbie? Something's a little off with you."

I was taken aback by the question. I thought we were talking about Tatyana. I guess she'd been observing me from afar.

"It isn't Debbie. I don't know what it is exactly. It feels like a combination of everything." Everything was mainly Nikola and Ben, but I wasn't about to tell her that.

"*Everything* being?" she prompted.

"Personal things combined with what seems like everyone at my counter losing their minds, more than usual."

"Yeah, well, if I didn't think you could handle your position I wouldn't have you in this role. I hired you because you're strong and determined."

I let my shoulders slump. "I don't feel so strong right now."

"Well you are. This is what I need you to do: Everything in your personal life needs to be just that, personal. Leave it at the door when you come to work. I know I make it sound easy, but that's what it takes to be in a leadership role." She hesitated briefly, as if considering whether or not to say something. "Did you know I've been separated from my husband for the past two months and that we just reconciled?"

Wow, I thought, *Sharee never gives out personal information.* "No, I had no idea. I'm so sorry."

"Thank you, but I didn't tell you to make you feel bad for me. I told you because even though I've been on an emotional roller coaster all this time, I never let it show. I couldn't because I set the example here."

I had to hand it to her. She was a pro. "You're right. I'm sorry."

"Being a good manager doesn't mean you have to be perfect. God knows I'm not. It's about knowing and overcoming your weaknesses before anyone else can see them."

"So, what about Tatyana?"

"What about her?" Sharee said, casually. "You're her manager and I know you'll make the right decision."

Now I get it. She hadn't called me back to talk about Tatyana. She'd wanted to talk about me. If Sharee could see something was bothering me, it was only a matter of time before the team would see it. She was right. I needed to nip this in the bud before it really started to affect my work.

"Now, go to your counter and be the Toy I know and love," she said, and turned back to her computer.

"Thanks, Sharee. You really made me feel better," I said, grateful I had such a good boss.

"Anytime, Toy. My door is always open to you."

On my way back to the counter, I decided to call an emergency meeting with the whole team after the store closed tonight. I absolutely hated having unplanned meetings but it was time my team got their shit together. Everyone was at work except for Ed, Biljana, and Tommy. I had Chance call and tell them it was mandatory that they in now. We were going to lay all the bullshit on the table, and then get back to business and whip this counter back to functioning the way it should.

The meeting had gone as planned. I let everyone know my expectations. They needed to take their jobs more seriously and with the upcoming event, kick up the energy several notches. Any unprofessional behavior and I'd have no choice but to write the offender up, and take further disciplinary action, if necessary.

Right before the meeting ended, I made one last announcement. "Here at work, I'm not your buddy. I'm your boss. So, if I seem a little less friendly, don't take it personally. I'm just doing my job."

I caught a glimpse of Biljana. *This works out perfectly,* I congratulated myself. *Now I don't have to play nice-nice with Biljana. I can keep my distance.*

After the meeting was over, everyone but Chance and I had left the room.

He approached me, biting his lower lip. "I have a huge favor to ask you."

I blinked. "That scares me. How huge?"

"Would you go to Tatyana's birthday party with me on Saturday night?"

Now I cringed. Chance knew I wasn't Tatyana's biggest fan and I didn't like mingling with my associates when it involved drinking.

"Please? Everyone is going. She even convinced Jean-Luc to come. I *cannot* go by myself!"

What a diva. God help Chance if he actually had to walk into a party without an entourage, or at minimum, a date.

"Isn't there someone else who could go with you?" I asked, knowing I wasn't Chance's only friend.

"Duh, but I need someone hot to walk in with. The only other girlfriend I'd bring is Aimee, and she's going to be out of town. I refuse to bring another guy, friend or not," he said, crossing his arms and poking out his chest.

I was flattered he considered me 'hot enough' to be seen with him, but I couldn't help but think how superficial he was being. *Hmm. If Tatyana invited everyone, that means Biljana will be there. I wonder if Nikola will be with her?* "Fine, but won't Tatyana be mad that you're bringing her boss?"

"Girl, she'll be wasted by nine o'clock. We won't even get there until eleven."

He had a point. I'd make sure I looked hot as hell that night, and then not even acknowledge Nikola's presence, that is, if he was there.

"Okay, I'll go." I heaved a heavy sigh, pretending I was being inconvenienced.

"Thank you, boo! Now I won't be pissed at you for ditching out on lunch with me today," he said, throwing his arms around me.

My hand went to my forehead. "Oh damn, I totally forgot. I'm so sorry."

"No problem, love."

I really, really hope Nikola is at this party. I'd love to see the look on that asshole's face when I walk past him, totally cool and unbothered.

I rounded the corner of the conference room and saw Biljana arguing on the phone with someone, but I couldn't make out what was being said because she was speaking in her native language. Still, I didn't have to know Macedonian to see she was fuming.

When she hung up the phone, I approached her. "Everything okay?"

"I'm fine," she hissed and walked off.

Wow. Where is the sweet young girl I hired? Then, I wondered, *Does she know something about Nikola and me?*

On the walk home, Nikola popped into my head as he'd been doing since I met him. *That son of a bitch!* Just the thought of him made me burn with desire, while at the same time, made my heart feel like it was breaking in two. It wasn't only the sexual chemistry we had. It was more. At least, silly me, I'd thought it was more.

When I was with him, I felt like nothing else in the world mattered. I wondered how it was even possible to have these feelings for someone so fast. I tried to convince myself that it was simply a major case of lust, but I wasn't that naive. In my teens and early twenties, I'd experienced lust with other men and this indescribable something, intense as it was, didn't qualify.

Then it hit me — more like smacked me in the face! What in God's name was I doing? Seeing Nikola at Tatyana's birthday party was *not* a good idea. What if I go to pieces in front of my team? My palms were sweating and my heart was beating out of my chest. I wished I could tell Chance I wanted out of our date, but I'd already ditched him for lunch! I couldn't bail on him twice in a row. But I couldn't imagine facing Nikola, either. *What do I do?*

Add to that, hearing from Ben out of the blue, an aggravating addition to my new chaotic mind frame. I felt like I was under a dark cloud that threatened to rain insanity. It was almost as if fate showed up to taunt me with him.

I'd always perceived a type of barrier around him. He just couldn't seem to fully open up to me. I wondered if he ever could. I knew love wasn't simple. I learned that from my parents. In spite of their obvious love for one another, their twenty-year marriage imploded from lack of communication, from keeping little secrets to telling half-truths. I worried that a life with Ben would be the same.

He'd always been very career-oriented and had made it clear to me, at the beginning of our relationship, that his "calling" always had to come first, or he'd never be happy with himself. He'd gone on to say that if people weren't happy with themselves, then they could never be happy in a relationship. I couldn't argue with that, but I didn't believe that a person should be defined by their career alone.

He was brilliant. It was actually one of the things that attracted me to him most. There was rarely a topic that he couldn't add something meaningful to. I always respected his drive and ambition, however it was also his Achilles heel.

I hadn't noticed it until his first year of practice. He was questioning everything about himself. He was confused as to whether or not he'd chosen the right path. So many of the friends he'd gone to school with as an undergrad had gone into business and finance without the oppressive, giant-size student loans that he'd amassed over the years, and were already making six figures. He was no longer the funny, idealistic guy I knew. He'd become hardened. Over time, his intellect also made him a bit of a know-it-all. He always had to one-up you in any conversation.

I'd tried to tell him that it was natural to have unrealistic expectations when you're young, and then realize nothing is as easy as it seemed. He hadn't wanted to hear it. Instead, he would argue with me or become depressed and pull away.

We had been living in separate apartments on the Gold Coast. We'd planned on moving into our own place as soon as he'd secured a position at the hospital. When my rental contract was up, instead of going ahead with our plans, he asked me to give him a little more time. I extended my lease to accommodate him.

One night after dinner at my place, I asked him if he wanted to set up property viewings with our realtor. We'd been discussing buying a townhome in Lincoln Park.

"I thought I told you I need more time." He glared at me.

After a couple seconds, I was able to force my voice past the knot that had formed in my throat. "Do you remember when you told me a man's actions speak louder than his words?"

He'd looked down and swirled the red wine in his glass.

"Well, your actions are very loud lately."

He rose from his chair and crossed the room.

"Ben, what is it?"

"I accepted a job in Boston," he said, not exactly looking me in the eye.

"Well, that's wonderful news!" I changed my tone to upbeat. "Boston's a great city! One of the girls I went to college with works out there. I bet Cesonne even has some management positions available in their Boston stores, so all I'd have to do is transfer."

"Toy..."

"In fact, I've been thinking about how nice it would be to get away from Chicago. A change would be just the —"

"Toy! I was talking about just me. *I'm* moving to Boston."

Shock, embarrassment and hurt were only a few of the feelings that exploded inside me. I was speechless.

After a silence so thick I thought I'd asphyxiate, he finally said, "I've been trying to tell you for weeks."

Anger overcame all the other emotions. I wondered if he'd tricked me into extending my lease so he could make a clean escape.

"For weeks? What do you mean, *weeks*?" My voice rose in spite of myself. "Just how many weeks, Ben? How long have you known? How long were you going to let me go on believing we were going to be together?"

He stared into his glass.

"I don't understand. How can you say you love me and care about me, and then do this? All this time you've been feeding me excuse after excuse, when what you were really doing was plotting your exit strategy!"

He finally looked up and met my eyes. "No, Toy. I do love you. It's me. I just don't know who I am anymore. I'm so disappointed in myself."

I softened a little and took a step toward him. "You're a young, talented *doctor* with the world at your feet."

He turned his back to me, retreating as usual.

"Nothing you do will ever satisfy you. Nothing! You'll always be trying to find yourself. That's nothing but a smoke screen for your incredible selfishness. It's *all* about you, isn't it?"

"You know, you're right," he agreed, bitterly. "I know I'm selfish, but if more people were selfish and didn't act simply on emotion, they might not only end up with the right person, they might be more fulfilled in general."

The 'right person' part stoked my anger to the boiling point. I continued to rant and rave in a voice that sounded strangely disembodied, as if it belonged to somebody else. I spewed every odious word I could think of until the only one left was, "Why?"

He shook his head and sighed. "Take care," he said, as if I was just some girl he'd had a dinner or two with. He shrugged his coat over his shoulders and walked out. The closing of the door was like a period; cold, dark and final. I stared at it for a minute, hoping he'd come running back and tell me it was all a mistake and he couldn't live without me. But of course, he didn't.

Numb, I walked down the hall that led to my bedroom, as a hollow pain gripped my chest. For a second, I thought I'd throw up. I flopped down on the bed and cried until my head was pounding.

Weeks had gone by and I hadn't heard anything from him. Finally, after a month of no contact I knew this time was different than the many times before. I promised myself I'd never let him back in, yet here I was, splaying myself wide open. I wished I didn't have to work the next day. In fact, I think I'd be fine staying in bed the next week with a box of Oreos and my DVR.

The next night at work was excruciating. The aisles were so dead that we could've done somersaults down them and no one would have noticed, and there was still another hour left until closing.

"Hey, Chance, Yvonne, Tommy," I called. "I think I'm going to cut you guys loose. It's really slow tonight." *Besides, I need some peace and quiet.*

"Thank God, I'm going crazy standing here," said Chance. "But, I wish I would've known earlier. I cancelled on two different guys who wanted to take me out to dinner."

"Well, you can always stay. I wouldn't want you to have cancelled on them in vain."

"No, I'm sure I'll have other offers before the night is over," he said, oblivious to my sarcasm.

"Hey, Toy. Can you sign out our gratis?" asked Tommy, handing me a form.

Gratis was free, full-size product, given to us in exchange for our commitment to sell, and could easily be mistaken for products we sold since there was practically no difference between it and live merchandise. The only thing that set the two apart was a small sticker labeled "No Retail Value" or "Not For Resale". This was the reason all counter managers had to review and "sign out" gratis their associates were taking out of the store.

The purpose of the freebies was to allow us to experience the products so that we could better promote them. *Whatever.* It was plain and simple bribery, but I was not about to complain. How else could I have accumulated over twenty thousand dollars in free perfume, makeup and skincare over the past five years, if it weren't for gratis?

I took the form from Tommy, grabbed a pen from the counter and started to sign off when I noticed it wasn't completed. In fact, it didn't list a single item he had in his bag. "Wait. Why is this form blank?"

Yvonne and Chance stood behind him, suddenly looking a little self-conscious, each with a form of their own in their hands.

Tommy shrugged. "You signed the last two sheets without having us fill them out. I figured it'd save you some time."

I'd been so distracted with everything lately, that I hadn't even realized I'd been signing blank forms. I took them from Chance and Yvonne, and sure enough, they were blank, too. This meant, the last couple weeks, my entire team had been taking whatever they wanted and I was scribbling my name on it! I squeezed my eyes shut, struggling to keep it together in front of them. *Okay, breathe, Toy. This may not be such a big deal after all.*

"Alright," I said. "This was my mistake. Going forward, no one takes anything out of the store until I've seen a *completed form* and I've compared the products to what you've listed. Got it?"

They bobbed their heads like children.

"I'm going to Sharee's office to pull our daily numbers and see how far we are from our goal. While I'm gone, you three fill out the forms so I can sign them when I get back," I instructed. "I'll have to talk to the rest of the team about this tomorrow."

"Will do, Captain," chirped Yvonne, but I could tell she was being overly enthusiastic.

I turned to head toward the office and noticed Chance give her the stink eye. *What was that all about?*

I returned to the counter ten minutes later to see the three of them still filling out their forms. "Did it get busy or something?"

"No," said Chance, not bothering to look up from the paper in front of him. Tommy and Yvonne appeared just as focused.

I walked around the counter, glanced over Chance's shoulder and nearly fell over.

"Chance, give me that," I said, snatching his form off the counter.

"Wait!" he whined. "I'm not finished!"

I stared at the sheet in disbelief. "You've written down twenty-two items and you're not finished?"

"No, I'm not. I've got five more pieces I need to log."

"Let me see that." I grabbed the clear plastic bag that was about to burst from the weight of its contents.

I pulled out each piece, methodically placing them one by one on the counter. Tommy and Yvonne stopped filling out their forms and watched.

"Two creams, two serums, and two eye creams? Really Chance?" I looked at him, eyes ablaze.

Cesonne's skincare collection was our most luxurious product group. It was also very expensive, which limited the number of testers we received. The least expensive item in the collection was the eye cream with a price tag of $1450.

By the time I finished emptying his bag, the counter was smothered in products. Four face masks, two eye masks, three face washes, two toners, and every single color of our newest lip plumper.

"This is a joke, right? Tell me this is some kind of joke, Chance," I said, my voice beginning to shake.

"What's the biggie?" he said, arms folded across his chest. "I can't push the products if I don't believe in them. That's the reason we get gratis, right? To try them."

"What's the *biggie*? The *biggie* is you've got close to $10,000 in product here, not to mention the fact that most of these are our last testers! How are we supposed to sell our products if we have nothing to demonstrate with? What are you thinking?" I demanded.

"I think you're *seriously* overreacting," he said, smacking his chewing gum.

"Watch it, Chance. In case you didn't notice, I'm not very happy right now. And, spit out the gum!" I blasted.

"What's up with you?" he huffed.

"I can't believe you took advantage of me like this. I forget to review gratis sheets for two weeks and suddenly you think it's okay to run away with the store? You've never taken this much before. Never!"

"Well, I figured if you weren't reviewing it, it didn't matter. I thought taking doubles was a good idea, just in case you decided to get strict or something," he looked at me pointedly, "which you *obviously* did!"

"Put it back. Put it *all* back!" I shrieked, attracting the neighboring counter's attention.

"Toy, nooo," he cried, gathering a few of the most expensive products into his arms and hugging them to his chest.

"Chance, you're on thin ice! Don't push me any further. You don't need a $2000 jar of cream, let alone two of them. This is just ridiculous. Put it all back, now! I'm going to have to make some guidelines before I let any of you take any more gratis." I glanced at the other two. "I'm scared to even think about what you two have taken the past couple weeks. This could put my job on the line."

Chance stomped his foot and turned on the tears. "What am I supposed to do? I'm halfway through all of my skincare and I don't have any of this season's new lip plumpers!" he moaned.

This time his tears weren't going to work.

"Get a stool and get over it," I said.

When the waterworks suddenly stopped, I knew I'd hit a nerve.

He wiped away a tear with a finger and widened his eyes. "Oh no, you didn't just say that."

"Oh, yes I did," I said, tossing every piece of gratis on the counter back into a bag.

Chance was very short. Now that we were adults he loved being petite, but in high school that wasn't the case. He'd detested his stature. His modeling aspirations were dashed because of it. Agency after agency had turned him down.

One day, during our senior year, Chance had been throwing one of his typical tantrums because I wouldn't let him "borrow" my homework. I'd been working on it for weeks. After he'd sailed off on me for not being a good friend, he finally asked me, "What am I supposed to do?" I told him to get a stool and get over it, clearly referring to his height. He didn't speak to me for three days, which was a record for us.

"You're cruel," he said through a fresh flood of tears.

"No, you were dishonest. I think it's time for you to go home for the night. We'll talk about this when I'm not so angry."

He plucked a tissue from a box. "Fine, I'll leave," he said, dabbing at his eyes. With great flourish, he gathered his personal items, walked away from the counter, and headed in the opposite direction of the employee exit toward the men's shoe department. *Good! A new pair of Louboutins might help him recover from his breakdown.*

What a little brat!

I pried my thoughts away from Chance and back to Tommy and Yvonne.

"Okay Tommy, let me see what you've got." I patted the counter.

He handed me his form. A rage rose so fast I thought my hair would catch fire. I crushed the sheet into a ball and tossed it into the garbage can. I gave Tommy a hard squint, then tore into his bag.

"Toy, I saw what happened with Chance, but this is different," he pleaded, before I could finish counting the ten bottles of $215 fragrance he was trying to have me sign out!

"I don't want to hear it, Tommy."

I slowly turned my attention to Yvonne, who met my glare with wide-eyed innocence. I knew that if both Chance and Tommy were doing this, there was no way Yvonne wasn't just as guilty.

"Yvonne," I smiled with eyes so full of fury she flinched. "Mind showing me your list, too?"

"Sure, Captain, but I think you'll be happy to see how frugal I was with my gratis," she beamed.

I breathed a sigh of relief. Maybe Yvonne had a little integrity after all.

My optimism was premature. I looked at her gratis sheet and gripped the counter to steady myself. Frugal? Had she really just said *frugal*?

"What the hell is wrong with you guys?" I yelled. "First, Chance thinks he can just clean out the entire stockroom, and then this?"

"I don't think mine is so bad," Yvonne shrugged. "It's only two pieces."

Yes, she only had two items all right, but they happened to be two serums that cost $1700 a bottle!

"Well, here's a clue, Yvonne. The pieces you chose are limited edition sizes. That means we'll never get them again." I enunciated, slowly: "And, you took *two*!"

A few silent seconds ticked by. While I fumed, Tommy walked to the other end of the counter with Yvonne in tow, and started straightening products.

"Well, Tommy. No more selling fragrances at Y Bar. Guess you're fucked," Yvonne said in a tone she thought was under her breath.

Tommy's head snapped in my direction. Our eyes locked. I eased up behind Yvonne.

"That was some fast and easy cash, too," she said, shaking her head.

"What's that, Yvonne?" I snapped.

Startled, she stammered, "Oh, n-nothing, Cap'!"

I glared at him. "Tommy, what's Yvonne talking about?"

"What do you mean?" he asked all innocent-like.

After a stare down with Tommy, I turned back to Yvonne. "What did you just say to Tommy? Something about 'selling fragrances at a club'?"

She broke down. "He needed the money, man!"

Yvonne wasn't good under pressure. In fact, she folded like a paper lantern.

"Drop it, Yvonne. You've started enough shit," growled Tommy.

"You ungrateful fucker!" she fired back. "I'm done covering for your penny-pinching ass!"

"Hey!" I cried, but they ignored me.

Tommy was furious. I'd never seen him this angry, not even with Jean-Luc. "I told you to drop it, but since you can't keep your fat mouth shut, maybe I should let Toy in on *your* little side gig?"

"I haven't done one thing wrong," said Yvonne, smugly.

"Well, if you consider returning gratis at other retailers for cash, 'nothing wrong', then you're a bigger idiot than I thought you were."

Yvonne stood there in silence. For once, she had nothing to say.

I stepped between the two of them.

"How about we recap for a moment? Sound good?" Not waiting for an answer, I continued, "Good! So, Tommy's been selling bottles of fragrances at Y Bar, and Yvonne, you've been exchanging gratis for cash. Tommy, I'm scared to even ask how much you're charging your *clientele*." Now, with a look, I demanded an answer.

Tommy remained quiet.

"Twenty bucks," blurted Yvonne.

"Yvonne!" cried Tommy.

"What?" she said, blinking her baby browns.

"Twenty dollars, Tommy? Nice. You're selling our fragrances for twenty dollars at a nightclub. *Classy*. And you, Yvonne. You've been going to our competitors returning things and getting cash back, is that right?"

She thought for a moment. Then, "Yeah, I think you got it right. Don't you think so, Tommy?"

Tommy squeezed his eyes shut.

"Is it just the two of you that's been pulling this or are there others involved?" My eyes shifted from Tommy, and then to Yvonne.

"Just us... that I know of," said Tommy, a little too casually.

I didn't believe him. Tommy wouldn't rat on anyone, and I knew that for a fact. Yvonne didn't *intentionally* tell on people, it just always worked out that way.

"Yvonne?" I demanded.

"What?" she said, her head already in the clouds somewhere.

"Focus, Yvonne. Is anyone else on the team doing this?"

"I doubt it. Chance is a product whore. He'd never get rid of anything. Tatyana's men buy her anything she wants. Um..." She hesitated a moment to think. "Jean-Luc's way too righteous. He'd never do anything he thought might be wrong. And I really don't talk to anyone else. So, no. I'm pretty sure it's just me and Tommy."

I knew if Tommy could've wrung Yvonne's neck at that moment, he would have.

"That's wonderful. I'm so glad the only enterprising geniuses are the two of you," I said, sarcastically. Even Yvonne caught it this time. "You both wait right here. I'm taking these products down to the basement stockroom." Entrance to this area required a passcode which lower-level employees didn't have.

I didn't know what to think about any of this. I should already have been on the phone with security, but I couldn't bring myself to do it. Not only did I care about Yvonne and Tommy, I knew I'd be in trouble, too. If I hadn't been so distracted, maybe none of this would've happened. Still, I'd been taken advantage of by my team and that really hurt.

A few minutes later, as I neared the counter, I could hear Tommy and Yvonne going back and forth.

"I'm sorry, man," whined Yvonne. "I thought Toy was cool."

"Toy *is* cool, Yvonne, but a boss can only be so cool. Now she's in a hot spot and it's all because of us. She could get in big trouble, you know."

"I don't know why I blurt things out, Tommy-boy, I just do. I'm sorry. I wasn't trying to be a narc, I just blow under pressure."

"Well, there's nothing we can do about it now. We're just fucked," he said, and chomped down on his thumbnail.

"I know. This is terrible. How am I going to be able to afford the lifestyle I've become accustomed to?" Yvonne said, like she'd just been dumped by a Rockefeller.

Tommy stopped his nail-biting and stared at her for a moment, then folded his arms on the counter and dropped his head on them.

I walked up to the register and checked the time on it.

"Toy, we're sorry. We really are," Yvonne whimpered. "Can we still leave early?"

Tommy looked up at Yvonne, amazed.

"You two have put me in a horrible position. What you guys did was not only wrong, it was unethical. But, since you had my signature, I'm guilty, too. I've decided not to go to security, but I won't forget this. First of all, nothing that you two told me tonight can ever be repeated —" I shot an icy stare at Yvonne, "*ever*. Second, you two will not take a single piece of gratis ever again."

"That's more than fair, Toy. I'm really sorry. I am," said Tommy, doing his best to look me in the eyes.

"Not even one piece, ever again?" Yvonne gasped.

"Would you prefer to be fired and possibly charged with theft?" I asked, watching her face go pale.

"No, I guess I'll take the deal."

She answered like she'd just made a plea bargain! Her demeanor almost made me lose my dignity.

Instead, I nodded, "Good choice. Now, why don't you two go ahead and leave? I'll close the registers and clean up. I could definitely use some quiet time after this."

"Okay, thanks again, Toy," Tommy said meekly, before walking away from the counter.

Yvonne, on the other hand, was as carefree as ever. "Yeah, thanks, Captain. See ya tomorrow."

All I could do was pray I'd made the right decision.

Chapter 9

The rest of the workweek went by so peacefully it almost scared me. I'd been super paranoid since discovering Tommy and Yvonne's charade, but so far security hadn't approached me. There was the usual bickering at the counter, but nothing I couldn't tolerate. There had been no major issues, so far. We were right on track for our goal with $45,000 in pre-sale and 75 appointments. The team had really jumped on board. When I left work that Friday evening all I had to focus on was looking sensational for my date with Ben. For once I could leave work at work.

The minute I walked in my front door I turned on some music, poured myself a nice glass of Chardonnay, and hopped in the shower. I was nervous. I couldn't believe in less than three hours I'd be looking into the eyes of the man I'd once thought I'd spend the rest of my life with.

Earlier in the week, I'd bought two dresses; one for Friday night and another for Saturday night. One was a black lace, plunge-neck, puffball Roberto Cavalli dress accessorized with my new, gold, lace-up Jimmy Choo heels and Ainsley cuff bracelet. The other was a red, bodycon Yves Saint Laurent dress with a criss-cross back and black peep-toe Louboutin boots. I tried on each outfit. They were both incredibly beautiful, but the Yves Saint Laurent was much sexier. The Roberto Cavalli dress was probably the better choice for seeing Ben after all this time.

It was 8:45 PM when I glanced into my full-length mirror. I curled my hair and let it fall in loose waves down my back. I smoked up my eyes with black liner and carefully applied a sheer coat of nude lipstick. I slipped out of my robe and into a sexy lace bra and panty set by Chantelle. It wasn't until I had the dress on did I realize how flattering it actually was. A girl can never really know how beautiful a dress is until she tries it on with her hair and makeup done. The fitting room never does a dress justice, or any outfit for that matter.

In spite of this, very few women shop the way I do. I can't endure dressing room torture. I walk into a boutique and pull items in my sizes off the rack that I think will look great. Then, I bypass the dressing room, go directly to the counter, and put them on my credit card. In the comfort and less-harsh lighting of my own home, I try on the clothes. Anything I don't like, I return with the tags still on, and the credit goes right back on my card. However, since I'm in sales myself, I always make sure to tell the sales associate my intentions from the get-go. I don't want to make them feel put-out.

I put on my shoes and cuff, which completed the look to perfection, just as I'd expected. I was still nervous about seeing Ben, but the wine was helping. I grabbed my coat and clutch, chugged what was left of the wine, and headed to the lobby. Once there, I asked the doorman to grab a taxi for me. The Peninsula wasn't far, but in this weather and these heels, I wasn't going to attempt to walk.

The doorman closed the door of the taxi behind me, and my heart started to race. I couldn't believe I was this nervous.

I walked into the hotel and took the elevator up to the floor where the bar was located. It was a busy Friday night, but even in this crowd I couldn't miss him. He looked good, *really* good. Age actually suited him. When I met Ben he'd appeared almost boyish but now he looked full on like a man. He hadn't seen me yet, so I had time to take him in as I walked up. He had on a crisp, baby blue button-up, with Balmain jeans, his favorite denim, Ferragamo dress shoes, and a Cartier watch I'd never seen before. I approached him, he smiled and stood up to greet me with a kiss on the cheek.

"Toy, you're breathtaking." His eyes lingered as if they were seeing me for the first time. "I called to tell you I'd walk you up, but you didn't answer."

"Oops, my phone is still on silent from work. It's fine. I'm a big girl. I can walk myself to the elevator," I laughed, trying to appear nonchalant even though my heart was beating out of my chest.

We were still standing awkwardly when he finally said, "Oh! Please, sit down." He gestured toward the couch.

I sat down and couldn't help but feel sad. We were acting like strangers. It was becoming uncomfortable now.

"I ordered you a Ketel and pineapple, I hope that's still your drink," he said, barely meeting my eyes.

"Yes, it is. Thank you." I was grateful the waitress walked up with our order right that minute. I really needed this drink.

"I knew we'd discussed wine, but I was thinking perhaps we needed something stronger since this is the first time we've seen each other in so long."

"Good call," I replied, and took a sip of my drink. I didn't know if I should be happy or completely pissed off. There had been so many nights I'd just wanted to talk to him about my day, ask him his opinion on something, and he'd denied me even that little bit of comfort.

"You're not yourself tonight," he noted.

"Not to be rude, but how should I be acting? Your popping back into my life out of nowhere is a little random, don't you think?"

"It is," he agreed. "Toy, I'm sorry I left like I did. I know it must have hurt. I'm so sorry for everything," he said, his eyes fixed on his scotch.

I didn't know what to say. Those old resentments I thought I'd buried were bubbling to the surface. I stayed quiet for fear I'd either cry or walk out of the bar.

"Do you know how beautiful you are?" He moved closer to me. "You've never tried to be one of those girls who strive to be what society says is beautiful. You just... are. I've always loved that about you. I've always loved you." He leaned in and whispered, "I still do."

I turned away. "Then why did you leave me?"

"I was honest with you when I left. I was dealing with terrible depression. I felt like a failure. I was having family issues I didn't want to stress you out with. I could go on and on giving you reasons why I left. Wouldn't you rather know why I came back?"

I spun back around, "Why Ben? Why did you decide to come back into my life just as I was starting to put the pieces back together?"

"Because I realized something that had never crossed my mind before."

"Which is?"

"You're my best friend, Toy. It took me losing you to realize how much you meant to me. I miss your laugh. I miss how you rub your feet together before you fall asleep. I miss watching your face when I'd get you worked up about something," he grinned, tentatively. "I miss *you*."

A tear slid down my cheek. "Not one call in almost a year, Ben. Not one."

"Please don't cry," He reached out a hand to wipe away the tear. "I didn't contact you at first because I was trying to believe I'd made the right decision. In my heart, I knew it wasn't true. Then, I did what I do with anything that complicates my life. I pretended you didn't exist. I tried so hard to forget you but somehow, you'd always pop into my head. I'd read a book and think, 'She'd love this.' Or I'd watch a movie and find myself thinking the same thing. Certain smells, foods I knew you loved, songs I would hear... all reminded me of you. There were so many nights I would've given anything to see you, even in that ugly T-shirt you always wore to bed," he laughed.

I smiled. He was referring to a T-shirt that I'd had since I was in the high school. It was huge, comfortable and hideous. I loved to sleep in it, but only when I was alone. One late night, Ben had surprised me. He stopped by with

Chinese food and I was wearing it. He said it was the ugliest shirt he'd ever seen. He laughed until he cried. After that, every now and then, I'd wear it when he'd stay over, just to mess with him.

I began to realize that I missed having someone who knew the small details about me. I missed the familiarity between us.

"I miss *us*, Toy," he said like a mind reader.

"I do too, but I don't know if I'm ready to trust that you won't break my heart again. Besides, you live in Boston now. Where does that leave us?"

"Bottom line is this. I miss you. You miss me. We live far apart but everything in life is temporary. We already have the most important part of any lasting relationship, which is friendship. I don't think we should waste any more time not being a part of each other's life."

"I don't even know what you're suggesting. You're confusing me. When we first met you said you didn't believe in long-distance relationships." I shook my head and sighed. "Look, why don't we just catch up tonight as old friends? You're here until Monday so that gives us time to talk about more serious things somewhere else, not here in the middle of a bar."

"Yes, ma'am," he grinned, and waved for the waitress to come over to our table. "Can we get another round and two lemon drops made with Ketel One?"

"Sure, I'll be right back with those for you, Dr. Bailey." She smiled at him and went to get the drinks.

"Dr. Bailey, huh?" I laughed.

"Hey, I've noticed it gets me better service when I go places," he said, a little sheepishly.

"I'm kidding. Maybe I should start calling you Dr. Bailey. Wouldn't that be a boost to your ego?"

"Only if you dress up like a sexy nurse when you say it," he whispered in my ear.

"Sorry, that's *not* a possibility tonight," I said with conviction.

A couple hours later, I was standing in Ben's hotel room in nothing but my black, lace thong.

I guess multiple shots of vodka make even the most impossible things, well... possible. I was still attracted to him and we'd always had good sex. But I couldn't help wondering how good it was going to be after my night with Nikola.

"How did I ever let you go?" Ben said, thickly, picking me up and carrying me to the bed. He started kissing my inner thigh and moved his way down to my toes. He'd always loved my feet and I loved the way he worshiped every inch of my body.

Almost a minute later, my mind finally caught up to his question. "I don't know, but you did." I was feeling incredibly drunk from all the vodka shots. "I hope you aren't just filling my head with sweet words to have sex with me," I said rather bluntly, thanks to the booze.

He looked up and shook his head. "We aren't going to have sex. I just want to lick you until you come over and over." And then he slipped his finger inside of me. I had to admit; we'd been lovers for so long that he knew my body better than anyone else. Still, Nikola was the first guy to give me multiple orgasms from actual intercourse, not oral. *Stop it Toy! Not him again? What the hell do I have to do to get Nikola out of my head?*

Next thing I knew, Ben was kissing me, and my head started to spin.

"I'm feeling dizzy," I mumbled, pushing him away.

"Are you okay?" He grabbed the water bottle from the nightstand.

"I feel so sick."

"Drink this, then we'll go to sleep." He twisted the cap off the bottle and handed it to me. I drained half of it and he chugged the rest. Then, he pulled me close to him. His smell, the way he held me, it all felt so natural, so... right.

I closed my eyes and wondered if this was how Nikola felt when he was in bed with Biljana, which I'd bet anything that was exactly where he was. The thought of them together, like Ben and I were now, created a dull ache in my head. *Stop, for crissakes!*

Don't ask me how, but I squelched the thought of them and drifted to sleep with the man I hadn't been able to stop thinking of for the past year.

I woke up the next morning with a painful headache. If memory served me correctly, Ben was a heavy sleeper. I slid out of bed and made my way to the bathroom. I looked in the mirror and groaned. Last night had accomplished nothing. I still didn't know how I felt about Ben. I was scared of getting hurt again and didn't even know if he truly wanted a commitment. Telling me he loved me was not enough. What bothered me most, I was still being bombarded with thoughts of Nikola, even when I was with Ben. Not a good sign. Everything felt more complicated than ever.

I stepped back into the bedroom and gathered my clothes. Ben woke up.

"You were going to leave without saying goodbye?" he said with puppy dog eyes, then sat up in bed. He ran a hand through his wavy hair as I admired him. I'd always loved his freckled face and green eyes.

I leaned down over him and brushed his wild hair with my fingers. He pulled my hand down to his mouth and kissed it.

"I didn't want to wake you," I explained.

"My alarm would be going off in a few minutes anyway. I have a conference in an hour."

"I have to get home and take a shower. I work in a few hours," I said, dreading the fact that I had to go in with this hangover.

As if once again reading my mind, he said, "Stop and buy some Gatorade and a banana on your way home, then take some Advil. And remember to drink a lot of water throughout the day."

"Thank you, doctor," I teased, and gave him a peck on the lips.

I missed his taking care of me. It felt good. But, how long would it last?

"Anything for my favorite patient. Let me throw on some clothes and I'll walk you down to the lobby," he said, getting out of bed.

"You don't have to."

"I know. I *want* to." He put his arms around my waist. "Can I see you tonight?"

I hesitated a moment. "Well, I have to go to a birthday party tonight. I told Chance I'd be his *date*, but he probably wouldn't mind if you tag along. You know how he loves an entourage. Besides, the minute we get there he'll be on a manhunt."

"I'd rather have you all to myself, but if I have to share you for a few hours, I'll make the sacrifice," he teased. Then, he kissed me long and soft on the mouth.

"You're so beautiful." He pulled away and gently slapped my butt. "This little cupcake ass of yours. God, I've missed it."

I laughed and picked up my coat and purse, then waited for him to slip into his clothes. When we reached the lobby, he pulled me close to him for another long kiss.

"I can't wait to see you tonight. Text me your new address. I'll meet you and we can take a cab to the party," he said, as we walked out of the hotel.

Ben escorted me to the first taxi in the line of cabs waiting in front of the hotel. He opened the door and I quickly got in, trying to evade the cold.

"Let's say 10:30 tonight, okay?" I said, shivering.

He fished a couple of bills out of his wallet, handed them to the driver, then leaned down to kiss me on the cheek. "10:30 it is."

I watched him walk back in the hotel. *He's such a gentleman. Ben would never leave me to find a taxi on my own, or pay for it.*

On the ride home, I found myself wondering if Nikola was as thoughtful as Ben. *Damn it! Not you again. Can't I just forget you exist? Wait a minute! What am I thinking? I pray you show up at that party, Nikola. Everyone always said that Ben and I were an attractive couple, and tonight we'll stroll in arm in arm. Now we'll see who's really in for the surprise!*

Chapter 10

I walked into work with a Red Bull in my hand. Thank God I only had three appointments. The thought of staying here any longer than I had to made my head throb. I still needed to take a nap in order to look alive tonight, let alone look good.

The minute I walked up to the counter, Tommy gave me a once over, followed by a mischievous smile.

"What?" I asked, a little more sharply than I'd intended.

Still grinning, he threw his hands up in the air. "Nothing."

I softened my tone. "No, really. What is it?"

"You just look like you had a long night. I'm not used to seeing you like this."

"I went out and had a glass of wine with a friend. No big deal. I just didn't sleep well, that's all," I lied, not sure why I was being untruthful with Tommy of all people. He came in hungover more often than not.

"If you say so," he chuckled.

He lost interest in my previous night's adventure when he saw a customer approach the fragrance bar. I groaned as I watched him and Jean-Luc approach the woman at the same time, so aggressively, she fled in the other direction.

Those two needed a serious talking to, but today it wasn't happening. I was way too burnt out.

"Toy, your appointment is here," called Fiona from the other end of the counter.

I turned around to see my favorite client, Mrs. Ibenski, waving at me. She was a wealthy, elderly lady who came in every few months to get her makeup done. She never spent less than $1500 each time she sat in my chair, but that wasn't why I liked her. She'd lived an adventurous life and I loved listening to all her stories. She'd been to places I'd never even considered; the Maldives, Antarctica, remote villages in South America, and tiny islands off the coast of Africa, to name a few.

"Hi, Mrs. Ibenski. How are you today?" I took her coat, draped it over a nearby table and patted the seat of my makeup chair.

"I'm very well, dear. I'm getting ready to go to Nassau this weekend. My bones can't handle this cold anymore." She loosened the angora ruffle scarf around her neck.

"I wish I were going somewhere warm," I said, wistfully, and poured some makeup remover on a cotton pad, then went to work on her face.

"A pretty young girl like you?" she playfully scolded. "You should have a string of young fellows lined up to take you on tropical vacations."

"It's not that easy," I groaned. "I don't think men are the way they were when you were dating."

She laughed. "Darling, men are men. Sure, some things are bound to have changed, but I assure you, they haven't as much as you think. Your soul mate is out there somewhere, just waiting to cross paths with you."

"Well, apparently he's still hopelessly lost," I shrugged. "The usual?"

She nodded with a chuckle.

I squeezed a dime-sized amount of cleanser onto a cotton pad.

"So, how's life been treating you, Mrs. Ibenski?"

"To tell you the truth, I'm a little lonesome, but that's to be expected. I'm getting by all right."

I knew she'd lost her husband last year.

"Can I ask you a question?"

"Sure, darling. Shoot."

"When you met your husband, did you know he was your soul mate?"

"Well..." she paused thoughtfully, "I was seventeen when I met Peter and we weren't married until I was twenty-one. I loved him with all my heart and had a wonderful life with him, a life that I may not have had with someone else. But, he wasn't my soul mate."

Her eyes began to twinkle. I knew she was must be replaying some kind of precious memory. That piqued my interest and my casual conversation starter turned into a full-on probe. "What do you mean?"

"After you spend your life with someone for over fifty years, sharing everything, having children and grandchildren, they become the love of your life because they've been your partner through all the ups and downs. You've developed a common history. That's different from being soul mates, you know?"

"Chin up," I said in order to finish blending her foundation. Sometimes having a conversation while doing makeup could be an artistic challenge. I was trying to follow what she was saying, but I didn't get it. She must've known because she went on.

"Young people sometimes marry the wrong person for what they think are the right reasons. I think the biggest fear they have when they're settling down is losing the spark, you know, the passion, and then living a dreadfully dull life with the person they married. Yet that's exactly what they choose. They find someone stable, someone with a good job and like-minded goals and they marry that stable person," she said, sagely. "Love is risky business and even though the relationship lacks excitement, they settle for the security of it. They're so preoccupied with convincing themselves this is the right person, they overlook the one who could be perfect for them. They make a decision based in fear and opt for safety rather than face the unknown."

"The unknown?"

"Yes. Falling in love is frightening. It's not comfortable and is probably the scariest, yet most exhilarating feeling of your life. When you're with that person, nothing else matters. And when you're not, nothing else seems as important as it did before."

Oh my God. Please tell me I'm not in love with Nikola, I thought, brushing some peach-colored blush on her cheeks. "But what if you think its love when it isn't? What if it's just new and exciting?"

"Oh Toy, love is the most complicated and confusing emotion in the world, but you'll recognize it. Do you know how many people I've known who were in love, but chose to talk themselves out of it for a reason just like the one you gave me? Or, on the other hand, convinced themselves they were in love because it was the 'right thing to do', then living the rest of their lives with regret?"

She was sitting in front of me, but I could see she was somewhere else.

"Did you talk yourself out of being with a man you loved?" I asked, hoping I wasn't prying.

She nodded her head.

"It was the summer before I married. My father's side of the family was incredibly wealthy, but my mother's wasn't as fortunate. Even so, my mother tried to appear as if she came from a family of means, when in fact, her family was quite the opposite. Oh, they weren't destitute, but they had to work hard for every dime.

"When I was a young girl, I spent every summer with my mother's parents in the countryside of Wisconsin. I always enjoyed the freedom they gave me. When I was with them I could just be me. I didn't have to be a debutante, watching every word I said and everything I did. They had a little cottage on the riverbank. I'd walk down to a sandbar and play, and when I was older, read for hours without ever being disturbed.

"It was during one of these long, lovely summers that I met Joseph. He was the grandson of a neighbor, a close friend of my grandfather's, who owned a cabin a few miles up the riverbank. The minute I was introduced to him I was smitten. He had blond, wavy hair, and the bluest eyes I'd ever seen.

"I was engaged to Peter, and he was enlisted in the Army and about to ship out to Europe in two weeks. He was the first man who was ever actually interested in my opinion."

As Mrs. Ibenski spoke, I could see everything she was describing as if I were watching a movie.

"We spent hours each day discussing everything from poetry to politics. We went on that way the entire two weeks. At night, I found myself falling asleep anticipating our next day together. He'd been a complete gentleman with me all summer, but I knew we'd developed deep feelings for one another. Of course, neither of us had the courage to do anything about it.

"Finally, two days before I was due to return to Chicago, he outright told me I couldn't marry someone else because he was in love with me. He said he'd known it from the moment he laid eyes on me. I didn't know what to say, and then he kissed me. It was so different than anytime Peter had ever kissed me. It was..."

"Like you felt alive for the first time?" I offered.

"Yes." Tears filled her faded, hazel eyes. "For the rest of that day we laughed and talked and kissed. I asked him to let me have the night to think about it all, even though I knew in my heart I couldn't stay with him. I remember him saying not to let fear of the unknown dictate my life."

"Why couldn't you stay if you loved him?" I asked, starting to feel a little weepy myself.

"Because I couldn't stand the thought hurting Peter and I feared disappointing everyone else. Whenever I had a thought of breaking off the engagement, I'd talk myself out of it. I convinced myself that it was just pre-wedding jitters and that it was impossible for me to fall in love with someone else so quickly. I knew my father would never approve of Joseph. He wanted to be a teacher, so in my father's eyes, he'd never have been good enough for me."

"How did you tell Joseph you weren't going to be with him?"

"I didn't," Mrs. Ibenski said, softly. "I left to go home the next morning without saying goodbye. I couldn't face him. I was a coward. After a few days, I was sick with grief and had no one to confide in. When I couldn't bear it anymore, I called my grandmother and told her I was taking a bus back to Wisconsin. A few hours later, I walked into the bus station where she was waiting for me.

"When she saw my face, she knew instantly why I'd come back. She took my hands in hers and told me Joseph was gone. He'd left the morning he'd discovered I'd left. I spent hours crying."

She paused and gently took the hand I was using to powder her face into hers. "Oh, Toy. If I could, I'd convince you to fall in love with someone who wants to know every detail about you and how you feel about everything. I'd tell you to find someone who instead of buying roses, picks a wildflower for you just to see your face light up. I'd tell you to fall in love with someone who reminds you of how wonderful you are when you least expect it, someone who wants to hold you close just to feel your breath against their skin, who can't wait to present you to his friends and family so they can share in the joy he's found in you. I'd tell you to fall in love with someone who loves all your imperfections and wouldn't have you any other way."

"Did Joseph love you like that?" I asked.

"Yes," she said, dropping her hand back into her lap. I watched her face take on a far-away expression.

After a second or two, she continued, "My mother came to pick me up and reassured me that Peter was the man for me." She closed her eyes as more tears formed.

I took a box of tissues from under the counter and set them in her lap.

"A couple of weeks later, my grandparents came to Chicago for the weekend. The first night they were there, my grandfather asked me to go for a walk with him after dinner. We'd just left the house when he told me they hadn't just come for a visit. There was something he had to tell me in person.

"I remember getting goose bumps because I *knew*, I just knew, it was something bad — about Joseph. And I was right. He'd been killed in action. I fell into my grandfather's arms, devastated. He held me tightly while I cried into his chest, and tried to console me by telling me Joseph had received a medal of honor for bravery. He charged and took out a machine-gun nest single-handedly, but died from his wounds." Her shoulders shook as a tremor went through her. "I can't help but wonder all these years if he did that because of me."

She dabbed at her eyes with a tissue, then straightened her back in the chair. "So, I married Peter as planned, and went on with my life.

"Years went by and every summer I thought of Joseph. I still do. Through all those years of marriage and three children, I never forgot our summer together. Those quiet moments on a tiny Wisconsin sandbar with him were more memorable than the most exotic places on earth I'd been with Peter.

"Some years later, I was going through my grandmother's things and I found an old letter addressed to me. One look at the masculine scrawl and I knew it was from Joseph. Why my grandmother kept it all those years, I'll never know.

"It was as if I was a teenager all over again. My heart raced as I opened it. It was a quote by Federico Garcia Lorca: *'To burn with desire and keep quiet about it is the greatest punishment we can bring on ourselves.'*

"I read it from time to time, but it wasn't really necessary. From the first time I saw them, the words set my heart on fire and will burn there forever. It makes me sad, but also reminds me that our summer together was real," she said, aggrieved.

"I'm sorry," I said, my voice scarcely above a whisper. "I can see it still upsets you."

I put down my makeup brush and wrapped my arms around her. "I'm so, so sorry, Mrs. Ibenski."

"It's alright, sweetheart. I'm glad I could share it with you. Even if Joseph had lived, I may not have spent my life with him, but the short time we had together made me grateful. It was the one time in my life that I had true, romantic love. Some people go their entire lives without ever experiencing love like that. I consider myself one of the lucky ones," she said, patting her eyes with a tissue.

Mrs. Ibenski looked in the mirror and laughed a little. "I'm afraid you may have to redo my face."

I picked up my brush and smiled back at her. "No worries."

I was really afraid now. I knew I didn't want to one day be regretting a choice I'd made sixty years ago. Was her Joseph my Nikola? Was Peter my Ben? There were definitely similarities in the stories, but there were quite a few differences, too. For instance, Nikola and I had an instant connection but he probably wanted no more from me than a fling, and Ben would probably make a great husband, if he could ever stop being so indecisive. Regardless of what Mrs. Ibenski said, men had changed since she was young, and for that matter, so had women.

And, what if she had chosen Joseph? What if he'd ditched the Army and they ran away somewhere together? There's no way to know how it would have turned out. There are always choices to make and most of the time, you never know which path will take you in the right direction. You pick one and hope for the best. How can you possibly know which was the right path when the grass on both of them was a beautiful, lush green?

I lightly touched her shoulder. "Do you mind if I ask you one last thing?"

"Go right ahead, sweetie."

"How do you know Joseph was actually the love of your life? Isn't there a saying 'Only unfulfilled love can be romantic'? Isn't fulfillment the death of desire?"

She considered my question for a moment, then said, "Unfulfilled love is something completely different than what I had with Joseph. Do you believe in love at first sight?"

"I-I don't know," I stammered, not sure what to believe in anymore.

"I think it's very rare," she said, her nose red from crying. "When you look into that person's eyes you understand the purpose of your being. It's as if you see yourself in them and there's a sudden and unmistakable understanding between the two of you." She put up a hand. "It sounds trite, I know."

It didn't sound trite. I just didn't know how to react. Her words moved me. They were beautiful but disturbing at the same time.

"Okay, enough of this chit-chat," she said, cheerily, "I'm ready for you to do your magic. Toy, make me beautiful."

I tapped my finger on my chin. "How does one improve upon perfection? You're asking me to do the impossible."

We laughed. I was thankful for the light moment but it only lasted a second. The thoughts Mrs. Ibenski provoked were racing so fast my head was swimming.

Chapter 11

I'd worked less than four hours and sold over $5000, so the counter was still on track for the event. I felt confident I wouldn't be in any trouble for leaving work a little early. I barely managed to finish my last two clients. It was almost 2 PM when the Advil started to wear off. The hangover was returning with a vengeance.

After cleaning my makeup brushes, I said my good-byes to the team. I grabbed my things from the locker room and darted out the employee entrance before anyone had time to stop me for small talk. I wanted to get home fast because I still had a little time to squeeze in a few hours of sleep before I had to get ready. I was determined to look incredible tonight.

I bolted upright in bed. An ear-splitting noise forced my hands over my ears. It took me a second to realize it was the ring tone I'd chosen for my alarm. I reached over angrily to grab my cell, still blaring short blasts, and knocked the phone to the floor. That noise! Why would I have chosen such an obnoxious sound to wake up to? I reached to the floor, catching myself before I fell off the bed, and silenced it.

After congratulating myself for not hurling the expensive piece of metal against the wall, I looked at the time. I'd slept nearly two hours. Good. I checked my texts and opened the one from Ben. He couldn't wait to see me.

I grabbed the Gatorade bottle on my nightstand and downed what was left of it, then lay back down half-listening to *Bridget Jones' Diary*. I'd seen the movie more times than I could count. I knew the dialogue by heart. There was something about it I found comforting. Maybe it was the music or maybe it was Bridget. She reminded me of myself; the ultimate optimist who was totally blown away when she realized her life was an emotional tsunami and her friends were completely insane. Whatever it was, the movie had a permanent place on my DVR.

Still sluggish, I forced myself out of bed and reached my arms over my head in a marathon stretch. Getting motivated was going to be a challenge.

I grabbed a towel from the linen closet, tossed it on the counter and stepped into the shower. I felt better the instant the hot water poured over my body. Thankful I had a few hours before Ben arrived, I took my sweet time.

I dried off leisurely and was reaching for the hairbrush when I caught a glimpse of myself in the mirror. I gasped. My face was puffy, my skin blotchy and I had dark purple rings under my eyes. I looked god-awful!

I went over to the large hallway closet and sifted through the hundreds of beauty products I stored there. Serums, masks, eye and face creams that I'd accumulated over the past few years had become a jumbled mess. I searched until I found a sea mud exfoliating mask and a brightening full-face cotton mask. I'd use them both. Could I fix my face in less than twenty minutes? I looked at my face again.

"We'll see," I said out loud.

I skipped dinner figuring it would be better not to risk a bloated stomach. Instead, I mixed myself a Ketel and pineapple cocktail. I found "My Faves" play-list on my iPhone, and dropped it into the sound dock. I walked to my bed-room and picked up the red Yves Saint Laurent dress I had lying on my bed, then pulled the black peep-toe Louboutin boots out of my closet. A little over an hour later I stood in front of my full-length mirror, admiring myself. God, this dress was stunning! And the shoes just added to it.

Mission accomplished. I am smokin' hot.

My doorbell rang a little after 10:00 PM. Ben, as always, was just a little late. It annoyed me when we first started dating, but after I'd seen how late he was to practically everything else, I'd gotten over it.

I ran a hand through my hair and opened the door. There he stood, his face partially obscured by the two-dozen red roses he was holding in a large, square vase.

"I hope the roses aren't too cliché," he said, placing the fragrant arrangement in my arms.

"Not at all." I closed my eyes and inhaled. I knew some people thought red roses were played out, but I loved them. Red roses and orchids would always be my favorite flowers. "They're beautiful. Come on in."

"I thought it would be a nice surprise," he said, kissing me on the cheek. "You're looking fantastic, as always."

I took in his beard, trimmed to a chic, designer stubble, just the way I liked it.

"Thank you. You look good, too," I ran a hand over his scruffy cheek. "I'll put these in the kitchen for now."

He followed me into the kitchen and looked around. I rearranged the roses while he walked into the living room.

"Wow, Toy. This place is incredible! I see you got the fireplace you wanted."

Do I detect a hint of regret in his voice? "Yeah, I decided if I couldn't have the guy I could still have the place," I said, a little sharply. "Let me show you my favorite room."

He followed me to the bath.

Ben did a survey, then commented, "This looks a lot like the bathroom in the hotel we stayed at in Jamaica."

"I know," I said, quietly. His eyes met mine. "That was our last vacation together."

"Not our last." He pulled me into his arms and kissed me deeply. "Do you remember how much fun we had in that tub?"

I could feel his erection growing when he pulled me closer to him. "How could I forget?" I breathed, suddenly excited myself.

Right as we were losing ourselves in each other, the doorbell rang.

"Don't answer it," he whispered, kissing my neck.

Reluctantly, I pulled away. "I have to. It's Chance."

I'd told Chance to drop by my apartment about a half an hour after Ben was supposed to be here to give me time to show him the place.

"I know," he said, his eyes still filled with lust, "but I don't have to like it."

"Waiting makes it more fun," I grinned.

He pretended to pout. "If you say so."

He followed me out of the bedroom. I answered the door. As expected, Chance was on the other side of it looking adorable in a Burberry fedora, with a Starbucks coffee in his hand.

"Hey girl, hey-ey," he sang and waltzed right in.

"Hi Chance. How are you, man?" Ben asked, reaching for Chance's hand.

Chance ignored it.

"Hello, *Benjamin.*" He side-stepped Ben and sat down on a stool in the kitchen. "I hadn't expected to see you again."

Chance had liked Ben at first, but changed his tune after the first few times Ben broke up with me.

"Okay," I said, hoping to warm the sudden chill in the room, "why don't we get going?"

"Good idea," agreed Ben.

"Ben, can you grab my white coat out of the front hall closet for me?" I asked, sweetly.

"Of course."

I took a peach colored lip gloss from my purse and standing in front of the hall mirror, applied some to my lower lip. Ben reached into the closet for my new white Dior double-breasted coat while Chance drained the last of my half-full cocktail on the counter.

"Oh," gasped Chance, "that coat is to die for!"

"I know. Isn't it gorgeous?" I gushed. "I've been dying to wear it."

While I put on my Dior cashmere gloves, Chance pulled three shot glasses from a cabinet and my vodka from the freezer.

"Chance, no!" I cried. "I'm already feeling a little tipsy from the one I just had. I think I made it too strong."

"Oh, come on. Don't be such a downer," he chided with one hand on his hip and the other pushing the shot toward me.

"I can't," I whined.

"Come on, Toy, let's take the shots. It'll loosen us all up," urged Ben.

I was surprised. Ben was never one for pre-gaming.

"Fine," I sighed, lifting the glass with a gloved hand.

"Cheers," we said, in unison.

"One more!" shouted Chance.

I gave them each a look and then, "What the hell," and held out my glass, thinking, *If I don't slow down with the drinks, this night is going to end sooner rather than later.*

On the way to the party, I sent a text to Tommy asking him to meet us at the door. He was working as security tonight. Good thing I did, too. When we got there, a long line had formed that reached halfway around the block. I *never* waited in lines at clubs, especially when it was 15 degrees outside!

"Toy!"

I looked above the sea of people to see Tommy waving an arm over his head. I grabbed Ben and Chance and headed for him.

"Nice coat," he said, kissing me on the cheek, then whispered in my ear, "Hey, can you spot me forty bucks until Friday?"

Leave it to Tommy to ask for a loan at the door of a club.

I nodded discretely. "Thanks for getting us in so quickly, babe. You remember Ben."

"Anytime," Tommy said, and grasped Ben's hand. "Good to see you." He slapped Chance on the back. "What's up, little man?"

"Hey, Tommy," cooed Chance, batting his lashes and smacking his gum.

"Come on guys, I'll take you to Tatyana's table," said Tommy. We fell in step behind him as I pulled two twenties from my purse and slipped them into Tommy's hand. It was all the cash I had on me and leave it to Tommy to get it before I even sat down.

We arrived at a low, black teak table surrounded by modular, dark leather sofas, and crowded with people. Some were dancing around it, some were standing and talking, but only three were seated: Jean-Luc, Biljana and Nikola. My heart began to race and the room temperature seemed to increase by at least twenty degrees.

"I didn't know this was a work party," mumbled Ben.

I leaned in and whispered in his ear, "Yeah, Chance talked me into it. Don't worry, we won't stay long."

The minute we walked up to the table I could see the shock register on Nikola's face. Then, I saw a glimmer of something else when he noticed Ben who was holding my hand. Confusion? Jealousy? I couldn't tell. What was obvious was that he hadn't expected me to be here tonight.

I noticed three bottles of Cristal in the champagne bucket. Hmm. I knew Tatyana couldn't afford this kind of bottle service. I looked around the VIP section and saw a man in a Gucci suit, probably in his early 50s, sitting at a nearby table with Tatyana standing by his side. He had his left hand around her waist and his wedding band in plain view.

What a philanderer. Now I know who's footing the bill.

Chance handed me a glass of champagne. It went down faster than I'd expected. Jean-Luc made a point of ignoring Chance and made small talk with Ben and me.

"Fuck this," mumbled Chance, just loud enough for all of us to hear him, then stormed off to the dance floor.

Everything this boy did was staged. Oh, sure. He was genuinely miffed at Jean-Luc's snub, but his actions were designed to draw as much attention to himself as he could. And, in ten minutes he'd be canoodling with someone else.

I forced my practiced smile to say hello to Biljana and Nikola, and introduced them to Ben, a real feat considering my nerves made my tongue feel like lead. After the brief intros, I tried my hardest to ignore Nikola. Nevertheless, he stared straight at me whenever I looked in his direction.

This wasn't how I'd imagined it. I'd wanted to walk in on Ben's arm, see Nikola and feel nothing. Instead, I felt sick seeing him with Biljana. I wanted to run from the room.

After a half hour or so I heard, "Babe, do you want me to get you another drink?"

"Huh?"

It was Ben. "Where were you just then?"

"What do you mean?" I asked, innocently.

"Seemed like you were a million miles away."

"Sorry, I was thinking about work. What did you ask me?"

"I asked if you want another drink," he enunciated, pointing to a bottle of Grey Goose vodka.

"Oh thanks, but no. I think I should probably have a bottle of water first. Those shots kind of got to me."

Yes, the shots definitely had an effect, but not as much as a certain guy seated across from me.

"Come on, one more drink won't hurt you. It's just what the doctor ordered," he said, already topping the vodka with pineapple juice.

He handed it to me and I grudgingly accepted it.

By now I was sweating and had to get out of my coat. I took it off slowly, hoping Nikola wouldn't be able to resist a look. It worked. I could see a hint of appreciation in his eyes as I handed the coat to Ben and smoothed my hands down the front of my tight dress.

Biljana was firing off something to him in their native tongue. Whatever she was saying couldn't have been very friendly, because when she finished, she jumped up and made her way through the mob of people crowding the VIP section. Nikola didn't chase her. Instead he made eye contact with me and took a sip of his drink.

"Ben?" called a familiar voice.

I turned my head to see where it was coming from. *Fiona.* And she was clearly very drunk by the way she stumbled up to us. She had a crazy look on her face, and I didn't know what to make of it.

Ben dropped his arm from around my waist and went pale as she approached him. "Hi, F-Fiona."

He'd actually stammered!

Hmm. Something's not right here.

He rubbed the back of his neck, something he did whenever he felt uncomfortable. I could feel the heat rushing through my body. She had some nerve saying hello to him while she ignored me.

"You didn't tell me you'd be in town this weekend. Are you two here together?" she asked, not even trying to hide her ire.

Since when did Ben need to update Fiona as to when he'd be in town?

He took a huge gulp of his drink and said, "I had a medical conference this weekend and yes, we are together." He shot me a semi-reassuring glance, then turned back to Fiona. "I didn't expect to see you here. You told me you hate the club scene."

And when did Fiona and Ben chat long enough for her to tell him she hated clubs? He'd hardly spoken two words to her the entire time we dated. Furthermore, how the hell did they suddenly know so much about one another? I could tell Fiona was genuinely confused at both seeing Ben *and* seeing us at the party together. Out of the corner of my eye, I glanced at Nikola who was taking it all in.

I cleared my throat loudly. "Is there something I'm missing here?"

Fiona smirked, then turned to him. "I don't know. Ben, is she missing anything?"

I slammed my glass on the table, but kept my voice under control. "Ben, what in the hell is she talking about?"

"Toy, let's not talk about this here. C'mon, let's go." He grabbed my coat.

The liquor amplified my anger that was growing by the millisecond. It was all I could do not to explode in front of Nikola.

"I'm sorry, Ben," Fiona said, snidely. "Did my showing up tonight ruin your special weekend? Since you don't feel like this is the right place to discuss it, I'll just do it for you." She turned to me and announced, haughtily, "We've been talking since he dumped you, Toy!"

Ben gasped, shock registering on his face.

I felt sick. So, this was why Fiona had suddenly put the chill on what I thought was our friendship.

"*Her*, Ben?" I cried, humiliated.

Ben looked at me with beseeching eyes, shaking his head. "Toy... I came back into town a few times after you and I broke up. Fiona and I..."

I could barely swallow past the lump in my throat. Not only was I finding out that both my boyfriend and former friend had betrayed me, but it was happening in front of Nikola, of all people.

I straightened, my spine tingling with rage. This wasn't happening. Not the Ben I knew. He wouldn't do this to me. Not with Fiona. I tossed down what was left of my drink and relished the heat of the vodka as it burned its way down. "Fiona and you, *what?*" I asked, not sure I wanted to hear the answer.

"Come on, let's get out of here. Please? We can talk somewhere else," he implored.

"What the fuck do you think happened, Toy?" laughed Fiona. "You're a big girl. Use your imagination."

A wave of calm washed over me. "That's *exactly* what I needed to hear," I said evenly, then slowly, deliberately, picked up Ben's drink and threw it in her face. Then, I snatched my coat from Ben and strolled away from the table. I only needed to hold back the tears until I was out of the club.

"You crazy bitch!" Fiona shrieked, grabbing napkins to wipe the liquid that dripped from her face.

I threw a dazzling smile over my shoulder and kept on walking.

"Toy! Wait!" called Ben, as he raced after me. I picked up my pace.

He grabbed my arm just as I had walked out the front door. I jerked it from his grasp and spun around to face him.

"I will never, *ever* forgive you," I hissed. "I trusted you. How could you do this to me? Of all the people in the world you could have chosen, you chose *her*?"

He took a step toward me. "Please, it's not what you th —"

I shoved him away. "I never want to see you again, *ever*!" I yelled, blinded by a sudden flow of tears.

"Let me get you a taxi. I could come with you if you'd let me. I don't want you to go home alone feeling like this. If you'd just let me explain!" he said, reaching out to me.

"Oh, now you give a damn about my feelings?" I asked, incredulous. "Really? Where were you the past year?"

"Toy, I'm going with you," he said, sternly, trying to throw an arm around my shoulder, but I deflected it.

"Security!" I screamed like I was being molested.

A huge bouncer in a suit, with a shaved head, made his way toward us.

"I'm a friend of Tommy's," I pointed both forefingers at Ben, "and *this* man is bothering me."

Ben's jaw dropped. He took a step back. "Are you fucking serious?"

"Very," I said, venomously.

The bouncer closed in on us, fixing a menacing look on Ben.

"You're unbelievable." He glanced at the bouncer, shook his head and stomped off down the street.

"You okay?" the bouncer asked, as he placed a gentle hand on my shoulder.

"Yeah," I sniffed. "Can you flag down a taxi for me?"

"Sure, hon." He held his hand up and a bright yellow Toyota immediately zeroed in to the curb. The bouncer helped me into the backseat as if he was tucking a baby into bed, shut the door and turned away.

A second later, the door flew open.

"Move over."

Nikola!

The bouncer spun around and bounded in our direction. Just before he got to us, Nikola slammed the door, shoved a twenty at the driver and we sped off.

"What do you think you're doing?" I shrieked.

"You are very drunk and upset. I will not let you leave by yourself. I saw what happened in there."

"Oh, this is rich. One jerk saving me from another," I derided. "Where's Biljana?"

"Do not worry about her. She left." He tried to put his arm around me.

"No!" I slid across the vinyl seat away from him. All of a sudden, my head began to spin.

"Where are you going?" asked the driver, who regarded us in the rear-view mirror.

Nikola gave him my address.

"Lady?" asked the driver, "is this where you want me to take you?"

"I guess."

"You sure?"

"Yes, she is sure," answered Nikola, annoyed. "Can you not hear?"

"It's okay," I slurred, attempting to reassure the driver.

I leaned into the door to get as far away from Nikola as I could, and glared at him. "You have some nerve after the way you treated me."

He reached out to touch my knee and I slapped his hand away.

"I am sorry, I really am. I tried to explain to Biljana that she and I were nothing more than friends and she went crazy. She was crying and telling me she is in love with me. I was in shock. I did not know what to do."

I looked at him warily. "Why were you shocked?"

"That she has such strong feelings for me. I told you, she and I fooled around from time to time, but she always knew what it was between us. Friends and that is all."

I giggled at first, and then exploded into a full-fledged fit of laughter.

"What is so funny?" he asked in confusion.

"Men! That's what. There's one universal trait you all seem to share. Blindness! When it comes to women, you're all freakin' blind!"

"What do you mean?"

"What men don't understand is that no matter what a woman says, if she's sleeping with a man, even sporadically, she's got high hopes that it'll turn into more. *All* women think this way. Just the way she looked at you the first time I saw you both together, the way she hooked her arm in yours, anyone could see she's crazy about you."

"Oh, come on," he scoffed.

Angry tears stung my eyes. "Listen," I said, "if there's something I know much better than you, it's how women think. I listen to women of all ethnicities and ages, all day, every day. I know women. I *am* a woman! Besides, that's no excuse for not bothering to call or text me after the night we spent together."

"I am trying to explain myself and you are not letting me finish." Then, a few seconds later, "Are you okay?"

I took a deep breath against a growing nausea. "I don't feel so good. My head is spinning," I said, and plopped over, my head falling in his lap.

"Fifty-dollar clean-up fee for vomit," the cabbie announced.

"Just drive! *Gomnar!*" Nikola retorted.

"What does 'gomnar' mean?

"Asshole."

I'd have laughed if I hadn't been so sick. I heard the cabbie grumble something to himself.

I tried to rise, but Nikola pressed a hand to my forehead. "It's okay. Alright," he soothed, stroking my hair with his fingers.

A little while later, we arrived at my apartment. Nikola helped me out of the taxi, then leaned back in to say something to the driver, and soon they were arguing. I headed toward my building. The week-old snow crunched beneath my shoes and before I knew it, my feet slipped out from under me. I fell down hard on my ass and slid at least a foot across the muddy, slushy sidewalk. Somehow I sat up, but when I gazed down at my gorgeous white Dior coat splattered with filth, I let out a long, pitiful wail.

That was the last thing I remembered.

Chapter 12

I woke up and the late morning sun was blazing through the half-open blinds. I winced at the glare and pried my eyes open. It took a second or two to realize I was in my own bedroom. My head was pounding and it hurt to even breathe. I was still in my dress from the night before, but my shoes were off and I was under a blanket. Then, in a flash, it all came flooding back, and I curled myself into a ball.

I'd made a total fool of myself at the club and Nikola had a front row seat to the entire scene. He must have thought I was a total psycho. I glanced down at the floor and saw my filthy coat. Oh, yeah. I'd fallen. I'm sure Nikola had turned around to witness that too. Was it humanly possible to feel any more disgusted with myself than I did right now? I wished I could go to sleep forever.

I was drifting back off when I heard footsteps coming toward my room. I sat up, disoriented.

"Toy, can I come in?"

He stayed the night?

I smoothed down my hair and prayed I didn't look as repulsive as I felt.

He stretched his arms as if he'd just woken up himself. "I did not mean to scare you. How are you feeling?"

"No, it's okay. I'd love to tell you I feel just wonderful, but I'd be lying." I dropped my face into my hands and through my fingers said, "I'm so embarrassed about last night."

After a second of silence, I looked up at him. "You stayed the night. Why?"

He sat down on the bed beside me. "Because you did not need to be alone."

"I would've been okay."

"Oh really? I guess you do not remember me carrying you unconscious into your building and up to your apartment last night. You were crying and telling me —"

I threw up a palm.

"It's okay. I don't want to know what I said. I'm already totally humiliated." Again, I turned away. I'd bet anything my face was red as a lobster. *I want to die, right now!*

"Do not worry about it. We have all had too much to drink and done things we regret. Considering how drunk you were, I would say you handled the entire situation very well," he said, kindly.

I cut my eyes at him. "Really?"

"Yes, really."

I smiled at his accent. He had such a deep voice but his words were soft. He brushed the hair out of my face with his fingers and I wondered again, how terrible I must look.

"I really need to take a shower. I feel gross," I mumbled, trying to ignore the way my heart skipped a beat when he inched closer.

"You are beautiful like this. I like it. Less makeup, more vulnerable……" He kissed my forehead.

He took me in his arms. For a little while, neither of us uttered a word.

I pulled away to look him in the eye. "I still don't know why you didn't call."

"I tried to explain myself to you last night, but you were not having it."

"I heard your explanation," I fibbed, trying to remember what he'd said in the cab. "You still could've said good-bye."

I slid farther away. I needed a little distance between us.

"You are right. I should have called, but I did not. I cannot change the fact that I made a mistake, Toy. When I left that night, I had planned on calling. I did not know what to do when Biljana reacted the way she did. I was confused and felt like I was not being fair to either of you."

I couldn't deal with this. Ben and Fiona. Nikola and Biljana. It was like a circus, and I was the sad-faced clown.

"You're right," I conceded. "It wouldn't have been and I shouldn't have slept with you as fast as I did. I don't know what came over me."

He grimaced. "You can believe me or not, but I really care about you. When I first met you, I felt something I have never felt before. Of course, I was attracted to you, but more than that, you were so sure of yourself. You were — are — beautiful, smart and sassy. I wanted to know everything about you. I still do."

He took my hands in his and squeezed them. My eyes filled with tears when I looked into his.

"Nikola, you don't know how much I'd like to just forget about everyone around us and be with you, but I can't. I won't share a man, and I won't allow myself to be the other woman. I'm sorry."

"I understand," he said, quietly.

My stomach turned upside down. I wanted so badly for him to tell me he would break off whatever he had with Biljana and be with me. Instead, he'd given up on us before we even had a chance to become an us.

I need to take a shower. Thank you for last night. Really." I touched his cheek with my hand and didn't wait for a response. I got out of bed, grabbed a pair of sweats and a T-shirt, and went into the bathroom. He'd let himself out last time just fine on his own. I was sure he could manage it once more. Besides, I didn't want him to see me cry all over again.

I looked in the mirror expecting to find mascara smeared all over my face but it wasn't. I didn't look hideous, just pale and tired. I groaned.

I probably cried all my makeup off and wiped it on the sleeve of my coat. Damn, I loved that coat.

I brushed my teeth and gargled with mouthwash, hoping the taste of stale booze would go away. I discarded my wrinkled dress and stepped into the shower.

There was something about a hangover that made me feel hyper sensuous and as the water hit my naked breasts, my skin turned to goose flesh and my nipples grew taut. Knowing that Nikola had just been sitting on my bed intensified the sensation.

All of a sudden, the shower door opened and in stepped Nikola, completely naked. Maybe I was hoping for it. Maybe I half-expected it. Whatever the reason, the intrusion hadn't startled me at all and I knew right then without a doubt, this was the most intense feeling I'd ever had with a man.

He looked at me longingly. "I do not want to say goodbye."

"I don't either, but Nikola, I can't do this," I said, my weak resolve swirling down the drain with the steamy water.

"I know, and you do not have to. I am going to tell Biljana, once and for all, she and I are finished. Done."

"I don't want you to do this because of me," I said, breathless in anticipation.

"I am ending it because it has long been over and really, never even began," he said with finality.

I looked up at him and wrapped my arms around his neck. Now we were skin to skin. He brought his mouth down to meet mine. Our tongues probed each other's mouths. I wanted him so badly it hurt. He moved his head down, his tongue trailed his fingers to my breasts. As he alternately took each of my erect nipples into his mouth, I let out a gasp.

I led him to the marble bench and kneeled in front of him. He wound his fingers in my hair as I took him into my mouth. The warm water cascaded over our bodies, heightening my already intense need.

His hips thrust forward. "Slow down," he said, and gently pushed me back.

I stood up and turned around. He moved in behind me. I bent forward, set my hands against the smooth marble wall and widened my legs. He kissed the back of my neck as he entered me.

He pushed slowly to begin with, until he was completely inside me, and then my desire took over. Instinctively, I moved my body with his. He moved faster with incredible urgency.

"Oh Nikola, yes!" I cried, delirious with lust.

I pulled an arm from the wall and touched myself as he reached around to squeeze my breasts to the point of exquisite, painful pleasure.

"Sit down," I ordered.

He sat on the bench and leaned back, his erection full and hard. I positioned myself over him, then sank slowly down the length of his shaft. I took his hand and one by one, slid each of his fingers in and out of my mouth. I rode him hard and slow, forward and back.

"I love being inside you," he cried, as his hands slid down my wet torso to my hips.

His moans increased my excitement to a fevered pitch. All at once, I cupped my breasts and pinched my nipples, then leaned forward and nipped his lower lip. It was just enough to push him over the edge.

"I am coming," he cried out, then covered my mouth with his. I felt him burst inside of me as I teetered on the brink of my own climax.

"Oh, God," I shrieked. "Me too."

After several long seconds of indescribable ecstasy, I pulled myself off him.

Breathless, he reached for my hand. "I do not want to go."

I held my face nose to nose with his.

"Good, because I was planning on keeping you hostage for the rest of the day." He punctuated his words with a long, lingering kiss.

We'd spent the better part of an hour making love in the bathroom, bedroom, and had finally ended up in the living room.

"Hey!" Nikola clapped his hands and rubbed them together. I'd never seen him so animated. "There is a Balkan grocery store a few blocks from here." He jerked a throw from the back of the couch, tossed it over me and tucked it down. "You stay warm. It will only take me a few minutes, and then I will cook for you."

"What?" I asked in surprise.

Nikola stood erect and put a palm to his chest. "I want to cook for you."

He threw on his clothes and must have flown there, because before I knew it, he was back. Still wrapped in the throw, I sat down on a bar stool and watched him prepare a breakfast feast more suited to a group of ten than just him and me.

"Do you cook?" he asked.

Jean-Luc had already filled me in on the myth held by most European men that typical American women didn't cook.

"I hate to disappoint you, but yes, I do," I laughed.

"Okay, like what?" he challenged.

"You know, macaroni and cheese, peanut butter and jelly sandwiches," I teased.

"Are you serious?" he said, wide-eyed.

I shook my head. "No, I'm not serious." I guess he hadn't quite mastered American irony. "I cook a lot of different things. In the morning, if I have time, I love to make chocolate or fruit filled crepes. I usually eat out for lunch because I'm at work. For dinner, I typically make baked chicken with different seasonings, or spicy pasta dishes — and I make a killer spinach soufflé. When Ben and I were dating I cooked a lot more."

Damn. Why'd I bring up Ben?

"It's hard to cook for one," I explained, awkwardly.

Nikola stiffened. "So that guy last night, Ben. You two were serious?"

"Yeah, we were together for a few years..." I winced, "a few *wasted* years, I might add."

My face must have reflected the freshness of the wound, because Nikola put the knife down and wrapped an arm around me.

"I do not know the history between the two of you, of course, but if that girl from last night was who he left you for, he is insane."

That made me smile. "Thanks. But that's not exactly what happened. I don't know the real story, but apparently, a while after he and I broke up, they started seeing each other. She and I were good friends at one point, which makes it hurt that much more." I wanted to change the subject. I'd been feeling so good and didn't want to ruin it.

He lifted my chin with a finger. "Hey, it is over. I am here with you now."

We studied each other for a second. "I know... I know it may sound silly, but when I'm with you, I'm caught between feeling incredibly happy and totally scared."

He turned and began unloading the bag of groceries. "What do you mean?" He glanced around. "Wait. Where are your frying pans?"

"In the cabinet, next to the stove."

I took a deep breath. "I don't know how to explain it. I guess I'm scared of how you make me feel... this feeling, you know? Like it's too good to be true." All at once, I felt completely exposed.

He found the frying pan and set it down on the stove to heat up. He crossed his arms thoughtfully and leaned against the counter. Then, kind of offhandedly he asked, Do you like poetry?"

"I guess. I mean, I like the cute poems I read on Instagram. Does that count?" I teased.

He grinned. "I love poetry because in most cases, so many feelings are expressed in such few words. It speaks to my soul."

"What's your favorite?" I asked, falling harder and harder for him by the minute.

"That is like asking me who is my favorite musician. I could never answer that because there are so many talented poets to choose from. There is so much beauty in the world," he said, spreading his arms wide. "Anyway, I asked you if you like poetry for a reason."

"Which is?"

"You said you are scared of how I make you feel. It reminded me of a line from a C.S. Lewis poem: 'To love at all is to be vulnerable'."

Did he just use the word 'love'?

He must've read my mind because his face turned red. "Not that I am saying we are in love," he quickly clarified.

"No, of course not," I reassured him, but couldn't stop the butterflies in my stomach.

"It is my favorite line from any of his poetry. These days I think people are afraid to give love a chance. They are afraid to be vulnerable. They complain about not being able to find love. How can you find love if you are scared of being naked in front of someone? When I say naked, I mean baring your inner self to another person."

Until this moment, I hadn't known what it was like to feel myself falling in love. I couldn't stop looking at him.

"What?" he asked, smiling sheepishly. "I know. I get passionate about poetry."

"I love it." I got up and went to him. I ran my hands through his silky hair and pulled his face to mine. I kissed him slowly. After a minute, I pulled away and returned to my seat.

"Maybe I should get passionate more often about subjects I love," he said, fast becoming hot and bothered.

"Maybe," I winked, and then headed to the bedroom for some clothes.

After a while, I walked back in the kitchen as he set several dishes along the island, buffet style; scrambled eggs with feta cheese, spicy, thick sausage sliced in quarter-inch circles, a course, red spread of some sort, a smooth white cheese spread, sesame-encrusted bread rings and pastries.

"This looks amazing," I gushed. "I've never had a Macedonian breakfast before."

"Chicago has a much bigger Serbian community than Macedonian, so this is more of a Serbian breakfast. One day I hope I can cook you an authentic Macedonian meal." He pointed to the sausage and said, *"soujuk"*. The cheese spread was *"kajmak"* and the red stuff, *"ajvar"*. I couldn't remember what he called the thick slices of warm bread or the stuffed pastries, but I'll never forget the taste of them.

I felt so relaxed, which was odd considering how enigmatic I found him. I was sitting here, my hair a tangled mess, not a stitch of makeup on, in my sweats, eating like a pig, yet I was at total ease. I hadn't been able to eat like this with Ben until we'd been dating for months.

"Have you ever been in love?" I asked, not sure I really wanted to know.

"Once. A long time ago. Back in my university days. It ended badly," he said, somewhat tersely.

I didn't probe, but I did wonder, *does all love, real love that is, end badly?*

Chapter 13

Nikola and I spent the rest of the day in bed, talking and making love for hours. Afterwards, we'd fallen asleep. When I opened my eyes the next day, natural light shimmered through the blinds, bathing the room in soft, golden sunlight. I thought it must be well after noon.

He was still asleep. With our bodies entwined, I took the opportunity to study him. His lashes were long, black and lacy; the kind wealthy women paid beaucoup bucks for. His skin, smooth and tan, was irresistible to me. I ran my hand over the contour of his body. I couldn't imagine ever getting tired of the feel of it. I closed my eyes and with my head on his chest, listened to the echo of his heartbeat, his deep, even breathing, and realized I could stay like this forever.

It dawned on me that this is what making love was. We were so in touch, so in sync, so passionate and intense, that when he was inside of me it felt like we were one. Even now, I was still aroused. With Nikola, I was insatiable.

Enveloped in an indescribable contentment, I drifted back to sleep.

I woke to the feel of his soft lips touching my forehead. I didn't know how much time had passed, but it felt kind of late in the afternoon.

"Are you awake, baby?" he whispered.

"I'm awake," I said, stretching.

"It is getting dark outside," he said.

"Yeah, what time is it, anyway?"

"I have not checked," he said, turning on his side to face me. "Why are you so worried about the time? Are you kicking me out?"

"No, I just don't want to cause any problems between you and Biljana," I said, and snuggled closer, pressing my cheek to his chest. "I know she's probably going crazy wondering where you are."

"Let her wonder. I am with you right now, and I do not want to think about her," he said, between provocative kisses. "It is not like we live together."

"Again?" I said in my sexiest voice. "You never get enough, do you?"

"I will never get enough of this," he said, and kissed my belly, "or these," my breasts, "and definitely not this." Then, he then kissed me deeply.

I was so turned on I could scarcely catch my breath. The sensation of him growing hard against my leg intensified my desire.

"I need you inside me," I said, breathlessly.

He turned me onto my stomach. I wrapped my hands around the bedpost, anticipating what I knew would happen next.

In an instant, he entered me, his body leaning heavily on mine. My back arched involuntarily each time he plunged inside me, creating an exquisite smacking sound that gave me chills.

"I cannot get enough of you," he said, thrusting himself in and out of me.

I moaned in response and squeezed the bedpost even tighter.

"Don't stop," I pleaded, feverishly.

"I am not. Do you feel how hard I am inside of you?" He tugged at my hair just enough to make me want more.

His rhythm grew in faster, more urgent motions.

"Pull my hair again," I said, "harder this time."

"You like being my naughty girl?" he breathed, heavily.

"I love it."

"Oh God, I am going to explode," he rasped, and I felt his whole body stiffen, and then weaken.

He rolled onto his back, completely spent.

"Sorry, I could not hold it any longer. That never happens to me. You turn me on so much," he panted.

"It's okay," I giggled. "You've more than proven yourself to me." I traced the hard line of his jaw with my finger.

"No, it is not okay," he said, turning on his side to kiss me passionately.

His lips trailed from my breasts to my stomach, then between my legs. I pulled his hair as he brought me to ecstasy with his tongue. An earthy moan escaped my mouth as I started my first of three orgasms in a row.

My body trembled with pleasure when he kissed my inner thigh one last time, before crawling up to lie beside me.

"That was incredible," I exhaled.

I turned over and curled myself into him. My breathing slowly returned to normal and before I knew it, we were both fast asleep.

I opened my eyes to find Nikola staring at me. I didn't know how much time had passed but it was completely dark outside.

"What?" I said, a little self-consciously.

"Nothing. I like watching you sleep. Do you have a problem with that?"

I raised an eyebrow. "If I did, would it matter?"

"No." He laughed and sat up, resting his back against the headboard.

I turned on my side and gazed up at him. "I'm glad you don't live with Biljana."

"Where did that come from?" he asked, not hiding his surprise.

I shrugged and gave him a crooked smile. "I don't know, the thought just popped into my head, and then came out my mouth."

He leaned down and kissed me on the forehead. "You are cute."

"I'm glad you think so," I said in my best little girl voice. "I don't want this night to end. I just want to stay here with you and forget about work, forget about the fact that she's in your life." My stomach clenched at the thought.

His face briefly tensed up. "Do not be like this. You always worry about so much. Enjoy the moment, *this* moment. Are you familiar with Horace? I have thought a lot about his work since meeting you."

"Well, I was kidding when I said I only read Instagram quotes," I giggled. "I remember reading some of his poetry in Lit back in college, but I wouldn't consider myself familiar. Why?"

"The Latin phrase *carpe diem* came from the 'Odes,' a collection of poetry by Horace."

"I remember the phrase…" I scratched my head. "Something about you only live once?"

Nikola grinned. "Not exactly, but you are close. It does not mean to ignore the future, but not to forget to live now. Take advantage of the life you have *today*. In *this* moment is where you will find life. Not in your hopes or worries for tomorrow."

"I don't know how to live like that. I always plan ahead. It's the way my mind works. I can't change that."

"You can change that." He pulled me closer. "You can begin right now, here with me."

"I still don't know if that's possible, but if it is, there's no one else I'd rather begin with." I rested a hand on his stubbled cheek.

"Okay, then we will get started." He playfully tossed the blankets off of us. "First, we take a bubble bath. I will grab some wine, you run the water," he said, and leapt out of bed.

I watched him walk out of the room butt naked and called out, "Grab the Kendall-Jackson Riesling!"

He turned around. "Not Red?"

"Whatever you want."

He shrugged. "Okay. Riesling it is."

I got out of bed, slipped on my favorite La Perla Primula robe and ran the bath. This was fun. I couldn't remember the last time I'd enjoyed myself so much.

A couple of minutes later, Nikola walked into the room with two wine glasses in one hand and the bottle of Kendall-Jackson in the other.

I raised a brow. "Where's the corkscrew?"

He blinked. "Oh, yes. Right," and started for the kitchen, then abruptly stopped. "You put your robe on?"

"Sure did," I cooed. "How else would you be able to watch me do this..." With two fingers, I undid the sash, and then shook my shoulders, causing the robe to slip to the floor.

"I think this is going to be an even longer night than I expected," he said, forgetting the wine altogether and heading straight for me.

He was right.

The following morning, I woke up and wiped the sleep from my eyes. Nikola was already dressed, which filled me with sadness. "Why didn't you wake me? I would've made you coffee."

"Because we were up so late. I know you have to go to work so I wanted to let you sleep in. I am actually late for work, but I will call you later, I promise," he said, leaning down to kiss me.

Damn it! I don't want to go back to work. Having two days off in a row in retail, especially a Sunday and Monday, was rare and although I was grateful for it, I wanted more.

I got up, wrapped a sheet around me and walked him to the door.

"Okay, I'll see you later."

He kissed me once more, and then he was gone. The minute the door shut my heart sank.

"Back to the real world," I griped, scooping my phone from the kitchen bar and turning it on.

At least that snake, Fiona, wasn't working today. I didn't know if I could keep myself from attacking and choking her.

I groaned when I saw I had three voicemails from Ben.

Screw him.

I also had about fifteen 911 texts from Chance, and two from Jean-Luc. I knew I'd see both Chance and Jean-Luc in less than two hours, so I'd wait to talk to them. After a few minutes, curiosity got the best of me and I listened to Ben's voicemails.

The first two were just Ben begging me to call him back. The last one was left early this morning. He was calling from the airport. He said he'd be back in town in two weeks and he needed the opportunity to talk with me in person. He swore he hadn't slept with Fiona, but that I deserved an explanation.

I thought about it for a second. *I've had enough of his lies and bullshit! No way is he going to worm his way back into my life.*

I grudgingly got ready for work. I was thankful Biljana was off today. I didn't want to face her. Although I felt fairly sure she didn't know about Nikola and me, I was fairly certain she sensed he was straying.

I walked up to the counter where Jean-Luc was placing cash in the register. He punched a few buttons and butted the drawer shut with his hip. I knew he must've gotten in early because opening the registers was the last step in the morning routine.

"Well, look who is here! My Blonde Ambition, who does not like to return phone calls or texts?" he said, with an arched brow, clearly irritated.

"I'm sorry. I turned my phone off." I kissed him on the cheek.

"It is okay, but in the future, if we ever attend another peasant gathering together, you will let me know when you get home, so I have no worries," he snipped.

I chuckled at his "peasant gathering" crack. That was Jean-Luc, always superior to everyone.

"Thank God Biljana's boyfriend got into the cab with you, or I would have," he smirked

I dropped the makeup brushes I was organizing. "What did you just say?"

"I think you heard me, baby." His eyes twinkled.

"Jean-Luc, I..."

He held up his hand. "There is no need to tell me to keep quiet. I am your friend, Toy. I will not say a word. I just hope you realize the dangerous little game you are playing."

"Did anyone else see him get in with me?" I asked, nervously biting my lip.

"Relax, Cherie. I checked to see who was around. Your secret is safe," he reassured. "So, *he* is the reason why your phone was off?"

"Yes," I said, my face suddenly growing hot.

"Did you enjoy yourself?" he said with a wink.

"What?"

"Did you *enjoy* yourself?"

"Yeah, Jean-Luc, I really did."

"Okay. Then, remove the embarrassment from your face."

"It shows, huh?" I frowned.

He sighed. "You know, as long as I have known you, I have never seen you act as *irrational* as you have these past few weeks, I assume since you had your first rendezvous with this man. But this new version of yourself, it is nice to see."

"What do you mean?" I asked, confused.

"You never let go, baby. You never stop to — how do you say — smell the roses. It is always about work and more work. Even when you were with Benjamin you still could not let go. Maybe you have found someone who taught you how?" He grinned.

"Maybe," I said, not sure if irrational was the descriptive word I wanted for myself.

"Come on, sweetie, we will grab some coffee now. Hurry, before the store opens." He took my hand. "Without the coffee, I cannot start my day, especially knowing a major fashion disaster will appear to me any minute now."

"Fine, Jean-Luc," I giggled. I knew he was referring to Tommy. That accent, especially when he was being insulting, killed me.

I guess I was pretty lucky to have people around me who, no matter what the circumstances, made me laugh.

When we returned to the counter, everyone working the morning shift had arrived; Tommy, Tatyana, Yvonne, and Ed. What a relief it was not having Fiona and Biljana here to contend with. When I'd written the schedule, I hadn't even known I'd be doing myself this favor.

An hour or so had gone by and the counter was getting busy. Tatyana and Ed both had clients in their chairs, Tommy was passing out fragrance samples to customers walking by, and Jean-Luc was communicating with an Asian customer, who spoke no English or French, through Google Translate on his phone.

Even a language barrier isn't enough to stop Jean-Luc! He seriously cracks me up.

My amusement was short-lived. It dissolved at the sound of Debbie's voice.

"Good morning, Toy. You're in luck, I'll be with you all day today to monitor your counter's progress for the event." She slung her coat and her grossly overloaded Gucci bag on the counter, taking up space we needed for product demonstrations. It was store policy that all employees and vendors check their coats and bags in with security before coming on the floor. Obviously, Debbie didn't get the memo.

I should call Loss Prevention on her ass, I thought.

Sharee approached the counter and met my eyes, then turned to Debbie. "Well hello. I didn't know you'd be in today."

"I don't think this place can afford for me not to be here today, do you?" Debbie said, waving a hand at my counter as if it were in gross disarray.

This insufferable bitch. Not only do I have to make sure we meet our daily goal and stay focused on pre-sell for the event, now I get to have Debbie micromanage my counter all day.

I'd be lucky if I got a quarter of my work done today. Instead, I'd be pulling reports for her, shuffling around product to where she thinks it looks more appealing, and pretending to be interested in the mindless small talk she liked to make.

Grrrrrr.

The phone rang twice and before I could pick it up, Yvonne beat me to it.

"Hello… this is Yvonne. Yeah, this is Cessone."

I'd explained to Yvonne a million times, "Yvonne, the proper telephone etiquette for Cesonne is, "Thank you for calling Cesonne at Norniesakmans Chicago, my name is, Yvonne. How may I help you today?" I'd even made her repeat it!

I glared at her, knowing Debbie would be riding me for this for the rest of the day.

Yvonne, without pressing the hold button on the phone, dropped the receiver on the counter and raced toward Debbie, Sharee and me.

"It's Frances! Like, "Frances of Cesonne" Frances," she gushed.

Debbie was already marching over to the phone when Yvonne called after her, "She wants to talk to Sharee."

Debbie stopped dead in her tracks, turned around and faced Yvonne. "I'm sure she didn't know *I* was here. Now, don't you have work to do?" She dismissed Yvonne with that patented shooing motion of hers, and picked up the phone.

Yvonne stared daggers at Debbie's back.

"Yvonne, I think your customer is ready for you," I kindly reminded her, and nodded toward the woman who'd been patiently waiting in a make-up chair.

"Thanks, Captain," she said, and stormed over to the client.

"Why does Debbie have to be so nasty?" mumbled Sharee.

I looked at her, surprised. *I guess even someone like Sharee can only take so much.*

Before I could say anything, Debbie cupped her hand over the phone's mouthpiece and practically yelled across the counter, "Sharee, come over here. Frances needs to speak with you."

Debbie, always the professional.

Sharee went to take the call. Debbie stood less than a foot away from her the entire time. The conversation went on for a while with Sharee mostly listening, uttering an occasional yes or no, and chuckling a few times, as if she and Frances were old friends.

I watched Debbie grow more agitated by the second.

When Sharee finally hung up, Debbie blurted out, "What did Frances have to talk with *you* about for so long?"

"Oh, about how preparation for the event was going," said Sharee, ignoring Debbie's tone.

"For ten minutes?" Debbie challenged. If she was a cartoon character, there'd have been smoke coming out her ears by now.

Tommy and I awkwardly milled around the two of them, not quite knowing what to do.

"Why don't we finish this conversation in my office?" Sharee calmly said to Debbie, tossing a glance in our direction.

Debbie, as if just realizing she was on the sales floor having this discussion, jerked her coat and bag from the counter.

"Let's go," she barked.

Sharee shot me one last wide-eyed look. I felt sorry for her. Debbie was a miserable excuse of a human being. Sharee was so much more qualified for regional director. But then, this was cosmetics, where more often than not it seemed, an imbecile scored a better gig than those who deserved it.

Chapter 14

The rest of the day went by quickly. Jean-Luc and Tatyana ended their shifts just as Chance started his. Debbie hadn't come back to the counter since Sharee and she left earlier — thank God! So, at a little after 5:00 PM, I was in a good mood. *A day without Debbie is like a day full of sunshine.* Chance, on the other hand, was a different story. He was still pissed off at me for leaving Tatyana's birthday party without telling him.

"You know, Chance, I'm sorry, but hunting you down on the dance floor wasn't exactly on the top of my priority list, especially when I'd just found out I'd been betrayed by both my boyfriend and my girlfriend."

"Your *boyfriend*? He hasn't been your boyfriend in forever, and how long have you and Fiona been on the outs?" He dropped his hand on his wrist. "Whatever."

I stuck my tongue in my cheek, debating on whether or not to let him have it. I struggled to keep my cool and said, "You know, I don't need this right now. I really don't," and walked away. Besides, I knew his bitchy attitude had a lot more to do with Jean-Luc than it did with me.

Later, after I'd calmed down, I'd sent him and Tommy to the stockroom to bring our new merchandise to the floor. They'd been gone about fifteen minutes when one of Chance's regular clients came in for her makeup appointment.

After seating her, I headed to the back. I opened the door, but stopped and listened when I overheard Chance talking about me.

"So, you heard Toy ditched me?"

"No, she didn't," scoffed Tommy. "She was fighting with Fiona and Ben."

"Yeah, right. Everyone's heard that part, but nobody seems to care that she left me at the club to fend for myself!" Chance sulked.

I bit my fist to keep from laughing out loud. *Fend for himself?*

"Come on, little man. She didn't do it on purpose. Besides, the French Douche Bag was there, wasn't he? And, how about Tatyana? You weren't there alone," Tommy snickered.

"Quit laughing at me. I was too, left alone. Tatyana was so fucking wasted she didn't even know her own name, and the 'French Douche Bag', as you so charmingly put it, left right after Toy made her grand exit."

"Well, if I hadn't been working, I would've chilled with you, bro."

"Yeah, thanks for that," Chance huffed.

I backed out, tapped loudly on the stockroom door and reentered.

"Chance, can you come to the counter? Cara's here for you," I announced, walking toward the two of them.

"Thank you," he said, snidely and shot past me.

I waited for the inevitable slam of the door behind him. He didn't disappoint me. I giggled.

"Man, he's pissed at you," grinned Tommy.

"Ya think?"

We laughed a little, then Tommy said, "I tried to explain, but he didn't want to hear it."

"He'll get over it," I said, shaking my head.

"I know, he's not one to carry a grudge for long. Anyway, I don't think you're the one he's upset with," Tommy said, slicing open a carton of stock with a box cutter.

"What do you mean?"

"He's got the hots for your golden boy."

I gave him a squint. "Golden boy?"

"You know who I mean. Jean-Luc." He cracked open another box and started unloading it.

"Okay." I watched him stack the contents, small, cellophane-wrapped boxes, on a shelf for a moment. "What makes you think Chance likes Jean-Luc?" I asked, suddenly realizing if Tommy could tell something was going on between them, so could the entire counter.

"Isn't it obvious? Chance is always bringing Jean-Luc coffee, offering to take him to lunch, and referring clients to him for fragrances sales, when you know damn well he can sell practically as good as Jean-Luc. You've never noticed Chance fawns all over him?"

"No," I lied. I wondered if he suspected more and gave him a prod. "Has Jean-Luc noticed?"

Tommy put the last box on the shelf and turned to look at me as if I'd just asked him if the moon was made of cheese.

"How do you think he's acting? He's so focused on sales, he wouldn't notice Giorgio Armani unless he was trying to buy a bottle of Cesonne."

Thank God! He doesn't know!

"Besides," he went on, "I don't get a straight *or* gay vibe from Jean-Luc. He's probably asexual. It's gonna be him and his right hand for life."

"Okay, okay," I turned away to hide my amusement. "I'm going back to the floor." I stopped at the door and over my shoulder said, "How much longer do you think you have back here?"

"Probably ten minutes."

"Cool, see you out there," I said, and headed for the counter.

I was pleased to see Yvonne and Chance both attentively working with clients.

A few minutes later, I was wiping down the counter when Jean-Luc walked up to me.

"Honey, why are *you* cleaning?" He shook his head in disbelief. "Are you not the manager?"

I put down the paper towel and spray bottle. "Are you not off the clock?" I said, mirroring his accent. "You were supposed to be gone an hour ago."

"I am on my way to Gucci and I thought I would stop and see how the counter is doing." He raised a Starbucks cup to his lips.

"It's doing very well and I appreciate your concern, but I am very capable of running the business."

He gazed at me, wounded.

"Fine," I sighed. "We've sold $600 since you left. Our daily goal has been met. And no, Tommy hasn't had any fragrances sales. Happy?"

He laughed and nearly choked on his coffee. "I love you, baby. You know me so well."

Before I could reply, Tommy was on my heels.

He gave Jean-Luc a cold once-over. "What're you doing here? I thought you were gone for the day, or at least I'd hoped."

"Don't worry. I am not staying. I am going to Gucci. You have heard of Gucci? As in the fashion house? Right?" Jean-Luc goaded.

Just as I was about to tell Jean-Luc to hit the dusty trail, I was stopped cold by two police officers fast approaching the counter. One was a short, Hispanic man in full police regalia. He pulled to a stop in front of Tommy, who was still beside me. The guy was a caricature of a badass Chicago cop: thumbs hooked on his belt, chest puffed out, and an exaggerated, wide-legged stance. When I glanced at his face, my eyes went straight to his overly tweezed eyebrows. Someone needed to point out that it wasn't a good look for him, but right now probably wasn't the best time.

The other officer was an older African-American man in a dark suit. If I had to bet, I'd put my money on him as the more intelligent of the two.

"Tommy Holsten?" asked Officer Dark Suit, flashing a gold badge.

"Yeah," Tommy answered, his face suddenly drained of color.

"You're under arrest for the distribution of an unlawful controlled substance."

Officer Brows whipped out his handcuffs and dangled them in front of Tommy.

Tommy knew the drill. He turned around slowly and put his hands behind his back, while Brows spouted his Miranda rights. Then, I heard the awful, corrugated sound of the cuffs closing and saw Tommy wince. I clamped a hand over my mouth.

"Toy, can you call Tatyana?" Tommy's voice was desperate, causing a terrible pang in my belly as they led him away.

"Don't worry, I'll do it," Jean-Luc chuckled, raising his cup, "As soon as I finish my latte I will call her."

I sucked in my breath and before I knew it, I'd elbowed Jean-Luc hard in the arm. "Stop it!" I hissed. I turned and called out, "Don't worry, Tommy. I'll call Tatyana!"

I nearly sprinted into the stockroom, whipped out my phone and scrolled through my contacts. I knew Loss Prevention would be racing down here any minute now, walkie-talkies in hand. They lived for this shit. The last thing I needed was to have them after me for making personal phone calls, especially calls regarding drugs and jail. I popped my head back out the door to make sure the coast was clear before I hit dial.

After calling Tatyana twice, leaving a frantic voice message once, and firing off a "CALL ME BACK, 911!" text, I went back to the counter.

I glowered at Jean-Luc, then turned my back on him and tapped the keyboard on the sleeping computer.

After a second or two, he stepped up beside me. "I apologize if you found my little joke distasteful, but I have no sympathy for such foolishness. He's clearly a moron, honey." Jean-Luc tossed his coffee cup in the trash and picked up a stack of fragrances strips. "I suppose I will go to Gucci another time. For now, the business needs me."

I glared at him. "Yeah, well you should be more than satisfied. He's really in for it now, and it's terrible enough without your nasty one-liners." My eyes stung with tears. "What did he ever do to you, anyway?" I spat, and turned away to hammer the computer keys.

Jean-Luc was no dummy. He backed away from me and strolled over to a couple of middle-aged women who were eyeballing our new fragrance display. I didn't bother telling him to go home. Let him work all night if he wanted. I didn't care.

I regained my composure — barely — and called, "Yvonne!"

She twisted her head in my direction. "Gotcha, Captain?" She saluted me with a hand badly in need of a manicure.

It was two hours later, and I still hadn't reached Tatyana. There was nothing I could do but wait. Poor Tommy.

A beautiful brunette, probably in her early 40s, walked up to Jean-Luc, and kissed his cheek. He seemed surprised. *"Que faites-vous ici?"*

"Je voulais vous voir," she replied.

French. Whenever I heard it, I wanted to kick myself for dropping the class in high school.

"Toy," he motioned me over, "meet the lovely Agathe. We met at the art museum yesterday. I told her where I worked. What good luck I ended up being here, yes?" Jean-Luc beamed. "Agathe, this is my good friend, Toy."

It didn't surprise me that this woman would be attracted to Jean-Luc. He was very handsome and always dressed to kill. What bothered me was the fact that he was still in denial about his sexuality, even after the Chance incident.

With that thought, I glanced across the counter to see Chance boring holes into Jean-Luc with his eyes.

"Toy, I think I will leave now." He pulled his jacket and scarf out from under the counter and offered his arm to the lady. "Au revoir."

Wow. What happened to "the business needs me"?

"Jean-Luc, please remember that we *do not* have our coats at the counter. It's Loss Prevention's policy, not mine," I said, still miffed. I had enough to worry about without security jumping my case for his stupid coat. "But, yeah. Au revoir."

"No problem, Cherie," he said, tossing the jacket over his shoulder with two fingers like the leading man in an old black and white movie, walking off screen with a dame.

I watched after him for a second, my ire giving way to wonder. The scene might be nearly perfect, if the she on his arm was a he.

I shook it off. I had bigger problems than Jean-Luc's sexual orientation. It was time for me to stomp out another flame. Tatyana wasn't answering her phone and I couldn't just let Tommy rot in jail.

"Chance?" I called, drawing my keys and phone from a drawer.

"Let me guess." He scrunched up his face. "You want me to stay late so you can go rescue Tommy?"

I gazed at him for a second. He turned away and started polishing a mirror.

"Awe, Chance..." I went to him, dropped my things on the counter and squeezed his shoulders. "I know you like Jean-Luc. All I can say is that everyone handles coming out in different ways. Maybe this is his way of doing it. Maybe he has to put the mask on one more time before he's convinced he's not that person."

"I know, but it still hurts. This is the first time I've actually *liked* someone in a long time." His voice began to tremble. "And, you've been so preoccupied lately. I don't know who to turn to or what to think about anything right now."

"Don't cry, sweetie. I know I haven't been the greatest friend lately. I think this event has really taken its toll on me. I'm sorry." I purposely left out Ben and my personal problems. This time it *was* all about Chance.

"I'll be okay. I think I'm starting to want something serious," he fretted. "I'm tired of the bar scene and just hooking up."

"You are?" I perked up. This wasn't the Chance I knew.

"Well, you don't have to look so shocked about it."

"Oh, sorry."

"Yeah, going to Rudi and Eddy's wedding a few weeks ago really made me realize how nice it would be to have a partner. They're always there for one another, they've got a beautiful home, and they're planning on adopting. I feel like if I don't get started soon, I may never have that." Again, tears filled his eyes.

I put my arms around him. "Yes, you will," then let him go and wiped a tear from his face. "You *can* have all of that, Chance. You just have to find the right person."

"If only Jean-Luc were the right one," he said, longingly. "I like him a lot."

I ran a hand through his hair. "I know you do, but you shouldn't wait for him. He hasn't even admitted he's gay."

"Yeah, it just sucks," he moaned.

"Come on now, babe. It'll all work out," I purred and gave him another good squeeze.

He sighed, "I hope you're right,"

"I am." I scooped my stuff from the counter. "But listen. I do need you to close for me, would you mind? I don't know how long this is going to take. I don't even know how to find out where Tommy's been taken. I have to get going."

"It'd be nice if Tatyana were here. I'm sure she'd know exactly what to do," he said, thoughtfully.

"Yeah, it really *would* be nice if she were here — or if she'd answer the damn phone! But she's not, so I guess I'll have to be Tommy's savior today," I said with zero enthusiasm.

"Okay, girl. Go do your heroine thing or whatever it is you're doing. Just don't forget to bring hand sanitizer with you." He curled his lip. "I heard prisons are nasty."

"I'm pretty sure he's in jail, Chance, not prison."

"What's the difference?"

"There's a big difference. Remind me to explain it to you sometime. I'll call you later."

"Keep me posted," he called as I headed out.

I glanced back at him on my way to the employee locker room. I'd never seen him act this way before. I wasn't sure if this was a case of his wanting what he couldn't have, or if he really *was* tired of the single life. Either way, I'd just have to wait and see how things worked out. Besides, I couldn't waste anymore precious time on Chance's problem right now with Tommy still cooling behind bars.

I opened my locker, set down my bag and pulled out my black, Henri Bendel cashmere gloves and scarf and black leather, Chanel boots. Finally, I slipped into my long, black and white, Chanel coat. Whoever said you couldn't look sexy in winter had obviously never been introduced to Chanel!

I picked my bag back up, slammed my locker shut, and walked through the locker room door. I was headed down the hallway to leave the building when I heard a deep, masculine voice shout from the security room.

"Hold up, Toy!"

I turned around to see a tall black guy with beady red eyes, in a security uniform, standing behind me on the opposite side of the Loss Prevention counter. I'd never seen him before, yet he knew *my* name. Where was the regular security guy, Clyde, who usually checked out employees in the evening?

I turned around and took a few steps toward him. "Yes?"

"I need to check your bag before you leave." His tone and the way he cocked his head put me on edge.

"Um, okay. Are you new?" I asked, politely.

"Not that it concerns you, but yes, I'm new. Open your bag for me," he said. It was an order, not a request.

That riled me. *Open your bag for me, PLEASE,* I wanted to correct him. Instead, I shrugged my purse off my shoulder, opened it wide, reached over and sat it on the counter directly in front of him. He rummaged through it like it was a bargain store basement bin.

"I just assumed you were new because I've never seen you before. I didn't mean to offend you," I mumbled, trying to make small talk.

"Man, she's good. She can go," said a voice I recognized with relief. Clyde, an ancient African-American man, who'd been part of the store's security team since Norniesakmans first opened, stepped up.

Everyone who knew Clyde would tell you he was a great guy. The one thing you could be sure of though, was Clyde knew everything that went on in the store. So much so, that if Norniesakmans had any smarts at all, they'd have had him sign a confidentiality agreement. He could probably write a trilogy about what went on in this place.

"I'll say when she's good, and until I'm through inspecting her bag, she's not good," the new guy said, putting a death grip on it.

He ransacked my bag for another minute while Clyde stood by glaring.

"Okay, you can go." He shoved my purse across the counter to me, "but here on out, bag checks will be mandatory when employees leave the building. It won't be random no more like it's been."

He strode past Clyde and plopped down into one of the chairs facing the several security monitors.

Clyde shook his gray head, flashing me an apologetic look. "Goodnight, Toy."

I shrugged. "Goodnight, Clyde."

I could tell Clyde and I were on the same page with this guy. *Who does he think he is, anyway? He knows my name, so he must've gone to HR and read everyone's file, looking for anyone who's been written up and may be a potential troublemaker. What a creep.* I hoped he was just filling in for someone, but judging by the way he spoke to Clyde, I had a feeling he was here to stay.

I trotted down two flights of stairs and just as I was about to exit the building, when I froze.

Wait! What if this new guy was brought in because of the gratis scam at my counter? What if he thinks I'm involved in their shenanigans?

I took the last flight and pushed through the door and into the street thinking of Tommy and Yvonne — and how much I'd love to hang them by their thumbs.

Chapter 15

I stepped out the back entrance and nearly laughed out loud. There stood the same flock of employees dressed in designer suits and skirts, smoking up a storm, without a bit of shame. It was as if smoking was part of their job description. Sold a pair of shoes today? Go have a smoke! Sold a dress? Go have a smoke! Made your goal today? Go have two smokes! Jeez!

So, what was I supposed to do about Tommy now? *Crap.* I bet our new security guy would know. I'd be damned if I was about to go back into the store, though. And, I certainly didn't want to have a chat with the new security goon.

Then it dawned on me. I didn't have to go in. I could call Clyde!

I pulled out my phone, selected "work" from my contacts and clicked on it. After asking for security and being transferred to three departments, none of which were the correct extension, I finally heard Clyde's voice on the line. *Whew. Thank God it's him and not the new sheriff in town.*

"Clyde, it's Toy," I said, and started coughing. No matter which way I turned, the haze of smoke followed.

"What's happening, Toy?" Clyde asked with a note of concern. "Are you okay?"

"Yes, yes. Just out here with the smokers. Listen, I know you saw Tommy get taken out of the store in handcuffs earlier. He has no family here, and I need to find out how to get him out of jail. I don't know where to start." I said in desperation.

"Well, let's see now, he was arrested here..." said Clyde.

"Yes," I said, exercising patience.

I loved Clyde, but he talked painfully slow. Sometimes I wished I could speed him up by grabbing his first word and pulling the rest out on a string. This was one of those times. I just wanted to find Tommy and go home.

"Well... then he's gotta be in District One."

"What's District One?"

"That'd be the police station where they'd be taking him for booking."

I was floored. He'd answered my question in less than five minutes. *Atta boy, Clyde!*

"Okay, so should I go there to get him?" I asked, anxious to get this show on the road.

"It ain't that simple. What was his charge?"

Oh no. I didn't want to tell store security that Tommy was in trouble for drugs, but what choice did I have? Tatyana was MIA. I didn't know anyone else who'd know how to handle a situation like this.

"I think the police officer said something about a controlled substance," I mumbled.

"Oh, Lord have mercy, that boy done done it now." I pictured Clyde shaking his head. "That's a felony, Toy. I hope he's got him a good damn lawyer."

"A felony? Oh, my God!" I felt my neck start to burn from the tension.

"He ain't getting out of there until he sees a judge. You might as well just go on home," said Clyde, now matter-of-fact. "He's staying at the Cook County Slammer tonight."

"There's nothing I can do?" I couldn't remember the last time I felt this helpless.

"You can call the jail tomorrow to find out when he's scheduled to go in front of the judge. And you can pray he keeps his mouth shut while he's in there," he instructed. "He doesn't need no fights at a time like this."

Clyde had a point. Tommy wasn't exactly the most passive guy I knew.

"Okay, Clyde. Thank you so much. I'm sorry if I took up your time. This is all such a big mess," I sighed.

"Yeah, but it ain't your mess, Toy," Clyde said, firmly. "He made his bed, now he's gotta sleep in it."

I wish I could feel that way, but I had a soft spot for Tommy. Despite always hitting me up for cash advances or favors, he was a nice guy and I suspected he'd had a difficult childhood. I'd also had a hunch that he might have a drug problem, but had never prodded him to find out.

"You're right, Clyde. I better let him deal with his own mess," I lied, knowing my involvement was far from over. "Thanks for your advice, I appreciate it."

"No problem, Toy. See you tomorrow?" he asked.

"You know it," I said.

"Alright, you have a good night."

"You too, Clyde. Bye." I stood there for a second. All I could do for now was to go home and hope for the best.

As I walked along Michigan Avenue I smiled to keep from crying. This day, like most days of late, had been completely ridiculous. I thought about all of the characters who'd filled my day. First, there was Debbie and the Frances phone call, next Tommy and Officer Brow, then Chance, Jean-Luc, and Jean-Luc's French Beauty and finally, Sheriff Hardass. I was afraid to say that it couldn't get any worse, because if the last few weeks had taught me anything, it's that when Murphy's Law is in high gear, anything can get worse!

I made it to my building. Mike the doorman said hello and handed me a bouquet of red roses. I looked at the card: "With love, Ben." They were beautiful, but not so beautiful that they'd make me forget what a dick he'd been.

I started toward the elevator and stopped. I spun around and walked back to the front desk.

"Do you have a special someone in your life who you could give these to?" I held out the bouquet.

"Uh, I th-think so," he stammered.

"Make it someone *very* special. This is over $300 in roses, my friend," I said, and shoved them into his arms

His mouth fell open.

"Don't forget to throw out the card," I called out before the elevator doors shut.

I put the key in the lock to open my front door, and let out a big fat sigh of relief. *Finally, the moment I've waited for all day.* I walked in, took off my coat and boots without bothering to put them away, and went to the bathroom and undressed.

I turned on the bath and let it run while I removed my makeup at the sink. Friday and Saturday night, combined with the two-day sex marathon, had taken its toll on me. It was recovery time. I tied my hair in a high knot, put a clay mask on my face, and sank into a tub of hot water. *Now this is what I call heaven.*

About fifteen minutes had passed when the doorbell rang.

Who in the hell is this, now? And, how could they have gotten past my doorman? I was seriously fed up with surprise visits.

I stepped out of the tub, wrapped myself in a towel, and marched to the front door. I put my eye to the peephole, but I couldn't see anyone.

"Who's there?"

No one answered. I stared at the door. Was it someone who'd rung the wrong doorbell?

I was halfway back to the bathroom when the bell sounded again.

"What the hell? Who is it?" I yelled, getting more agitated by the second. Water dripped from the ends of my hair onto the floor.

Finally, "It's Fiona."

Fiona? *Fiona? What could she possibly have to say to me?*

"What do *you* want?" I asked, sharply.

"Just a few minutes to talk to you," she pleaded. "I want to apologize."

Should I even waste my time hearing her out?

"Please, Toy?"

Fine! I threw open the door, and stood squarely in the doorway. I didn't care that I was soaking wet in a towel and had a mud mask on. All I could think of when I looked at her was how good it had felt to throw that drink in her face. *Too bad I don't have one handy now,* I thought.

"I don't want your apology," I spat.

"If you'd just let me a have few minutes, please!" she said, giving me the sad eyes routine. "I know you'll be glad you did."

I wasn't about to give in. "I'm sure nothing from out of your mouth could make me feel better. I'm tired and frankly, if I never had to see you again, it'd be too soon."

"One minute is all I need." She was practically begging me.

"One minute? Is that all? Where were you when I needed one minute of your precious time? When I'd just lost Ben? Oh yeah. You did give me a minute, didn't you? You took a minute to make me feel like his leaving was all my fault. Come to think of it, you've always tried to make me feel like shit. And, not just about Ben, but about everything!" I fumed.

"Nothing happened between Ben and me," she said, and turned to walk away.

"Pfft, yeah, right," I said, and crossed my arms.

She spun back around to face me. "No, Toy. I mean it. Will you listen?" she said, a tinge of anger in her voice.

"You've got sixty seconds before I slam the door in your face."

Fiona's eyes looked past me expectantly, but I wasn't about to let her get too cozy. I stood in the doorway like Gibraltar.

She let out a sigh of exasperation and said, "Look, right after you two broke up I texted him a few times and mentioned that even though you two were over,

I'd like to be friends. After exchanging a few more texts, he told me he didn't think it was a good idea. He said he didn't want to hurt you.

"I let a few months go by and texted him again. I used you as a reason to contact him. I told him you'd gotten a new place and you were dating someone else."

I went rigid. "You told him I was dating someone?"

"Will you let me finish?" she snapped.

She had balls. I guess she didn't realize how much I wanted to strangle her.

I bit down hard. "Go ahead."

"He didn't answer immediately. A couple months later, he texted me back telling me he'd be in Chicago for a medical conference. I asked him if he wanted to have coffee and talk. He agreed and so we met."

"You never even liked Ben. You used to tell me I could do better!" I said, my anger giving way to hurt.

"Yeah, well things change," she mumbled.

"Yeah, they sure do," I snapped, the anger I'd quelled rising again, quickly.

"Toy, you said you'd let me finish," she said, quietly.

I nodded and she went on.

"So, we met for coffee at the Starbucks on Chestnut. It wasn't a big deal. Just small talk and him wanting to know how you were. It lasted about thirty minutes, then he had to go. Later that night, I called him and said I had something important to tell him about you, but I could only do it in person, something I hadn't been able to say earlier that day. He offered to meet me in the lobby, but I said he was being overcautious. I convinced him we were both mature adults and should talk in his room.

"He was waiting outside his door when I got there. I asked if I could use his bathroom. He let me in. When I went into the bathroom, I stripped down to the lingerie I was wearing underneath, came out and tried to kiss him," she said, carefully avoiding my gaze.

"Pathetic," I snorted.

"Apparently, he thought so too."

For a fraction of a second, I almost felt sorry for her. *Almost.*

"He told me to get dressed. I was so ashamed. I didn't wait around to be chastised by him. I texted him the next day and apologized for my inappropriate behavior.

"He said he still loved you. I told him I was sorry and that I hoped we could be friends. He said okay, but when I'd text him, his responses became shorter and they were always, always about you," she said, tears welling up in her eyes. "And, okay, you're right. I *am* pathetic."

"Why are you telling me all of this?"

"Because I care about you, Toy," Fiona said, then grimaced. "And, I'm sorry about Saturday night. You know how I hate clubs because I can't handle my liquor? I almost always end up making an ass of myself or put my foot in my mouth. I was in love with the *idea* of Ben, not Ben himself. I've always wanted to have a guy like Ben for myself. That's why I tried dating a couple of his friends. I got caught up in stupid envy and just lost it. And, the alcohol sure didn't help," she said, swallowing hard. "Please Toy, let me make it up to you. I know we seldom get a second chance in life, but could you find it in your heart to let me try and be the friend I should've been?"

Tears were now spilling down her face.

"I need time to process all of this," I said, softening a bit.

She nodded, and then walked away.

I closed my door, made my way back to the bathroom, and tested the bath water with two fingers. *Lukewarm...yuck!*

"Guess I'll just shower," I muttered.

I felt terrible. I hated what Fiona had done but I could still remember when she'd been a close girlfriend of mine. Life sure takes some strange turns.

You never knew when that seemingly meaningless lunch, the one where you and your girlfriend ate, drank and laughed for hours, would be your last; when that person would no longer be the first person you text in the morning or the first person you called for reassurance when you're unsure of a decision you made.

A tear slid down my face. I guess I'd never really grieved the loss of our friendship. I'd been so stricken over losing Ben, I hadn't let myself feel the hurt of losing Fiona.

I wiped away the tear and pulled myself together. Maybe I would give her another chance.

I grabbed my phone from the nightstand and fell into bed. I pulled up my last conversation with Ben and composed a new text.

Me: *When are you back in town? I think we need to talk.*
He responded immediately: *Next Sunday. I'd like that.*
Me: *K, Sunday. Afternoon work?*
Ben: *Sure does. 2 PM?*
Me: *Starbucks by my work?*
Ben: *Perfect...and Toy, thanks for giving me a chance to talk to you.*
Me: *You're welcome, good night.*
Him: *Goodnight;)*

Just as I was about to put my phone down another text popped up. *Nikola!* I actually had butterflies in my stomach.

Him: *Just wanted you to know I'm thinking of you. Goodnight beautiful.*
Me: *;) Goodnight.*

He texted me! I felt like I was sixteen and had just been asked to prom by the star quarterback. I wanted to text him more, but I decided to play it cool instead. No need to show him all of my cards.

I restarted *Bridget*, more as a reflex, but paid less attention to it than I normally did. My mind was swirling around the Ben and Nikola situation I'd inexplicably become involved in.

The next morning, I intended to stop by the front desk to have a talk with Mike, the only doorman to let just about anyone up to my apartment without so much as a call. When I got to the lobby, the supervisor was manning the desk. As angry as I was at Mike, I didn't want to get him in trouble, so I kept on walking. I'd catch him tonight.

I pulled the hood of my Fendi coat down tightly over my head and walked against the cutting gusts. Chicago wasn't called The *Windy City* for no good reason. My face froze and my eyes watered.

I entered the building, walked up the stairs and paused at the employee entrance. I heard an obnoxious and familiar laugh. I stepped through and sure enough, there was Debbie in the hallway that separated the locker room from the security monitoring room, leaning against the security counter, giggling like an adolescent.

What's so funny? God, she was annoying!

I had barely finished the thought when I locked eyes with a pair of beady ones bulging from the face of Sheriff Hardass. *Just my luck! I couldn't have walked in at a worse time.*

I stood dumbfounded.

As usual, Debbie was a walking fashion catastrophe. She stood there wearing a Hermes T-shirt; black Topshop leggings, which revealed a disgusting camel toe; and Versace gladiator boots. Gladiator boots in winter? *I'll bet she thinks she looks like a runway model.* Someone needed to tell her she wasn't nineteen with a twenty-one-inch waistline. It was also a shame that such a beautiful shirt and pair of boots could be made to look so cheap. There was something pathetic about how she bought designer *everything* — and didn't have a clue as to how to wear it.

"Toy, I'll meet you at your counter a little later. Pretend I'm not here right now, okay?" Debbie mandated, without even looking at me.

"Sure, Debbie, no problem."

That was her not-so-subtle way of telling me not to ask her any questions. As if there was anything she could enlighten me on! She didn't know anything about my business, and was the laziest person I knew, not to mention an incredible, egotistical bitch with a personality more obnoxious than an alarm clock blaring at 5:00 AM.

Well, at least Sheriff Hardass wasn't messing with me. Instead, he acted like I wasn't even there. I hoped it'd stay that way.

I walked into the locker room and hung up my coat. I wondered what Debbie was doing here an hour before the store opened. She never came in this early unless corporate was in town or an event was taking place. *Debbie better not be conspiring with the Sheriff to bust somebody on my team before the big event. She knows I need everyone to pull it off.*

I put my things in my locker, checked myself in the mirror, and exited out of the room. Both she and the sheriff were now gone. I went down the long hallway to the sales floor.

When I reached my counter, I turned on the computer, then went to the mailroom where all of yesterday's sales were printed and waiting for the counter managers to pick up in the morning. I collected my papers and was just about to leave the room when a pair of voices caught my attention.

Debbie's insufferable voice carried across the hall from Sharee's office. I tiptoed back into the mailroom and pretended to go through the past few months' sales results in case anyone came by and wondered why I was standing there.

In response to what Debbie had said, I heard: "I'm so glad we had the chance to talk a few minutes before Sharee came in. I learn so much from you, Debbie."

Fiona! Back in true brown nose form.

"It just comes to me naturally, Fiona. I myself didn't go to college. I worked my way up the ladder to get where I am now," said Debbie with faux modesty.

I couldn't stop my eyes from rolling like a marble in a roulette wheel. It was an involuntary reaction to the both of them. *But why are the two of them meeting this early?*

"That's incredible. I had no idea you never went to college!" Fiona spread it on thick.

"Everyone's shocked when I tell them that," Debbie boasted.

Not me!

"Well, I want you to know that things will change at the counter once Toy's gone," Fiona said, conspiratorially. "She pretends she's got everything under control when she's in front of you, but it's all an act."

That little witch!

"I'm well aware of everything that goes on at your counter. I still have a few other people I need to interview for Toy's position, just because it's HR protocol, but you're my top candidate. Oh, and *Sharee* has to be in the loop in order to follow corporate policy, although I don't think it's necessary to have her in the decision-making process since it is *my* call in the end."

"Do you think Sharee will cause a problem with my promotion?" Fiona asked, nervously.

"No way," laughed Debbie, as if Sharee was nothing.

"Thank you so much, Debbie," Fiona concluded her ass kissing.

I thought about putting my foot across Sharee's office door so Fiona would trip over it when she walked out, but decided against it. Then it hit me: Was Debbie preparing Fiona for my position because I was getting promoted, or was there another reason? I was suddenly paranoid.

Less than a minute later, Fiona walked out of Sharee's office. She was grinning from ear to ear. I walked out of the mailroom and watched shock register on her face.

"You're here early," I said, giving her a Cheshire Cat smile.

"Well it *is* getting close to the event. I think everyone should be working extended hours," she recovered quickly.

"Don't worry, Fiona. The event will come off without a hitch." I looked at her pointedly. "I have *complete control* of my team and my counter."

Her mouth fell open.

Yeah, let her wonder whether I overheard her or not, the little snake!

Then, with a quick, "See you on the floor, Toy," she scurried away.

"Toy, just the person I wanted to see."

I took my time turning around. "Oh, hi Debbie."

With an obviously fake smile, Debbie began. "Listen, Sharee and I discussed it, and we feel you're definitely ready for that promotion." Then, she took on an equally false somber expression. "Of course, it still depends on your event results. If you don't make your goal, it could go the opposite way — a demotion.

I remained poker-faced. "Of course," I said.

So, this was her angle. If for some reason I didn't make the event goal, she'd screw me over completely. *Not gonna happen.*

"So, we're interviewing for your replacement."

"That's great news."

"I told you when I hired you that under my leadership, you'd go far with this company," she said, amazing me with her gall.

"Yes, you sure did." What an egomaniac. *Sharee* was the one who'd hired and mentored me. Not Debbie.

"Okay, I'm running late for a mani-pedi appointment, so I have to hop to," she said, holding up her claws. "Keep up the good work. Remember, this event has to be phenomenal. *Own it*, Toy."

I put on my best cheerleader voice. "You got it, Debbie. You can count on me to do my best."

The second she turned away I dropped the stupid smile. Maybe she'd get hit by a bus on her way there. No matter, I was relieved not to have to spend another minute with her — today, anyway.

Around 5:00 PM, I was at the sink cleaning my makeup brushes. I was thinking about how I'd almost forgiven Fiona when Ed rushed up.

"I need to speak to you, like immediately," he whispered, sharply.

"Are you alright?"

"I can't talk about this here," he said, looking both ways like some kind of B movie spy. "Can we step outside?"

"Okay," I said, laying the brushes down. Was there ever a day I could leave on time?

I followed him to the furniture store in the mall that was nearly always empty. In spite of the fact that I knew what he had to tell me wasn't nearly as serious as he was making it out to be, I had to pretend to care. It was one of the cons of being a manager.

"Okay, the *only* reason I'm not taking this straight to HR and Sharee is because, while it happened during work hours, it technically didn't happen *at* work," he said, punctuating his words with bounteous hand gestures.

"Okay, go on." I said, impatiently.

"So, this morning, I went to grab a coffee across the street at Corner Bakery because I don't like the coffee here. I had to use the bathroom, and, well, there were only two stalls and one was *occupied*," he said, his eyes widening.

"Well, what's so earth-shattering about that?"

"One stall was occupied by *two people*!" he said with barely restrained amusement.

"That's just gross, but luckily, not my problem."

"I'm not done. So, I quietly stood up on the toilet in my stall and poked my head over the partition, but before you think I'm some kind of pervert, let me explain." He was practically bubbling over with glee.

I deliberately my watch.

"I think anyone in my position would've done the same thing. Who wouldn't with the noises that were coming out of there?"

He had to be, hands down, the nosiest person I'd ever known. "That's not really an explanation and I wouldn't, that's who!"

"I know, I know. But I haven't gotten to the best part yet!"

"Gee. I can't wait to hear this," I said, my patience stretching.

"It was Jean-Luc and Chance!" Ed tattled, euphorically. "Chance was going down on him, Toy!"

I sucked in a lungful of air, and exhaled, "No!"

Those two couldn't have been so stupid as to do something like that on their break in a public bathroom. Not to mention a bathroom next to our store!

I gave him a deadly stare. "Are you *positive* it was them?"

"Um, a hundred percent!" Ed put his right hand on his heart, and his left hand in the air. "May I be struck by lightning if I'm lying. I even watched for a couple of minutes. But, only to be really sure it was them."

"Of course," I said, sardonically.

"What are we going to do?"

Before I could respond, he started a rant. "I've been trying to tell you Jean-Luc is gay!"

After all this time, it was official. Jean-Luc was gay.

Ed continued, "But what the F? We can't afford any more drama at the counter before the event. We're already down a person with Tommy in jail. Did you hear? His bail is $100,000."

I cringed when I heard that. I had so much on my mind that I'd forgotten to call about Tommy! Oh my God!

I pulled myself together and said, "First off, *we* aren't going to do anything. I'll address this with both of them. You need to keep this to yourself because it really doesn't put you in the best light. This didn't happen at work, and you'll make yourself look like a pervert." I wagged a menacing finger at him. "So, Ed, don't repeat this."

"Okay, I won't say a word." He made a zipper motion across his lips.

I didn't believe him, but said anyway, "I'm going to hold you to that." I gave him ice-cold eyes, and then walked away.

What the hell were Chance and Jean-Luc thinking? I was going to have to do some major damage control because of this.

When I got back to the counter, Jean-Luc and Chance were with clients. *Damn it.* I really wanted to go home, but I had to talk to them, like now! I couldn't have Ed go running to upper management, complaining that he'd come to me with this and I did nothing about it. They'd done the nasty on a *break*, so technically it had happened on company time. However, it hadn't occurred on work premises — so, they hadn't *exactly* broken any rules. This was such a greay area. Still, if the rumor got out, it would make top billing in the gossip circuit, which could be damaging to my team and me. This counter didn't need any more negative attention.

I checked my phone. My mood went from darkness to daylight in less than a second when I saw a text.

Nikola: *We said 9:30, but will 8:00 work instead?*
Me: *Even better, we can hang out longer;)*
Him: *See you then, sexy.*

The anger and anxiety I felt from what Ed had just told me melted away. I actually felt giddy. *Is this what it's like to be in love? If so, I don't think I've ever experienced it before.*

I stepped over to Ed and assured him I would address the incident with Chance and Jean-Luc outside of work. I told him I probably wouldn't have time to do it today, but it would happen very soon. He seemed fine with it, but I still didn't trust him.

I was gathering my things when I noticed Biljana texting on the floor. None of us were supposed to have our cell phones out in the open in front of clients, but I did allow their use discreetly behind the counter, as long as it was business related. I felt uncomfortable saying anything to her, but I couldn't let my personal feelings get in the way of my duty.

"Biljana?"

"Yes?" she replied without looking up.

"If you want to text, please make sure it's behind the counter where customers can't see. The only exception is if you're texting a client. Otherwise, step off the floor, okay?"

"I'm sorry," she blushed, and put her phone in her sweater pocket. "Toy?"

"Yes?"

"Could I stay until closing tonight, instead of working until six? Niko canceled our plans."

I felt my stomach clench. *Nikola had plans with her?*

"Sure, no problem," I said, feeling both angry and sad.

"Thank you. I appreciate it," she smiled.

Something was different about Biljana. I could feel it. I still didn't think she had the lowdown on Nikola and me, but I was sure she knew he was seeing *someone*. Women just *know*. I hoped I wasn't right and Biljana's nervous energy around me was just her reacting to my "no more buddy-buddy" announcement in the meeting.

I had to get out of there. The counter drama, Biljana — it was all too much. Now, instead of looking forward to relaxing with Nikola, I was dreading an awkward conversation about Biljana, and I still had to find out what was going on with Tommy.

Maybe I could get in touch with Tatyana. Maybe she could help Tommy. And, how am I going to confront Jean-Luc and Chance? Should I do it with them together or individually? How is Jean-Luc going to react now that he has no way of denying he's gay?

I practically flew off the floor and out of the building, my mind racing madly.

Chapter 16

I shut my locker, slung my Fendi bag over my arm, and let out a sigh. I dreaded having to lay eyes on Sheriff Hardass, let alone go through his inspection. I disliked him so much that I still hadn't bothered to find out what his real name was. I didn't want to know. There was something about him that bothered me, an underhanded manner that gave me the creeps.

When I walked out of the locker room, I was giddy with relief. From across the hall, the eyes that met mine weren't cruel and callous, but warm and friendly.

"How you doin', Toy?" he asked.

"Clyde," I breathed, "I'm so glad it's you."

"That bad, huh?"

"Oh, yeah."

"Uh-huh, I've heard he isn't making too many friends around here."

"Well, you saw the way he treated me the other night?"

"Yep. Sure did. Don't worry. I doubt he'll be here long. In all my years, I've seen plenty of people with his attitude come and go just as fast. You just can't pay them no mind," he said, slowly getting up from his chair.

"Jerks like him just drive me nuts. He's Loss Prevention, not the FBI."

"You crack me up, Toy," laughed Clyde. "Let me just peek into that bag, you know, for the camera's sake."

"Oh, I almost forgot!" I slid the purse off my shoulder and opened it for him.

"You're good," he said after a cursory inspection, then walked back to his chair and turned around. "So, how's old Tommy doing?"

"I'm about to find out," I said, and pulled out my cell.

"You tell that boy I said he needs to calm down. One-a these days he's gonna get himself mixed up in something nobody can save his sorry butt from."

"I'll relay the message, but I'm not sure it'll make any difference. Thanks, Clyde. Have a good night."

"Night, Toy."

I walked down the stairs, out the employee entrance and past the smoker circle. I pulled off my glove and dialed Tatyana. After the third ring, she finally answered.

"*Da*?"

"Tatyana, it's Toy," I said, tucking the phone between my chin and shoulder so I could slip my glove back on. It was freezing!

"I know who it is. What do you need?" she said, rudely.

"Did you get my messages? Tommy's in jail."

"No, he is not. I picked him up from the station a few hours ago."

"What? Why didn't one of you call me? I was freaking out," I huffed, beyond exasperated.

"Relax. He is sleeping and I told him I would let you know he was okay."

And now, I was pissed. "Don't tell me to relax. If he told you to tell me, then why didn't you?"

"Look, we are not at work right now. I do not answer to you. Call his phone and leave a message."

Before I could respond, the phone went dead.

"Bitch!" I spat and glared at the phone for a second, then shoved it into my pocket. I took a deep breath and exhaled. *Well, at least Tommy's out of jail. I'll call him tomorrow morning when he isn't with his watchdog.*

Later that evening, I was engrossed in a rerun episode of *Will and Grace* when the phone rang. After the fifth ring, I groaned and grabbed the phone. When I saw it was Ben, I nearly fumbled it.

"Hello?" I said, a little too urgently.

"You answered." His voice exhibited relief.

"Yes, I did. Why wouldn't I? I told you I'd meet you when you were back in town."

"I don't know. Just insecure, I guess. I hate the way things ended between us," he said, sadly.

"Yeah, well I guess we don't really have a good history when it comes to endings, do we?" This came out sharper than I'd intended.

"No, we don't," he conceded.

My pulse quickened with anger. "I don't know what to say, Ben. I have no idea if I really know you anymore."

"What do you mean?" he said, raising his voice. "You know me. You're the only person who does."

"Really? How can I be sure? The Ben I thought I knew wouldn't have walked out on me. He wouldn't have talked to Fiona behind my back or hit the ignore button on his phone when I called, over and over and over," I said, my voice starting to shake.

He let out an audible sigh. "I know, babe. I know how wrong I was. I do."

"How do you think it feels to find out you were back in town, not once, but multiple times and you agreed to see Fiona, of all people?"

"I'm sorry, Toy, but I swear, nothing happened between us. She said you were dating someone and when I heard that I just lost it," he lamented.

"My God, Ben. Why would you believe her? Why didn't you just ask me?"

I knew I was being hard on him, but it was like everything I had bottled up since our breakup was gushing over. I had no control over it.

"I don't know. I was scared that you'd just hang up on me if I called you, after the way I treated you. I don't know what I can do to make up for it. Everything you said that day was true. I was scared. Ever since I can remember, I had this plan for my life and then all of a sudden, I was regretting the choices I'd made. I didn't know what to do. I was torn between doing something completely different or moving into another field of medicine altogether. Then, there was you," he said, softly.

"Yeah, then there was me," I echoed, bitterly. "Who you tossed aside like I was nothing."

"That's not true, Toy. You're far from nothing. You're everything to me. Everything..." His voice broke. "It's just... I can't... imagine my life without you."

He was choked up!

"I could have the perfect job, a hot car, a huge house, but none of it would matter if you weren't there to share it with me. I just want another chance. I couldn't blame you if you told me to go to hell, but please don't, please," he pleaded. "Give me one more chance, Toy. I'm so sorry."

"Oh, Ben!" Now I was crying. With the back of my hand, I wiped the tears from my eyes. I had to admit I still loved him, but I was afraid. "I know you're sorry. I believe you, I just don't know if things can ever be the same," I said between sniffles.

"It can be the same, even better. I know it can, if you're willing to give us another chance. I swear I'll make it up to you."

"I just... I don't know," I wavered.

"Well, don't answer right now then," he said, pulling himself together, again. "Try not to worry about anything. When we see each other we can talk, okay?"

He'd always had a way of reassuring me and making me feel like everything would be okay. But I wasn't so sure this time.

"Toy?" Ben broke the silence. "Are you still there?"

"Yes, yes. I'm here," I said, still caught up in my thoughts.

"Damn, I'm getting paged. Can I call you tomorrow?"

"Sure, but make it after 9:00 PM. I work late tomorrow."

"Sounds good. I love you, Toy."

"I know," was the best I could muster at the moment.

"Bye, babe."

"Bye."

I sat there for a second. I still loved Ben, I couldn't deny that. Then, I thought of Nikola and how he made me feel. I wasn't sure if any other man could ever make me feel the way he did. But was it love, or just sheer lust?

Less than an hour later, I was back on the couch, scrolling through pictures on Chance's Instagram. I was trying to keep my mind off the fact that Nikola originally had a date with Biljana tonight. Maybe she wasn't telling the truth. From what Nikola had told me, she had a tendency to exaggerate situations. Maybe she'd asked him to meet up, he'd said no, and she considered that cancelled plans.

I was already showered and dressed casually-cute in anticipation of Nikola's visit. Casual-cute is a term I use to describe the way a woman wants her guy to think she always looks while lounging at home. You know, a messy, but sexy ponytail and yoga pants paired with a tight T-shirt, tinted moisturizer to give your face a flawless, natural looking finish, and just a little mascara as a finishing touch. The goal was to make it seem like the look was entirely natural and effortless, when it really takes a minimum of an hour's worth of work to achieve.

It was a little past 8:00 PM when Nikola arrived.

"Hi," he said, and kissed me on the cheek. He stepped inside, leaned down and removed his shoes. He pushed them to the side with a toe, and then looked up to meet my eyes.

"What is wrong?" he asked. "You look upset."

I guess I hadn't done a complete job of covering the puffy, red-eyed mess I'd become after talking with Ben. The last thing I needed for Nikola to know was that I had just been crying over my ex-boyfriend.

"Nothing. Just a long day at work," I white-lied.

"Me too. But hey, now I am here. And I happen to be great at relieving stress, too," he said with a playful look it his eye. He lifted me up and headed for the bedroom.

I playfully jostled his hair. "You are so bad."

"Not as bad as you think," he said, and plunked me down on the bed. "Turn over. I will massage you."

"Oh, a massage? Is that what you call it?" I batted my eyes.

"Seriously. Turn over. I am really good at it. I have been doing it since I was very young. I used to rub my baba's shoulders."

I gave him a perplexed look.

"Grandmother," he explained.

I turned over. When he placed his large hands on my back, I immediately knew he was an expert. This guy never failed to satisfy.

His strong hands kneaded the back of my neck with firm, deep strokes.

"Your baba, is she back in your country?" I asked, my words muffled by the pillow.

"Yes," he said. "I think she is the person I miss the most."

"Do you talk often?"

"I talk with her once a week, but it is not enough. I am going to try to go back home the end of December and stay a while," he said.

I grew quiet. *What is "a while?"* I wondered. The thought of him being so far away immediately made me sad.

"Not for very long. Maybe six weeks or so," he said, as if reading my thoughts.

I lay quiet for a long time while he released all the tension and stress from the day through his touch.

He dropped over on his side and I turned to face him.

"I have to ask you something that's been bothering me."

"What is wrong?" he asked, crinkling his forehead.

"Biljana told me you two had plans tonight," I said, searching his eyes.

He rolled over on his back and sighed. "Biljana, I feel, is in her own world. She called this morning and asked me if we could have an early dinner because she wanted to talk to me. I said yes at first. When I hung up and thought it through, I felt it was a bad idea. So, I called her back and cancelled. I do not want to lead her on."

Relief washed over me. "I'm so glad to hear that."

"Stop worrying. I only want you. What are you going to do when I leave for Macedonia next month?" He traced the tip of my nose with a finger.

"I don't want to think about you leaving." I reached over and playfully grabbed a fistful of his hair. "Come here."

He leaned in and kissed my forehead, my cheeks, and finally my mouth.

"I want you inside me," I whispered between kisses.

He stood up and pulled his shirt off, tossing it aside. I took in his dark, tanned skin and the ripple of his muscles. His arms and chest were magnificently sculpted, but even more impressive was his six-pack. *God, what a turn on!*

"Take everything off, except your panties," he said, unzipping his pants and letting them drop to the floor.

A moment later, I stood before him, near naked. He gently sat me down on the bed and pulled my hips to the edge of it.

He dropped to his knees in front of me and licked me slowly, up and down, until I couldn't take anymore.

"Stop," I pleaded. "I told you, I want you inside of me."

I pulled his boxers off and then fell back on the bed.

He crawled on top.

"Say it again," he whispered.

"I want you inside of me."

I could feel his erection hard against my inner thigh, so close…

"Say my name when you say it," he said, tugging my hair with a steady pressure.

"Nikola, I want you inside of me. Please, put it in, I need you so badly," I begged, wanting him more than ever.

He pulled my panties to the side. "Is this what you wanted?" he asked, easing himself in.

"Mmm, hmm," I moaned, running my fingers through his silky hair.

I squeezed my legs closer together, causing more friction.

"You drive me crazy," he groaned.

He rocked himself, back and forth, in and out of me, slowly and deliberately.

"Come inside of me, Nikola, now!" I clawed at his back. I could feel him get rock hard before the release.

"I'm coming!" He trembled with pleasure for a long few seconds, until all at once, his body went slack.

"Oh my God, that was incredible," I said, my breath coming in gasps, having climaxed as well.

"*You* are incredible." He fell from me onto his back.

After a moment of recovery, I teased, "Tired?"

"Who would not be?" He arched an eyebrow. "You are insatiable."

"Only with you."

Less than an hour later we were soaking in the tub. Enveloped in his arms, all I could think about was how I wished we could just fly away to a tropical island together. Away from Biljana, Ben, everything.

"What are you thinking?" he asked, kissing my neck.

"Just that I wish we could always be like this."

"How do you mean?"

"Just enjoying each other. No stress. No expectations. I can't explain it. I just feel so content when we're together."

He went quiet, lost in thought.

"What's wrong?" I asked, squeezing his hand.

He sighed, "I feel guilty about Biljana. But, I do not share her feelings. When I cancelled on her, I told her she could not continue to think of me other than her friend."

"You did?" I reached over the side of the tub for my towel.

He shook his head. "Yes. She did not take it well. She started crying. She wants to talk to me in person tomorrow."

I stepped out of the tub and started to dry off.

"Are you going to meet her?"

"I think I should. She is so adamant about talking to me face-to-face," he shrugged.

At least he didn't look happy about it. "You're right." Even though I hated the thought of them being together, I knew he was only doing what was fair, since they'd known each other for so long.

"I know what you meant earlier when you said you could not explain how it felt when we are together," he said, still sitting in the tub of now lukewarm water.

"You do?"

"Yes. I have never felt like this with anyone else. It is like a calmness comes over me when we are together."

"Me too." I dropped the towel on the counter.

All of a sudden, he bolted from the tub, water flying everywhere, and wrapped his arms around me.

"You're all wet!" I gasped, looking over my shoulder at him.

"I think about you so much that sometimes I feel like you have put a spell on me, with those light eyes of yours." He turned me around to face him.

"Oh, c'mon," I giggled.

"I do." He brought his forehead down to meet mine. "If I contacted you as much as I think about you, we would not be standing here together right now. You would think I was a stalker and tell me to get out of your life."

"I don't think I could ever tell you to get out of my life," I said, softly.

He tilted my chin. I searched his eyes.

"I am in love with you," he said, then he kissed me; a deep, long lingering kiss.

My heart was pounding. On one hand, this was all happening so fast. But on the other, I'd always heard when you meet the right person, you just know it.

After the kiss ended, I looked up at him lovingly. "I think I'm in love with you, too."

We woke up early the next morning and decided to get some coffee at Le Cafe. We bundled up before walking out into the freezing cold. I tied my Burberry scarf around my neck, then turned to wrap his Gucci scarf around his.

Nikola looked down into my face. "I love your eyes, your nose, and — well everything." He bent his head to peck my lips.

"Thank you, you're not so bad yourself." I ran my hands down his lapels.

"Ready?"

"Let's go," I said, and linked my arm in his.

We brushed the snow off us before crossing the threshold of Le Cafe. We said hi to Mattie, grabbed our drinks, peeled off our outerwear and sat down together. God, I loved being with him.

"Do you know, in my country, it is said only women with light eyes can put a spell or a curse on you?" he said with a crooked smile.

I giggled. "Are you serious?"

"It is folklore and I did not believe in it," he grinned, "but the way you make me feel is starting to convince me. I did not think people could fall in love as fast as I have with you."

My heart fluttered and my stomach turned a somersault. *Is this real? Is this gorgeous, exotic, incredibly sexy man really, seriously in love with me?*

We were walking hand in hand, back to my apartment. A woman, head down, tightly bundled up was walking in the other direction, toward us. When we were close enough to make eye contact, she looked up and gasped, "Toy?" Her eyes moved from me to Nikola.

Ohhh shit! This isn't good. I could feel Nikola tense when he saw her. He dropped my hand.

"Hi, Tatyana," I said, as nonchalantly as I could manage.

"I would ask you to introduce me to your friend but I think we have already met," she said, coyly, her eyes still fixed on Nikola.

"Yes. We have met."

His tone was cold, almost menacing. It worried me and it was pretty obvious it unnerved Tatyana, too.

She quickly shifted her gaze to me. "Well, I am running late. Ciao," she said, and hurried on.

"Peasant whore," Nikola muttered.

His comment shocked me. "What did you say?"

"Did you see how she was looking at us?" His seethed. "Who is she to look at me or you like that? Ukranian whore, just like them all."

"Yes, but don't you think calling her a whore is a little extreme?"

Sure, Tatyana was no angel. In truth, she was probably only a step up the ladder from actually being a prostitute. But I didn't like it when men called women derogatory names, especially men I associated with. *Red flag!*

"No, I do not." he snapped. "I do not like being corrected, Toy. Especially by women."

Was he kidding me right now?

We walked the rest of the way home in silence. Instead of worrying Tatyana might tell Biljana about seeing Nikola and me together, my mind went in an entirely different direction. I'd never seen this side of Nikola before, and I didn't like it.

We rode the elevator to my floor without uttering a word, and the minute we entered my apartment, he said, "I had better go. I have a lot of things I need to do," and gave me a quick kiss on the cheek.

"I understand. I'll talk to you later," I said, holding the door open. He walked back out.

"Ciao," he said.

"Do all Europeans say 'Ciao' to say good-bye?" I half-kidded, as he headed for the elevator.

"I cannot speak for all of Europe," he shot back over his shoulder.

I closed the door and leaned my head against it.

Wow. One minute I was getting coffee with my dream guy and the next, I was standing alone in my apartment wondering if I'd just walked home with Lucifer! The name he'd called Tatyana still disturbed me.

My text tone sounded. *Maybe it's Nikola apologizing for his rotten behavior?*

I glanced at the phone screen and rolled my eyes. *This should be good.* I clicked on the message.

Tatyana: *I see we are more alike than I thought.*

Me: *We are nothing alike.*

Her: *Oh, yes. More than you know. But do not worry, I would not dare ruin the princess' reputation. Your secret is safe with me...*

I could almost hear her accent. *"Da... I vould not dare ruin zee princess' reputation..."*

I didn't respond any further, but was relieved to read her last sentence. I believed her when she said she wouldn't say anything. For some reason, I figured in Tatyana's screwed up code of behavior, she'd consider it rude to tell on me. She probably loved the fact that I was doing something similar to what I'd lectured her about.

I shuddered. How had I managed to get myself into this situation? Better yet, would I be able to get out of it without everyone involved getting hurt?

Chapter 17

I lay in bed, bundled up in my down comforter, relaxing for the first time all day. For once I was thankful it was so crazy busy at work today, which resulted in minimal contact with Biljana and Tatyana. And now I could snuggle up to some *Bridget Jones.*

I was at the part where Bridget discovers Daniel is cheating on her. No matter how many times I've watched this scene, I always want to wring Daniel's neck. I think I related to it. One minute you think you've found Prince Charming and the next you discover he's the Prince of Darkness.

My phone went off. Without reaching for it, I turned my head and looked at the screen. It was Nikola. My mind reeled back to the unnerving behavior he'd displayed this morning. I let it ring a few more times before I picked up.

"Hello?"

"I need to see you," he blurted out.

"Um, sure. Is something wrong?"

"Yes. But I will tell you about it when I see you. I will be there in half an hour."

"That soon?" I threw the comforter aside and leaped out of bed. I was a wreck!

"Yes, is that okay?" he said, but it really wasn't a question.

"It's just — I haven't showered," I said, struggling to keep my voice even.

"Who cares? Do not be so insecure," he scoffed.

Insecure? Who does he think he is? I resisted an urge to click the phone off.

"You are always beautiful," he added, just in time to save himself from being on the other end of a dial tone.

"Okay, I'll see you soon," I conceded.

"Perfect."

"Okay, bye."

What's so urgent that he has to see me right now? Did Tatyana tell Biljana after all? The thought set my nerves on edge.

I stepped into the bathroom and looked at myself in the full-length mirror. *Gross.* I had the same makeup on from that morning, my hair was in a messy knot on top of my head, and I was wearing Ben's favorite ugly T-shirt. I only had minutes to perform what would be tantamount to a miracle.

I quickly undressed, leaving my clothes in a pile on the floor. I filled the sink and took a sponge bath, only now I called it a whore's bath. It was a term Yvonne used and one that, crude as it was, refused to leave my head.

I brushed my teeth, sprayed my hair with dry shampoo, then twisted it into a messy topknot bun. I slapped some tinted moisturizer on my face and coated my lashes with mascara.

I glanced at the clock on the wall and whined, *"Five minutes!"*

I dug a pair of faded AG blue jeans from the hamper, gave them a quick snap to release some of the wrinkles, shoved my legs into them and pulled my softest, sexiest Scoop sweater out of the drawer and over my head, all in less than two minutes. Whew! This was the fastest I'd gotten dressed in like — well, ever. The clothes weren't what I'd have chosen under normal circumstances.

I'd just started to straighten the covers on my bed when I heard a knock on the front door.

"Damn it," I growled. *Did I even have a doorman anymore?*

He wasn't kidding about that thirty minutes. I picked a pillow up off the floor, tossed it on my bed, and then made my way to the door.

I opened the door. My heart skipped a beat at the sight of him. Snowflakes still clung to the wide shoulders of his black Ralph Lauren wool coat. His eyes were glassy and red. He looked like he'd been crying. Something was definitely wrong.

"Come in," I said, trying to sound casual.

He walked in and without a word, took me in his arms. We stayed that way for a minute before he let me go. He slipped off his shoes and ran his fingers through his now damp hair.

We walked into the kitchen. "Tell me what's going on." I helped him out of his coat and threw it over the back of one of the pub chairs at the island. He took a seat in the other and propped his head on his hands.

"You're worrying me," I frowned. "What's the matter?"

"So much I do not even know where to start." His shoulders slumped. "Do you have anything to drink?"

"I have a bottle of Middle Sister Moscato, but that's it."

"Can I have a glass?"

"Sure." I moved quickly. The suspense was torturing me.

While I grabbed a couple of glasses from the wine rack, he walked into the living room and sat before the dying embers in the fireplace. I poured up the Moscato.

I took the two glasses, walked over to where he was, and sat down beside him. "Here."

"Thank you." He took the wine and practically downed the entire glass in one swig. He stared at the glowing coals for a few seconds, then: "This is where we were first together. Right here." He ran a hand over the Oriental rug. "Do you know that I watched you sleep almost an hour that night before I left?"

"You did?" I sat down beside him and tried to catch his gaze.

"Yes. You were so beautiful. You look like an angel when you sleep," he said, still staring at the fire.

"Look at me," I said, caressing his shoulder.

He turned his head slowly. He leaned in avoiding my readied lips, and kissed my forehead. Before I could look up, he pulled my face to his chest and whispered into my hair, "God, this is killing me."

My stomach clenched. "What's wrong?"

"Biljana is pregnant."

"What?" I couldn't have been more shocked if someone told me a loved one had passed away. I pulled away from him.

He grimaced. "She told me tonight. She said she wanted to tell me for weeks now, but I was acting strangely."

"Oh, my God. No, God! This can't be happening," I gasped, tears stinging my eyes. I stood up.

"I do not know what to say," he mumbled.

After a pause, I wiped away the tears. "I thought you two weren't having sex!"

"We are not, Toy. It happened before I met you," he lamented.

"Well then, there's nothing left to say," I said, coldly, and turned my back to him.

He rose and placed a hand on my shoulder. "I do not want this to end between us Toy, but I cannot leave her. Not pregnant. What kind of man would I be? I just want you to know that this time we spent together meant so much to me."

I brushed his hand away and spun around. "I guess this *was* all too good to be true!"

Tears were welling in his eyes. "I did not mean for it to end this way."

"Yeah, well. It did. What can we do about it now? It's done." I struggled to keep my voice even. "Thank you for coming over and telling me all of this in person, really."

He stared at me and I could see the hurt he was feeling. "Toy, stop acting as if this is no big deal. Talk to me." He took a step toward me. "Of course, I was going to tell you this in person."

"I don't know how to act. This is just so… unfair."

My body began to shake. He wrapped his arms around me, held me close, and the dam broke. I sobbed into his chest.

He lifted my face. When our eyes met, for the first time in my life, I understood grief. He kissed a tear from my cheek. He held me for a little while, and then gently broke our embrace.

"I should go," Nikola said, his voice thick with emotion. He snatched his coat from the chair.

"I know," I whispered, turning to walk away.

"Toy?"

I stopped. "Yeah?"

"I have never had such strong feelings like this before, and I know I never will again." He forced a smile, his eyes glistening. And then he was gone.

I ran to my room, threw myself on the bed and sobbed until my pillow was soaked.

"I'll never see him again," I cried out loud, inconsolable.

It felt like hours had passed when my tears finally ebbed. I closed my eyes against the throbbing in my head, praying for sleep. My mind raced through assorted scenes of Nikola and me; the thrill of the first time we met, our intense conversations, the silly ones too, the passion of the first time we'd made love, and the rapture of that last time, neither of us knowing it would all be over in a day. The thought of never being with him again caused a hollow ache in my soul.

I clicked the DVR back on. The expression misery loves company came to mind with painful acuity as I watched my old friend *Bridget* let love make a fool of her again.

The next morning was horrible. I went into work early hoping it would help clear my mind. I also needed to have a long talk with Jean-Luc and Chance before Ed came in. I was happy to see Clyde and not that other jackass. I wasn't in the mood for anyone's shit today.

I approached my counter and saw Chance sitting in a makeup chair, in front of a mirror, a cup of coffee in one hand, a lip-gloss in the other.

"Chance, you're in early," I said, not bothering to hide my surprise.

"Well, I wanted to see you, and you're so busy lately, it seems like I should make an appointment. I checked the schedule and knew you were opening, so here I am," he said, never lifting his eyes from his own reflection.

"Well, I'm glad you're here," I said, flatly.

"What's going on with you anyway? Is it still the Fiona and Ben thingy?" He dropped the gloss and swiveled the makeup chair to face me.

"Partially. This event has me stressed out, and yes, the Ben and Fiona *thingy* didn't help."

"Girl, you've got to stop worrying about this damn job. I know you'll make the event goal. I have complete confidence in you."

"Complete confidence"... truth or pep talk? I wondered.

Chance continued, "As far as Fiona goes, she's *always* been jealous of you, as she *should* be. You're fierce, boo." He pursed his shiny lips.

The silly expression made me smile. Chance never failed to amuse me. I dreaded the fact that I had to lower the boom.

"Thanks, babe," I said, and gave him a hug.

"Hey! Why don't we have a girl's night in? I'll bring some wine, we'll order takeout and watch chick flicks." He clapped his hands together.

"Actually, that sounds great. Let's do it tonight," I said. It would be a relief to have Chance over to keep my mind off my problems.

He polished off his cup of coffee and uttered, "Perf!"

I cleared my throat and said, "I do need to talk to you about something else, though."

"Oh?" he stood and propped a hand on the counter.

"Ed saw you and Jean-Luc in a compromising position," I said, careful to keep my voice neutral.

He raised an eyebrow. "Compromising position?"

"Ed saw you two in a bathroom stall across the street at Corner Bakery." I intensified my gaze. "Yes, Chance, *compromising*," I enunciated. "We went to the same high school and I know my vocabulary can't be much more extensive than yours."

"Oh yeah, that..." he winced.

"Yeah, that. Why would you two do something so private in a public bathroom, not to mention while you were on company time. Aside from that, why are you messing around with him when you know he's still claiming he's straight?"

"Because I think I'm in love," he said, tears glistening in his eyes.

I shook my head. Chance cried about everything.

"Wait a minute. You think you're in love with Jean-Luc? Really?"

"Yes," he lamented.

Then I remembered. After I stormed out of Tatyana's birthday party and Jean-Luc left, it infuriated Chance right into the arms of his new sugar daddy.

Still maintaining a neutral stance, I asked, "Well, what about Henry? You told me you've been spending a lot of time with him lately."

Henry was a wealthy sixty-something-year-old entrepreneur who owned upscale gay bars in Chicago, LA and New York. He owned a Bentley, a Rolls, and a Lamborghini, and had several homes across the United States, including one in an exclusive northern suburb. He had fallen head over heels for Chance and Chance had fallen head over heels for Henry's bank account.

"Um, maybe I embellished how much time we were spending together." he said, carefully avoiding my gaze.

"What do you mean embellished?" Most people would consider Chance's embellishments to be straight up lies.

"I've seen him a few times, but I'm not that into him. He on the other hand, is obsessed with me," he smirked. "I've actually been spending every night with… well, with Jean-Luc."

He must have seen the fire in my eyes.

"Before you say anything, I would've told you, but Jean-Luc made me promise not to tell anyone."

Just as I was about to lay into him about hiding all of this from me, I realized I'd been doing the same thing to him. Then, it dawned on me. If you had to lie about your love life to the people you cared about most, your relationship probably wasn't all it was supposed to be.

"Chance, I'm just worried you're going to get hurt. I've never actually seen you *really* into anyone. I want Jean-Luc to be happy, but you and I both know he's still in the closet with the door barricaded shut."

"Don't you think I know that? Look, I'm willing to give him the time he needs to come out. When you love someone, you've got to make sacrifices, Toy."

"Fine," I relented. Sometimes I just wanted to slap him. "I can't choose who you date, but will you two stop having sex during work hours? I don't need Ed bringing this to HR."

"But Toy, it's so much fun sneaking off on a break and — " he raved, until he noticed the frosty look on my face. "Okay. Yes, I promise it'll never happen again."

"Thank you."

"Oh, yeah! Henry is throwing a party next Saturday after our event. You're coming," he ordered.

"Oh, no. You know how exhausted I'm going to be. There's no way I'll feel like getting dressed up again after fifteen-plus hours of work."

"Which is why Henry is throwing it at his condo. It's just a few blocks away and it'll be totally low key."

Nothing with Chance ever ended low key.

He took my hand in both of his. "Please," he pleaded, poking out his bottom lip.

"No, Chance. I just can't," I asserted, and took my hand back.

"You mean you can, but you won't. Come on, pretty please? I really want Jean-Luc to come. I know he'll come if you're there. I'd do it for you," he whined.

I can't believe him. He's trying to get Jean-Luc to come to Henry's party so he can make both of them jealous! How does he always convince me to go out when I don't want to?

"Low key, huh?"

"Girl, would this face lie?" He batted his lashes.

"Yes, as a matter of fact, it does it all the time," I smiled, not altogether kidding.

He clapped his hands together, laughing. "I know, but not this time. I promise."

I laughed, too. What would my life be like without Chance?

"Henry's also having the entire party catered. I told him I wouldn't come if it wasn't."

"My God, you're a brat! Is there anything Henry won't do for you?"

"Hmm..." He thought for a moment. "No. I just wish it were Jean-Luc and not him. Do you know how hard it is to let Henry go down on me?"

"No, and please — no details! I don't want to imagine you with anyone like that, let alone some old fart," I cringed.

We stared at each other for several seconds. His hopeful, childlike eyes won the contest. I blinked and said, "Okay. I guess I can make it."

"Really?"

I nodded.

"Promise you won't ditch out on me at the last minute?"

"I won't. I promise."

Chance hugged me and squealed with delight. "This party will be just what you need to loosen up."

As if on cue, Jean-Luc made his appearance.

"Party?" Jean-Luc raised a brow.

"You should come. Toy's on board," pleaded Chance.

"Yeah, I'm *super* excited," I said, sarcastically.

"She really is." Chance shot me a look. "Henry said I could invite as many people as I want."

"Okay then. The three of us can all go together. I'd love to have you on my arm, baby," Jean-Luc said, and suggestively, looked me up and down. "You know we would be a power couple, Cherie."

"Whatever, Jean-Luc," I grinned. After a pause, I turned deadly serious. "Now, there's something I need to talk to you about, Jean-Luc."

Chance cleared his throat. When I glanced at him, his eyes were begging me not to say anything.

"Something wrong, Cherie?" asked Jean-Luc.

"Oh no," I evaded. "I just wanted to get your input on the design I came up with for the event's floor plan before I present it to Sharee."

"Sure, but don't worry. You are my Blonde Ambition. Everything will be perfect as always," Jean-Luc said, and kissed my cheek.

"I told her the same thing," Chance added.

"Okay, I will go get the coffee. When I return, I will help you finish the floor plan." He turned to Chance. "Did you want to come along?"

"Sure," said Chance, unable to hide his delight.

"Thanks, guys." I watched the two of them walk away, Chance incandescent next to the object of his desire. I struggled with whether or not I really should talk to Jean-Luc about the restroom incident, or to just let Chance handle it. The mere thought of yanking him out of the closet like that made my stomach churn. Still, I'd told Ed I would take care of it, so there was no going back now.

And, Chance. Maybe he did love Jean-Luc. I only hoped that their love story would end a happier one than mine, but so far, it wasn't looking too good. First, Chance, who I'd never known to be faithful to one person. Then, Jean-Luc, who couldn't even admit he was gay. Their entire relationship, if you could call it that, was based primarily on deception. Still, Chance was the best friend I'd ever had. For that reason, I felt obligated to find out whether Jean-Luc was using him or not.

A few minutes later, Chance and Jean-Luc returned with the coffee. I grabbed mine, took a sip and swallowed hard, preparing myself for the task at hand.

"Jean-Luc, can you help me grab something from the stockroom?"

"Of course, my dear!"

We walked in silence, coffees in hand, until we reached the door to the stockroom.

Jean-Luc turned to face me. "Cherie, you don't really need help. Chance told me you know what happened. I don't want to discuss it, but rest assured, it will never happen again," he said. He managed to meet my gaze, but the shame in his eyes was like a blind that blocked the light between us.

I began, "Jean-Luc. Is there anything you'd like to tell me?

"Like what?"

"Well, like, what's going on between you and Chance? I mean, the truth."

He straightened. "Come on, baby. This isn't 1955. This is 2017. Just because I experimented does not mean I am a gay. I prefer to call it straight-strayed."

"Yeah, I'm sure straight men stray, maybe even with another man, but a full-blown affair?

"I suppose that depends upon what you consider an affair," he jeered. "I do not feel the need to explain to you what goes on in my personal life. I said it would not happen again. That should be enough. Would you like to take this further, maybe to HR, or should we collect the supplies? I should like to return to the counter.

I knew what he was getting at and it was time to give up.

"Yeah, sure. You go back and hold down the fort for me, okay? I'm going to the mailroom." I said, and headed that way.

How do you win with a guy like this?

I was walking past Sharee's office when I heard what sounded like a heated conversation. I stood quietly for a moment, and sipped my coffee.

"I'm sick of this, Debbie. I usually don't complain, but this is too much," said Sharee, perturbed.

"Oh, loosen up, Sharee, said Debbie, indifferently. "It's not a big deal. It's not like it's going to affect your position if Toy doesn't get what she wants."

Sharee was adamant. "Toy deserves the National Makeup Artist position, not Fiona. She's earned it. Fiona can have the counter manager role, as planned. It's only fair."

With my mouth full of coffee, I gasped. A spasmodic cough racked my body. Semi-hot brown liquid spewed and dribbled over my chin. I caught it with my free hand. Still strangling, I stifled the cough and strained to hear the rest.

"Look," Debbie's voice sounded menacing. "*I* think Fiona is more capable of handling a national position than Toy is. Toy can stay in the role she's in. And, may I remind you that you don't call the shots — *I do*."

"I won't let you do it. I'll go to Frances," Sharee resolved.

I shook the coffee from my hand. My heart slammed against my ribcage. I should really have gotten out of there before they caught me eavesdropping, but this was just too much to walk away from!

"Don't fuck with me, Sharee," seethed Debbie. "Make no mistake. I didn't get where I am without knowing the right people. If you push me, Toy may not even keep her role as counter manager."

The hand that held my coffee started to tremble.

"Fine." After a short silence, she added. "You really don't care about anyone, do you? I can't help but wonder how you sleep at night."

"Don't worry about me, Sharee. I sleep like a baby. Just do what I tell you so *you* won't have anything to lose sleep over. Are we clear?"

"Crystal."

I ducked into the mailroom just before Debbie walked out, banging Sharee's door closed behind her in triumph.

The only thing that hadn't shocked me about the entire conversation was Debbie trying to promote Fiona instead of me. If you kissed the right ass, no matter how talented you were—or weren't—you could get a promotion. People fell up in this industry and it seemed Fiona would be no exception!

I stood frozen in the mailroom. So many questions were rocketing through my head. Could Sharee stop Debbie from giving my promotion to Fiona? Would she try? If Frances found out what Debbie was up to, would she take it upon herself to intervene? Should I tell Sharee what I'd overheard? *Why in the hell is Debbie so set against me?*

Chapter 18

The day wore on and it was business as usual in my department. I was standing outside the counter demonstrating some lip colors on the back of my hand for a customer, when I was nearly run over.

"Out of the way!" roared Sheriff Hardass.

I looked up to see him, and not far behind, Annie, a chubby brunette girl who'd joined the Loss Prevention team a few months earlier.

"About five-feet-two, grey hair, about a hundred pounds," she barked into her walkie-talkie. "Suspect shoved a bottle of nail polish down the front of her blouse." Her face was red as a fire engine and pouring sweat. It must be hard being the new mall cop in town.

"What's happening? Is it a celebrity?" asked Jean-Luc, whipping around the counter to get a closer look.

"From what I can tell, looks like some old broad's getting her ass nailed by that new hard-on in security," said Yvonne, eloquent as always, while standing on her tiptoes, trying for a better view.

"Villagers," balked Jean-Luc, disgusted. "What kind of a person steals from a store like this? Do people not understand this is *luxury* we are selling? Go to Wal-Mart if you must steal!"

"Jean-Luc," I sighed. He really was by far, the biggest snob I'd ever met, and his salary hadn't even broken 60k a year.

"Wait a second. That's Mrs. Banks!" Chance cried. "She's been suspected of stealing for years. Why would they even bother with her? She spends a fortune in this place. So, she pinches a little something for herself every now and then. What's the big deal?"

I gave him an arctic glare.

He threw his palms up. "What?"

I turned my back to him.

Before I knew it, my entire team was standing in the main aisle watching the elderly lady get hauled away, the Sheriff with her right arm and Annie with her left. Mrs. Banks was screaming, "I want to see the store manager, now! Do you know who I am? You won't get away with this!"

I watched them until they were nearly to the back of the store. Finally, I tore my eyes away and announced, "Okay. Come on guys. Show's over. Let's get back to work."

I knew shoplifting cost the company a lot of money, and even the elderly should be held accountable for their actions, but knowing she'd been grabbed like a tackle dummy at a Chicago Bears training camp by a gung-ho, wannabe sheriff, was enough to win her my sympathy. I didn't know if what they'd just done was even legal!

"Awe, Toy. It's deader in here than my grandpa's dick. Can't we just wait around until the cops get here?" pleaded Yvonne.

I watched the client I'd been showing lipstick to turn five shades of red before she looked at me aghast and stalked off.

I grabbed Yvonne's hand and pulled her back behind the counter. "Yvonne, what have I told you about your language?"

"Sorry, Toy," she said, picki[illegible]at what was left of her red nail polish. "I wasn't thinking."

"That's the problem, you need to *start* thinking. What if that client tells Sharee? Or worse — customer service! What then?"

She looked up at me like a kid who'd been caught with her hand in the cookie jar.

"I'll try to keep a lid on it, cool?"

"No, it's not *cool*. If your behavior doesn't start improving I'm going to be forced to take disciplinary action. Do you understand?"

It was hard to keep a serious expression when dealing with Yvonne. Granted, she had the mouth [illegible] 'runken sailor, but she was so damned lovable.

She nodded and made h[illegible] over to Chance. I wondered just how long the two of them co[illegible]ch other entertained exchanging crude stories.

The floor had begun to settle down when a semi-familiar face appeared. It was Officer Brows. The sensible officer who'd accompanied him on their last visit was nowhere in sight. Brows rested a hip against the counter and scanned the store. "Got a call they apprehended a shoplifter here. This must be my lucky week. Can you tell me where the holding room is?"

I looked around, not sure if he was talking to me or to someone else. "Are you asking me?"

His head snapped in my direction. "Yes, I am. Where would I need to go?" he asked, eagerly.

What a dork. Who gets excited about arresting an old woman?

I pointed, "Through those double doors, walk down the hall. It's the last door on the right."

Apparently, his lofty position made a simple "thank you" entirely unnecessary. I gaped as I watched him practically run to the holding room. He'd probably been a loser in high school, and then became a cop to boost his low self-esteem.

My thoughts were interrupted by Jean-Luc.

"Honey, you have a call," he said, holding up the counter phone.

Wow, I'm really out of it today! I didn't even hear it ring...

"Who is it?" I asked quietly.

"It is your favorite villager." He said, loud enough to make sure the person on the line heard him.

I jerked the phone out of his hand. "This is Toy."

"Hi, Toy, it's Tommy."

A wave of relief washed over me. "Oh my God, how are you?"

"I'm okay. Listen, I'm just calling so you won't worry. I don't wanna discuss my case over the phone, but I'll be in touch."

"That's fine. Make sure you call Human Resources and request a leave of absence to keep your job secure. I need you for the event."

Jean-Luc stood in front of me disapprovingly and interjected, "Do not tell him that. If he loses the position, it is his problem."

I waved him away.

"Will do. Hopefully, I'll be able to make it," Tommy said, hesitantly.

"Thank you. Take care, will you please?"

I disconnected and turned around to see Jean-Luc standing a few feet away from me.

He took a step toward me with outstretched arms, "Cherie—"

"Don't Cherie me! And, don't ever interrupt me when I'm on the phone. Your behavior is going to change. You will no longer do whatever you want at this counter," I snarled. "Do you understand?"

He flinched at my tone of voice. "Yes."

"It had better, because I'm done with your arrogance!"

He didn't say another word. Instead, with his nostrils flared, he gathered his things and clocked out for the day.

I knew he must be really perturbed to leave exactly when he was scheduled to. He always stayed late to make extra sales. As I watched him leave, I started to feel bad thinking that maybe my frustration over Nikola had pushed me over the edge, but then I thought about Tommy. He was at his lowest point and Jean-Luc couldn't have cared less. On second thought, Jean-Luc had it coming.

I glanced at my watch. Time to go. I was tempted to stay until close. I didn't want to go home. The thought of walking into my apartment to the bottle of Moscato Nikola and I would never finish, was enough to bring me to tears. I hoped Chance was still planning on us having girl's night, but the way he and Jean-Luc had been secretly (ha-ha) flirting all day, I was beginning to doubt it.

It was only 9:00 PM, but I'd crawled into bed early, right after, as I'd expected, Chance rain-checked on me. I heard my texting chirp and looked at it. *Hmmm, Ben.*

Him: *Can you talk?*

Me: *Yeah.*

Hardly a second passed when my phone rang.

"Hi," I bubbled, surprised at myself. I was actually happy to hear his voice.

"Hi there. How've you been?"

"Hmm, so-so. Been working a lot preparing for yet *another* event. You know how it goes."

"Yeah, I've been busy, too. I'm so ready to come back to Chicago," he sighed.

"I think it'll be good for us to talk openly about everything. You know, air everything out face-to-face," I said. *You'll be a welcome distraction.*

"I can talk as openly as you'd like. I'll bare everything, even my body," he teased.

"Funny," I said, my thoughts drifting to Nikola.

"What's wrong? You don't sound like yourself."

I had to hand it to him. He really did know me. It was nice to feel this kind of closeness again.

"I don't know where to start. It's just been a crazy few weeks, you know? You and me, Fiona, work drama, and more of that than the norm," I added.

"I was going to say, when isn't it a soap opera there?"

"Yeah, but not always to this degree. I put in a request for three weeks off after the event. Ordinarily they wouldn't approve it because of the holidays coming up, but I haven't had any serious time off this year with the constant parade of events."

"Good for you. For once, you'll get to have a real holiday."

We talked some more until I noticed nearly an hour had gone by. "Wow, we've been on the phone for a while," I pointed out.

"Remember when we first started dating?" Ben asked. "We'd talk for hours. Seemed like minutes, then."

"Yes," I said. "I miss those days."

"We can still have times like that."

"I don't know..." *Could I ever be content with any man after Nikola?*

"We can, Toy. If you'll let us."

Did I really want Ben back or was he my rebound from Nikola? After a pause, I said, "I have a lot to consider, Ben. For now though, I think I'd better go to sleep. I've got such a busy week ahead of me. See you this weekend?"

"Absolutely. Sleep well, Toy. Goodnight."

"Goodnight, Ben."

I laid my phone down beside me and curled into myself, sadness wholly consuming me. Try as I might, I couldn't banish Nikola from my head. I really believed he loved me. The fact that he was with Biljana out of a sense of duty made this all the more painful. I thought of Mrs. Ibenski and panic set in. *Have I lost my soul mate just as she had? Will I spend the rest of my life comparing every man I meet to Nikola?*

I thought of that old Tennyson line: "Tis better to have loved and lost, than to never have loved at all." *You know what? F-U Tennyson!*

The rest of the week had mercifully flown by, one day blending into the next, with me slaving each day from open to close. Otherwise, I don't think my heart could've survived the sadness, or my head the anxiety.

It was Friday, the day before the big event, *finally*. Despite the fact that Debbie had been at my counter all week "organizing", we'd still managed to have some productive days.

Frances, the founder of Cesonne, was making an appearance after store closing that night. The thought frayed my already raw nerves. She was internationally known for her red lipsticks and had created the line so that there was "a shade of red lipstick for every woman". Already an accomplished diva, she'd just recently added Best-Selling Author to her list of achievements.

The event area was gorgeous. There was a huge, black marble desk and red leather chair for Frances's signing. Behind the desk were two towers filled with boxed sets, which contained her best-selling lipstick, Red #11, and her book, *With Love and Red Lipstick, Frances*. Our buying office had sent us a little over $150,000 worth of merchandise for the event. I was more than pleased with my team for booking our appointment slots solid and having over $80,000 rung up in presale for our select clients. It had taken every single person on the team to make this happen, but we'd done it.

I had about an hour before the store closed and Frances arrived. I hadn't eaten all day, so I went to grab a sandwich at L'Appetito. It was only a couple of blocks away and their sandwiches were to die for!

While waiting for my sandwich to be made, I heard someone call out, "Hi, Toy!"

I turned around and was a little surprised to see Biljana who'd left the store more than two hours ago, sitting with an attractive African-American guy I'd never seen before. I wanted to pretend like I hadn't heard her, but the familiar way he looked at her caught my attention.

I walked over to them and said, "Hi Biljana, how's it going?"

"Good, *very* good," she giggled, not bothering to introduce me to her friend.

"That's nice. So, how's the coffee here?" I asked. "I've never tried it.".

"It is good, but Macedonian coffee is much better," she said, shooting her friend a sly smile.

"So, I take it you're not recommending it, then?"

"Nothing compares to Moroccan coffee," said her friend, who reached out and touched her with a finger.

I fought to keep my face passive. These two seemed awfully cozy with each other.

"That's what you need, Biljana. Come on. I know a place that serves the best Moroccan coffee in Chicago," he said, as if I wasn't even there.

"Well, I've never had either." I turned to Biljana, "Maybe you could bring me a bag. You know, the event starts tomorrow."

After an awkward silence, I stuck out my hand. "Oh, I'm Toy, by the way."

He took it. "Daniel," he said.

"Yes," she giggled. "How rude of me. Well?"

"Well," I said. "I gotta get back. Nice to meet you, Daniel. See you tomorrow, Biljana."

She ignored me and whispered something in her friend's ear.

I took that as my cue to leave.

On the walk back to work, my mind was racing. Was it acceptable for women in Macedonia to hang out with other men when they were pregnant by someone they were supposedly committed to? Somehow, I doubted it. It couldn't be in Macedonia or anywhere else, for that matter.

I pulled my phone out of my coat pocket and scrolled down to Nikola's name. I started to call and tell him, and then stopped. It wasn't my place to get involved in his and Biljana's relationship. Besides, there wasn't any proof.

If what was going on was true, it would all come out anyway. I just hoped he'd discover it in time...

Overcome with emptiness, I shoved the phone back into my pocket.

When I arrived back at work, Frances's entourage was already there, inspecting the main aisle where the event would be taking place. There were six of them, four men and two women. The newly-minted-MBA men were dressed impeccably in Yves Saint Laurent suits and the Frances-wannabe women were clad in Chanel tweed suit dresses. And, surprise! Debbie was nowhere in sight. I went to my counter and made myself look busy while waiting for them to approach me.

I'd just finished cleaning the makeup brushes when Sharee rushed up.

"Frances just arrived! She'll be heading over here any minute now," she said, doing a quick inspection of the counter and nodding her satisfaction.

Frances was in her mid-50s and still a stunner. German, with shoulder length brown hair, huge green eyes and large enough breasts to wonder "Did she or didn't she?" At thirty-one-years old she'd created Cesonne Cosmetics. Her empire had started with only one red lipstick. She sincerely believed that all women could, and should, wear red lipstick, and that's how she marketed it.

Frances pulled ahead of her competitors in the cosmetics industry when she began to create limited edition shades, finishes and textures of red lipstick for celebrities. She did private consultations to create their perfect reddish hue, then named the lipstick after them. Her gimmick created a cult following. It became so successful that now she only created three celebrity shades per year, and there was always a waiting list. Last year Amber Heard, Eva Green, and Sanaa Lathan were branded. We'd sold out of those three, company-wide, the month they were launched.

I blinked my eyes and the next second, Frances herself was standing before us.

Debbie made her usual eleventh hour appearance. "Toy, come over here, sweetie," she beckoned with outstretched arms.

Sweetie? Good acting job, Debbie.

"Frances, I'd like to introduce you to — " Debbie started.

Frances cut Debbie off by crossing in front of her. "Toy, of course." She took both of my hands in hers. "I've heard nothing but fabulous things about you from Sharee." She made a show of looking me over. I felt like I was being presented to the Queen of England on national television.

"Thank you. It's such a pleasure to meet you. I'm sure you hear this all the time, but your lipsticks are incredible — and everything else you've created," I gushed. "I'm really very honored to be part of your team."

She smiled, but her silence was deafening. You could hear a pin drop in the room as she continued to observe me. A dark panic engulfed me. *Did I say something wrong? Is my lipstick smeared? Wrong shade of red?*

My life had just started to pass before my eyes, when I heard Frances say, "You are an ambitious one, aren't you?"

I didn't know what to say. I was scared and exhilarated all at the same time.

After a beat and hoping for the best, I offered, "Yes, I suppose."

"I personally hired Toy because I was confident she'd be an excellent team leader," interjected Debbie.

I noticed Sharee's face had suddenly colored.

"That is interesting," said Frances. She dropped my hands to turn and face Debbie.

"Pardon me?" Debbie blinked.

"I said that is *interesting*." Frances looked her dead in the eye. "Is my English not clear?"

Whoa. This is getting interesting.

"No, of course not, Frances. You're English is perfect. I was just curious as to what you meant by 'interesting'," Debbie uttered, her plastic smile never wavering.

"I just returned from a meeting with Human Resources and we were reviewing Toy's performance. According to the paperwork, it was Sharee who hired her, no?" Frances arched an eyebrow.

Debbie's face went pale. A flicker of fear flashed in her eyes, but she kept her composure.

"But, I was the one who —" Debbie countered, only to be cut off by Frances once again.

"Sharee, will you come over here?" She motioned Sharee forward and threw an arm around her. "You, my dear, have an eye for talent. The key to being a good manager is realizing you are only as good as the people you hire." Frances ever-so-slightly angled her head in my direction. "Fabulous work on your part."

"Thank you, Frances," said Sharee, poised as always.

"Toy, lovely meeting you. I look forward to our event tomorrow. Thank you for all of your hard work." She turned and startled me with a kiss on both cheeks. "Now go home and get some beauty rest."

"Thank you, Frances. H-have a good night," I said, shocked that I was being dismissed so early. Usually I'd be stuck here until long after midnight, the night before an event.

Debbie moved away to the side, still retaining the manufactured smile. She was doing a better job at keeping it together than I'd have given her credit for.

Just when I thought Frances had forgotten her, she said, "Debbie, can you stay here with my assistant to wait for my flowers? I can't work tomorrow without some natural beauty to gaze at. They will be coming sometime tonight, special delivery. You don't mind, do you?"

Debbie stood with her mouth agape as Frances linked arms with Sharee, and the two of them strolled off together. I wasn't going to wait and see if Frances might change her mind. I put it in gear and headed for the locker room, risking a glance over my shoulder, only to see Frances laughing with Sharee. And, I thought I'd heard her mention something about dinner.

I didn't dare to lock eyes with Debbie. I'd seen and overheard, but as of yet, never felt her full wrath. I wasn't about to risk it now. I moved on to get my coat, but found myself worrying about Sharee. Debbie was evil to the bone. Even though it wasn't Sharee who'd made her look like a fool in front of everyone, I was sure Debbie would go after her since Frances was untouchable.

Sheriff Hardass was standing sentry at the employee exit. I refused to acknowledge him with a greeting and simply opened my bag. This time he gave a casual glance inside, then nodded his head toward the exit.

"Creep," I grumbled under my breath and headed down the stairs.

Crap. I forgot my scarf!

I turned around and grudgingly made my way back up the stairs. I expected to see the new security guard standing at the door. He wasn't, but, I could hear a muffled voice saying, "Don't worry, baby. It'll all work out," but I couldn't decide from where.

I began tiptoeing toward the locker room and glanced across the hall into security, and there was Sheriff Hardass, whispering into the phone with his back to me. I prayed he'd stay that way.

Who the heck is he calling "baby"? I wondered, and bit my lip to stifle an audible "eww"!

I slipped into the locker room, grabbed my scarf from the bottom of the locker, and eased back into the hallway.

This time when I passed by, he came in loud and clear "We can't be talking about this now. Stop trippin' bae."

Who in the hell is he talking to that would distract him from a chance to swing his weight around? Work was getting stranger by the minute.

I quietly made my way back down the stairs and out the door without him noticing.

"Whew," I breathed.

One more day and I'll have a three-week vacation, I reminded myself. *Just one more day...*

I'd made it to the first block on the way home when the text tone on my phone went off. *Anyone but work!*

I jerked the phone from my pocket, saw it was Ben: *Good luck with your event tomorrow, babeJ*

I slowed my step and smiled.

Me: *You remembered?*
Him: *I remembered. I'm pulling a double at the hospital but wanted to shoot you a quick text. Can't wait to see you Sunday. Gotta go. xo*
Me: *Thank you... xo:)*

Still smiling, I tucked the phone back into my pocket. I was impressed that he'd not only remembered my event but had actually wished me good luck. In all the time we'd dated he'd never done that. *Maybe he's actually starting to see my job as more than just lipstick!*

I burst into my apartment, threw the keys on the kitchen counter and grabbed a bottle of water from the fridge. I would've preferred merlot, but I knew I had to be up at 4:00 AM. Instead I opted for a soothing cup of chamomile tea.

I tossed and turned all night, then was jarred awake by the blaring alarm. "Ugh," I grunted and hit the snooze button.

I never slept well before events, jolting awake every hour on the hour out of fear my alarm would fail and I'd oversleep. *Just ten more minutes*, I wished and flipped to my other side.

I was just dozing off again when my phone started ringing. I knew it could only be one person this early in the morning.

"Good morning, Sunshine!" sang Chance.

Was there ever a morning that Chance didn't sound overly chipper?

"Hey, babe," I mumbled, my words thick with sleep.

"Ewe, you sound like shit, girl."

"Chance, I just opened my eyes. I haven't gotten out of bed yet. Why the hell are you even up? It takes you like thirty minutes to get ready," I said, thinking how nice it'd be to not have to spend two hours every morning to make myself presentable.

"Because I stayed at Jean-Luc's last night. I've actually been staying with him a lot lately. Sorry about not coming over the other night. He and I were busy, if you know what I mean, and I couldn't tear myself away," he giggled.

"Yeah, I figured. It's fine, I needed the rest anyway."

"I left before he woke up this morning, and when I got home I couldn't sleep, so I decided to shower and get dressed. Now I'm on my way to your apartment to bring you a coffee," he chirped.

"You're on your way? *Now?*"

"Actually, I'm already here at your door. Let me in," he said, oblivious to my at-this-hour tone.

"Of course, you are. Okay, I'm dragging my sleepy ass out of bed. Bye," I growled, threw my blanket aside, and slipped into my robe. Did my doorman *ever* monitor the people coming and going in the building? This was really becoming a nuisance.

I opened the door to find Chance all giddy looking. He made a theatrical jump to the side and screamed, "Surprise!" revealing, in a crouching position...Ben?

Ben wore his own goofy grin, and held a Starbucks coffee in his hand.

I didn't know what to say. Ben had never been the type to just "pop in" out of nowhere. I smelled a rat with the name Chance written all over it.

"Oh wow, what a surprise. Come in," I said, imagining various ways to bring about Chance's demise. Sometimes he just didn't think. Couldn't he have given me the heads-up at least enough to drag a comb through my hair?

"Hi. I'm sorry for just showing up like this. I wanted to wish you good luck before your event in person, so I ran it by Chance and he thought it'd be a nice surprise," said Ben, anxiously.

Well, this one sure came out of left field. This was Ben's idea? And he was nervous. Actually, I'd never seen him so nervous. It was kind of cute.

"Thank you. It was really thoughtful of you to do this, but you didn't have to come over this early just for that," I said, leading them both into the living room.

"Here's your mocha, girl," said Chance. He took the drink from Ben, handed it off to me, and frantically headed for the front door. "Oh my God, I think I left my wallet at your front desk! I'll be right back."

Before I could say anything, Chance was already out the door. I took a seat at one end of the couch while Ben took a seat on the other.

Ben and I locked eyes and I couldn't help but to laugh at Chance. There was always some sort of crisis going on with him.

Ben ran his hand through his hair nervously. "Toy, this past year has been both the best and worst year of my life. Obviously, it was the worst, because you weren't with me. But it was the best because it made me realize that my life doesn't have meaning without you to share it with. I love you. I don't want to spend another minute of my life without you in it."

He lifted himself from the couch, came over and assumed the kneeling position in front of me.

"Will you marry me?" he proposed and opened a small, black leather box. Inside was a simple, elegant princess cut diamond ring.

I was beginning to feel light headed.

"Toy?" Ben prodded.

"I just feel..."

My heart was racing. If this had happened a year ago — just one year ago — it would've been the easiest decision of my life. But so much had changed since then. I'd changed. Could anything ever be the same after Nikola?

"I - I need a few minutes,"

I tried to stand up, but instantly felt dizzy.

"I don't feel good," I said, slowly sitting back down.

Ben was by my side in an instant. I was fighting off a wave of nausea as he helped me lay down on the couch and prop up my feet.

"Just close your eyes, Toy," he said, softly, before his lips brushed my forehead. "I'm not going anywhere."

My heartbeat began to slow down as I shut my eyes and drifted along the flow of consciousness, just above sleep.

Chapter 19

Chance burst through the front door, and I heard him cry, "Toy! Oh my God, Oh my God! Call a doctor!"

And then, Ben, "Chance, I *am* a doctor. Relax. She's going to be okay."

I slowly opened my eyes. It took me a second or two to focus, but when I could, I saw Chance pacing back and forth, and Ben sitting on the couch beside me.

"What happened?" I slurred, still woozy. A wave of nausea passed through me.

"You stood up so quickly that it caused your blood pressure to drop," said Ben.

"I walked in and saw you were just laying there and I thought you were dead! All I could think was how could this be happening to *me*? My best friend dying on the day of our biggest event!"

"Hey, Chance," Ben said in his doctor voice, "why don't you go get Toy some Ginger Ale and crackers?"

"Yeah, I guess I could do that." He started for the door, then turned back around. "Like goldfish crackers, or what?"

Ben tried to look serious. "Let's shoot for saltines."

"Okay. See you in a few minutes," said Chance, whipping the long end of his Burberry scarf over his shoulder.

I heard the front door shut and looked up at Ben. "I need to get dressed."

"Hold on, Champ," he teased.

When I started to sit up, Ben gently put his hand on my arm. "Seriously. It's better for you to lay down a few minutes and get up slowly. I don't want you to throw up. That's why I sent Chance to the store," and then added, "Well, that was one of the reasons. He needed to calm down."

I'd have laughed, but my head was aching. "Yeah, he can get a little hysterical." I put a hand to my forehead. "Ugh, I should already be dressed by now. How long am I going to feel this way?"

"It shouldn't be too long. The worst thing you can do is push yourself too fast," Ben cautioned. "You need to rest for now."

"Oh my God! This can't be happening. On the day of my event!" I wanted to cry.

"Toy, close your eyes and relax. Chance will be back any minute, and then we'll calm your stomach. You'll make the event. Better late than never," he said, caressing my hand.

I must have dozed off because when I opened my eyes, I was covered with a blanket. I sat up slowly. My eyes were drawn to the coffee table where a slowly bubbling glass of Ginger Ale sat with an open package of saltines. Not far from them was the ring Ben had just proposed to me with.

He was asleep on the other end of the couch. His usually short hair had grown into a mass of thick, brown curls and it looked like he hadn't shaved in a couple of days. It felt so easy — so natural, to have him with me right now.

I eased out from under the blanket, trying not to wake him, and stood up. I felt so weak that I sat right back down. I moved closer to Ben and put my head in my lap.

"Babe, are you okay? I guess it's not a good idea to propose to a woman before 5:00 AM, huh?" Ben smiled. "I just know how important today is to you and wanted to make it even more special."

"You don't know how much it means to me to hear you say that."

He ran his fingers through my hair. "It's true. These last few weeks have been a living hell for me. Knowing you thought I'd sunk so low as to sleep with Fiona nearly killed me. It really did."

"I'm sorry. I didn't know what to think. The entire thing just seemed so suspicious, so when she insinuated you two had been together, it seemed true," I said, weakly.

"I talked to her, but only to keep some sort of connection to you. I know it sounds pathetic, especially when I was the one who ended it, but it's the truth." His voice grew slightly tense. "And Toy, there's one last thing I need to tell you."

"Okay," I said. *Please don't let it be something terrible you did with another woman. I can't handle any more surprises.*

He took my hand. "Fiona *did* come up to my hotel room once. She said she needed to talk to me about something really important. I let her in my room, then she asked to use the bathroom. When she came out, she was dressed in lingerie and threw herself at me. I pushed her off and told her to get dressed and get out."

I struggled to keep a straight face as I listened to him tell me the exact same story Fiona had. Still, I was happy to hear their stories matched!

"I just want you to know that nothing happened with her, or anyone else for that matter," he said, firmly.

"You didn't sleep with anyone while we were apart?" I asked, then immediately regretted the question, knowing it was none of my business.

"I went out on a couple dates, but no, I didn't. They weren't you."

I was suddenly overwhelmed by a mixture of emotions: guilt, anger and regret. I couldn't take back the past year, and some of it, I wasn't sure I even wanted to.

He took note of my silence. "Look, I don't care what you did while we weren't together. I just care about what happens from this moment on."

I looked down at my hand in his. Lately, my life had been nothing but chaos. Now, sitting next to me was a man I knew and loved, offering to give me stability and to love me for the rest of my life. Yet, I was still unsure.

I glanced at the ring again and was swept back to one of Ben and my first dates. We were walking past Tiffany's and he pointed out a gaudy six carat diamond solitaire in the window, joked that I was "high maintenance" and when I did become engaged, that'd be the kind of ring I'd expect. I'd laughed at him and told him he didn't know me at all.

Then, as we were about to walk away, I saw it. A princess cut diamond accented by an understated platinum and diamond band. I'd been smitten with it.

I looked up at him in confusion. "If this was all spur of the moment planning, how did you happen to have the very ring I told you I wanted so long ago?"

"Because I bought it a few days after we saw it in the window of Tiffany's," he smiled.

"What?" My heart fluttered and I all but forgot about my throbbing and churning stomach. "You've had it this entire time?"

"Yes. You've always been the one. I knew from the moment we met. Nothing matters to me anymore, Toy, nothing. Not without you."

I looked into his eyes and was overcome with love.

"Yes," I said, softly.

"Yes?"

"Yes, I'll marry you."

He reached over to the table and picked up the tiny box, opened it, and pulled out the ring. He slipped it on my finger and as he did, I realized that something had been missing from my life this past year. It wasn't just him. It was us. I missed being us.

"I love you," I said, and leaned in to kiss him.

"I love you too, so much."

We kissed and I felt the same heady feeling as when we'd first met. I looked at the solitaire, its platinum band stippled with pavé diamonds, and smiled up at him. "I'm engaged."

Then a thought occurred to me. I glanced around the room. *Where's Chance?*

"Don't worry, we're alone. I told Chance I'd take care of you," said Ben, as if knowing what I was thinking.

"Well then, come take care of me."

I made it into work by 8:30 AM, feeling like I'd been up for days. When I reached the counter, to my surprise, I found the team, sans Tommy and Fiona, all eagerly waiting for me. Fiona was probably running late on purpose, just to piss me off.

"Congratulations!" they cried in unison. Chance clapped his hands together, while Yvonne jumped up and down.

"Thanks, guys," I said, flashing the ring, then hugging each of them in turn.

When I got to Biljana, I examined her facial expression to gauge her reaction to the news of my engagement. Her face gave no clue one way or another.

I got to Chance and narrowed my eyes. I'd called him when I was getting dressed to tell him I'd accepted Ben's proposal. "It's a good thing I didn't want to keep this a secret."

He looked at me with that guilty, childlike look, but before he could open his mouth to explain, I pulled him into a hug. "I'm kidding, babe."

"Come on, baby, let's see the rock." Jean-Luc wiggled his fingers excitedly, gesturing for a closer look.

I held out my hand. He took it and examined the diamond intently.

"Would you like a loupe?" I joked.

"It *is* from Tiffany's, right?" asked Ed, snootily.

Jean-Luc dismissed Ed with the toss of his hand. "Baby, he did a phenomenal job! Magnificent color and clarity." He grinned at me. "French-set." He tilted my hand. "And this has to be *at least* two carats."

"I don't know how many carats it is, but it is beautiful, isn't it?" I gushed.

"You fuckin' hit the jackpot, man. A *doctor!* I knew you had it in ya, Captain," lauded Yvonne.

I was so happy I didn't bother to correct her language. "Thanks, Yvonne. But it's not about the money."

"Yeah, right," she snorted. "I've always said that a man can have the looks, the personality, and the cock, but if he doesn't have the dough to go with it, he's not gettin' this papaya."

My jaw went slack.

Jean-Luc regarded her with disgust. "Must you always speak such filth? This is a moment that is to be treasured in Toy's life. May we *please* leave the village talk for later? *Dieu aide moi, je suis entouré par des paysans,*" he snobbed.

I understood enough French to know he was again complaining about being surrounded by peasants.

Yvonne must have figured it out, too, because she glared at Jean-Luc and barked like a drill sergeant, "Go fuck yourself, Jean-Luc!"

Jean-Luc's eyes narrowed to slits, but before he could respond, I stepped between them.

"Come on guys, this is a very special day. We have Frances here and we're going to show her what this team is made of. No more swearing or arguing, and enough about my engagement. We're about to make Cesonne history!" I wanted to laugh at how corny I sounded. Did I mention that cheerleading captain is also part of a cosmetics business manager's job description?

I glanced behind Chance and saw Tommy approaching the counter. He had dark circles under his eyes and looked like he hadn't slept in a week.

Before I had time to warn Jean-Luc not to antagonize Tommy, he called out, "Who let you out of your cage?"

"Jean-Luc!" I cried.

"What?" he returned.

I cut him a dirty look and turned my attention to Tommy.

"I'm so happy you're here," I said, hugging him tightly. I really was glad. Tommy was a few years older than me, but his vulnerability made him seem more like a troubled little brother.

"How was it in county? I hear it's pretty rough in there and you have to watch your back — er, that is, your back*side*," Yvonne hooted.

"Yvonne!" I said, sharply.

"What? It's a joke. You know I'm joking, right Tommy boy?"

"Yeah, it's cool," he muttered.

"All that matters is, you're still part of this team," I said, trying to lift his spirits.

"Thanks, but I have a court date in two weeks, then I don't know what'll happen," he moaned.

"Well you're here today and we're *all* glad," I said, glaring at Jean-Luc.

"Yes, thrilled," jeered Jean-Luc.

I clapped twice. "Okay everyone. Now that Tommy's here, let's gather around for a quick team meeting."

With a pained look on his face, Chance took a seat in the makeup chair and pointed to his neck. Yvonne went to work massaging him. I rolled my eyes and grinned. He was such a delicate thing. Biljana, Tatyana, and Tommy sat on the glass counter, and Jean-Luc leaned over it.

I put on my game face and said, "Jean-Luc, you and Tommy bring up as many large shopping bags as you can carry. Chance and Biljana, make sure all register areas are stocked. Yvonne and Ed, when Fiona decides to grace us with her presence, you three make sure each makeup station has a minimum of three #11 red lipsticks. Tatyana, you and I will check in our freelancers."

Before I could ask if anyone had questions, they scattered in different directions. I guess they understood. This place was like a nut house, with tons of glitter dumped on it to camouflage the insanity, but I had to admit I loved it.

I picked up my clipboard and skimmed the names of all the freelancers coming in to set up their stations for the event. I liked to do this because it gave me an idea of how busy the day would be. It was extremely difficult to find good freelancers, and when you did, they were usually a little coocoo. There are a few things about freelance makeup artists that most people outside the industry don't know.

They are independent contractors hired to work special events and provide extra support for the counter. Being IC means they aren't store employees, so there are always gray areas when it comes to what they can and can't do. Although I appreciated what they did, managing them was like working two jobs simultaneously.

I had to sign them in and out to verify they actually worked their scheduled shifts and wrote down their *true* sales for the day, break up the inevitable catfights, and deal with the endless customer complaints regarding "overly aggressive salespeople". I've even had a freelancer roll her eyes and say, "You're *really* not going to buy anything after I spent all this time with you?" when a client said no to her sales pitch!

I scanned the roster of freelancers and two names stood out from the rest to warn me of the shit storm that awaited me, and two names stood out from the rest to warn me of the shit storm ahead: Isabelle, the Brazilian and Adina, the Israeli. The two women were phenomenal salespeople, but they nitpicked and bickered over everything. One time they almost came to fists over, of all things, whose box of tissue was whose. I was constantly being tapped on the shoulder by one of them, requesting a private conversation about something the other had done. It was like babysitting two bratty toddlers, but I had a soft spot for them. They were passionate about what they did.

I glanced up from my clipboard to see Officer Brows patrolling the periphery, and had myself a chuckle. He'd obviously lowered his standards to do crowd control and pick up some extra weekend bucks.

I was back to perusing the roster when Tatyana approached me.

"I hear the lucky guy is Ben," Tatyana snipped.

"Yes, it's Ben," I replied, without looking up.

"Well, I wish you both the best," she said without an ounce of sincerity. "I just hope you made right decision."

That got my attention. I slapped the clipboard down on the counter. "What are you getting at?"

"I think you know," she said, cattily.

"Not that it's any of your business, but as a matter of fact, I'm more than sure I've made the right decision. I'm positive. Happy?"

Even as the words spilled from my mouth, I had a gut feeling that what I was saying wasn't altogether true.

Tatyana lowered her eyes and rested her hand on mine. I relaxed. I understood she wasn't taunting me.

"Toy, it is okay to lie to the world, but never lie to yourself." She gave a deep nod and walked away.

I stood stunned. Tears stung at my eyes. I would never have thought of Tatyana as a person who could stir up this kind of emotion in me. I guess there actually was a heart lurking somewhere underneath those enormous boobs.

I quickly dabbed my eyes with a tissue and pulled myself together just in time to see Chance and Biljana approach the counter.

"Babe, before everyone gets here, can Biljana and I go on a ten to have a smoke?" Chance said in his little boy voice.

Now I can add "smoking" to Biljana's laissez-faire pregnancy habits... I hope Biljana isn't smoking. Stop it, Toy. It's not your affair.

"Yeah, but please hurry," I said, knowing Chance's ten minutes could last thirty.

"Okey-dokey," he said, and practically skipped away with Biljana in tow.

Just as they left, Fiona showed up, clocking in like nothing was wrong.

"Um... hi," I said, to prompt an explanation.

"Hi," Fiona mumbled.

"Excuse me, but you're late. Did I miss something? Like — a phone call?" I said, peeved.

"My alarm didn't go off," she said, casually.

"We're talking about this later. This is unacceptable on the day of an event. Understood?"

"Yep." She popped the 'p'. *God she's obnoxious.*

"Okay, go find Yvonne and Ed. See if they need help with the makeup stations. After that, make sure all of the freelancers have checked their personal belongings in with security. No wallets or purses. And they can't have anything but water at their stations. No coffee. No soda. *Only water.*"

Fiona's expression, before she walked away, made it clear it was killing her to have to take orders rather than give them.

In the next instant, the freelancers came pouring in, filling the main aisle with artistry tables and director's chairs. The store was coming to life.

My name rang out from every direction. "Toy, where's the cotton?", "Toy, where's the alcohol?", "Toy, someone stole my mirror!", "Why is her location better than mine, Toy?", "You said we'd have more chairs!", "Can I take a quick bathroom break?", "I thought coffee wasn't allowed on the floor, Toy — Francesca has a cup, why can't I?"

I solved the problems and answered the questions as best I could while simultaneously checking in more freelancers. I was just about done with check-ins, when Yvonne came up to me.

"Holy fuckin' shit," she said, taking in the more than forty freelancers prepping each of their stations. "It *is* a war zone today, man!"

Against my will, I laughed, "Yvonne!" and handed her a bag of extra mirrors to pass out.

"Oh, Toy. I looked in the stockroom for those additional, free gifts with purchase. I couldn't find them. Do you think you could take a look in the basement stockroom?"

Damn. I can't afford to be off the floor. Only management was allowed in the basement stockroom because that's where we kept all of our most expensive stock and testers. *Better now than later when I'll be swamped with customers,* I rationalized. I found Tatyana and asked her to finish checking in the freelancers while I ran downstairs.

I stopped for a moment and watched with excitement as the throng burst through the doors and spilled into the aisles. Women of all colors, shapes and sizes — carrying lap dogs and dragging children — deluged the counters, plopped into makeup chairs and disappeared into back rooms for facials. And in the background, Officer Brows' head was rapidly pivoting right and left, on the alert for any minor infraction that might require his intervention. The event was in full swing. Let the sales begin!

Moments later, I typed my key code into the lock pad to get into the downstairs stockroom, but it didn't work. *What the hell?* I tried again and... *still invalid. Damn it!* I needed to make this quick. *Wait. I wonder if Sharee's code will work?* She'd given the override to me to use for emergency purposes only. *I think she'd consider this an emergency.*

I punched in her four-digit code and sure enough, the door quietly slid a couple inches open. Since her code worked and mine didn't, someone must've put an access restriction on the lock. Only an executive could do that, but it didn't make sense to deny access on the day of an event.

I pushed the door open, took two steps in, and froze. I couldn't have been more horrified had I barged in on a murder.

There were Debbie and Sheriff Hardass! Her back was against the far wall; her blouse was unbuttoned and her skirt was pushed up. He was practically slobbering all over her.

They were clearly so preoccupied they hadn't heard me enter the room because they continued their repugnant groping without hesitation. At that point, the hydraulic arm silently pulled the door shut. *Now what?* If I pushed down on the bar that opened the door, it was almost certain I'd attract their attention. But I couldn't just stand there — at some point they'd see me. And these were two people I didn't want to piss off. *Damn it! I guess the best I can hope for is they finish up and leave sooner than later.*

I tiptoed over to a 4'x 4' stack of boxes, crouched down behind them, and began praying this nightmare would be over quickly. *I must have the worst luck in the universe. How do I end up in these situations?*

"Jerry, we've got to stop," Debbie managed between gaspy moans.

Sheriff's name is Jerry? I guess even assholes have names, but *Jerry*? I would've never guessed. Frances will be here soon and I've got to be presentable to greet that hoity-toity bitch," Debbie said in a shrill, whiney tone that I assumed was her sexy voice. It may have turned Jerry on, but to me, it was further proof that Debbie and sexy didn't run in the same circle.

"Come on. I'll make it quick, promise."

"I don't know," she said, hesitantly, "Is letting off a load worth this kind of risk?"

Debbie. Always the lady.

"We won't get caught," Jerry said, smugly. "I've got this room on lockdown."

God, if you get me out of this one...

"What about the problem I said I needed help with? If you handle it for me, I promise I'll surprise you on the drive home tonight. Okay, Daddy?" Debbie did her sad version of cooing.

I wanted to vomit.

"Daddy" let out a resigned sigh. "Okay then. What's the problem?"

"It's Sharee, an arrest isn't enough. I have to get creative. All I need is a little help from you and I can be rid of her for good."

What? I peeked in between the boxes and saw that Debbie still hadn't pulled her skirt all the way down, but her breasts had been put away. *God is merciful...*

"So, what do you want me to do?"

"Well, I don't want her to just go to jail — I want to muddy her name *forever*. If she's caught with drugs, she's finished! Even stealing wouldn't ruin her like drugs will."

My mouth dropped. *This evil bitch has no soul.*

"I get what you're saying," he said with a villainous grin. "So, what'd you have in mind?"

I leaned closer to hear every word and almost knocked over the stack of boxes while leaning closer to hear every word. My heart nearly stopped.

"Wait till you see what I've got!" Debbie pulled a pair of latex gloves out of her blazer pocket and put them on. She then produced a 5"x 5" plastic bag from her other pocket. It was filled with white powder.

"I fished an empty sandwich bag out of Sharee's trash can a couple weeks ago. It's got her fingerprints on it. And now it's filled with coke. At some point today, Sharee and Frances will go to lunch. I'll sneak into Sharee's office and tape this to the underside of her bottom desk drawer." Debbie put the coke back into her pocket and removed the gloves as she continued.

"When Sharee returns from lunch, tell her you need to have a word in private, and escort her to the holding room. Inform her you've received an anonymous tip that she's distributing drugs at work, and you need to search her office. I know Sharee. She'll call your bluff and tell you to go right ahead. Bring Clyde along as a witness. You'll find the bag I planted and that's that. She's outta here, outta this industry, and shit outta luck — for good."

"What if it don't go down like that?" Jerry raised a cautious eyebrow.

"No sweat. I have a backup plan that'll make Tommy look like the informant and Sharee as his source. It'll easily give the cops probable cause for a search warrant." Debbie grinned, proudly. "But I'm betting you won't need one."

"Damn, you're not only sexy, you're brilliant as hell."

"You think I did good, Daddy?" she said, batting her uneven false eyelashes.

I jerked my head back around to make sure they didn't see me.

"I sure do," he said, followed by a slurpy kiss.

Sweat beaded on my forehead. This was too much, even for Debbie. I couldn't let her get away with this. I leaned back, pulled my knees up to my chest, and began to strategize.

I almost went through the ceiling when I heard the stockroom door open.

"I'm telling you, man, Toy was coming down here...Whoa! What the fuck!" cried Yvonne.

"Debbie?" shrieked Sharee. "Jerry?"

"Thank God you're here," I cried, and jumped out from behind the boxes, toppling them over.

Debbie stood across the room, attempting to smooth down her skirt, while Jerry stood frozen.

"Toy? What's going on here?" Sharee's disbelieving eyes flicked back and forth from me to them.

Before I could speak, Debbie started barking orders. "Yvonne, go back to the counter. Keep your mouth shut about anything you *think* you saw in here or you'll be at the unemployment office come Monday. Sharee, Frances will be here any minute, so you go and make sure the Green Room is ready. Toy, you stay here. I think we need to have a little chat."

I couldn't believe it. Even when she was clearly busted, Debbie still managed to keep her cool and take control. Or so she thought...

"Debbie, the only person on the unemployment line after today is going to be you!" Sharee stared her down. "You think you can get away with anything, don't you? Well not this time. You're done. I won't allow you to bully your way out of this one."

Debbie laughed, but it was a nervous laugh. Jerry just stood there, cauterizing me with those beady, red eyes.

Debbie made another attempt to assert her authority. "Sharee, just do what I said. We'll talk about this later. Toy, stay. We need to —"

"Absolutely not," Sharee overruled her. "Yvonne, go get the store manager and call LP. Tell them we need them down here *now*!"

"You got it," said Yvonne, turning toward the door.

"Yvonne, I wouldn't do that if I were you," Debbie screamed, finally losing her cool.

I couldn't stand it anymore. "Sharee, Debbie was going to set you up. She has cocaine! She was going to plant it in your office!"

Sharee's face darkened, but somehow, she maintained her composure. "Yvonne, call LP first and tell them we need the police here. *Go*!"

Yvonne shot out the door.

"That's ridiculous," snorted Debbie.

"No, I don't think it is, Debbie," Sharee spat. "Actually, it sounds exactly like something you'd do."

Debbie glared at Sharee, then me. "I'm warning both of you, we have connections." She gestured from herself to Jerry. "You fuck with us and this will only be the beginning of you constantly looking over your shoulder."

I realized that this entire time Jerry hadn't uttered a single word.

"Any *beginning* that doesn't include seeing you squeezed into clothes three sizes too small, I welcome. Your threats don't scare me anymore, Debbie," said Sharee, coolly.

Before Debbie could respond, the door swung open. In paraded Officer Brows, Andrew Kenny, our store manager, with Clyde and Yvonne bringing up the rear.

"Officer Brows?" I blurted, then clamped both hands over my mouth. He regarded me for a second. Then, I pointed at Debbie. "Check her pocket! She's got cocaine!"

The expression on Debbie's face was priceless. To be a woman of so many words, she just stood there sucking air.

Officer Brows moved closer to Debbie. "Do you mind emptying your pockets, just so we can clear all of this up?"

Debbie looked to Jerry. He casually shrugged his shoulders and said, "This all you," sending her into a rage.

"Fine," she said, pulling out the bag I'd seen earlier. "But it's not mine, it's Jerry's! He set this whole thing up —"

"Now you know that's a damn lie!" He lunged at her.

"I'm going to need backup," Brows barked into his radio, before attempting to separate the two of them, with Clyde on his heels. Jerry was big, but Brows outweighed him and soon had him pinned to the floor. Clyde easily restrained Debbie and I couldn't help but notice the look of satisfaction on his face.

A few minutes later, Debbie and Jerry were in handcuffs and I felt like I'd just won the lotto.

"Good-bye, Debbie," I waived, merrily.

Debbie and Jerry continued flinging accusations at each other as they were being walked out.

"Thank God that puta is toast!" Yvonne said, wiping her brow.

Sharee and I looked at Yvonne, and then burst into laughter. For once, Sharee let loose. The three of us waved our arms in the air and shimmied our hips like background singers, when Yvonne broke into, and Sharee and I joined in with, *"Ding Dong, the merry-oh, sing it high, sing it low. Let them know, the Wicked Witch is dead!"*

I thought, *could it be humanly possible for this day to get any stranger? Wait! This is the cosmetics business. Of course, it can!*

Chapter 20

I tapped my foot impatiently. I was sitting across from a young police officer whose totally buff physique challenged the chest buttons of his uniform. Officer Iosco had been assigned to interrogate me about the stockroom incident. After Debbie and Jerry were arrested, I thought I'd be free to work my event. *Wrong!* I'd been sitting in the store's holding room for over an hour! I glanced up at the clock on the wall for the umpteenth time.

"I think this is all the information I need for now. If I have any more questions, I'll get in touch with you." He held up a sheet of paper. "Is this a good number for you?"

"Yeah. It's my cell."

"Okay, well thanks again." He stood and crossed the room.

"You're welcome." I quickly rose from the table. *If I don't hurry, I might miss Frances's arrival!*

"Oh, and if you ever need someone to talk to..." He handed me his card and softened his voice sympathetically. "I know you endured a really traumatic experience. Maybe we could talk about it over coffee sometime."

I studied the card for a second, for his benefit. "Thanks, Officer Iosco. I'll keep that in mind."

His attempt to use therapy as a way to get me out on a date was pretty obvious. It was hard to imagine he hadn't noticed the ring on my finger — or maybe he didn't care. Nothing surprised me these days.

He pushed open the door. I walked by him and smiled, then rushed back my counter.

It wasn't an easy task to push through the mob of people who were lined up to purchase Frances's book and lipstick. My eyes finally caught a familiar face. Chance stood at the front of the line, clipboard in hand, smacking loudly on his gum. His eyes met mine. I watched his Adam's apple bob hard as he swallowed the gum.

"Toy! Oh my God, what are you doing here?" he cried, dramatically.

"What do you mean?" I asked.

"Sharee said you'd probably be going home after everything that happened. Then she placed me up here with this dorky clipboard. I mean, there are plenty of people, less important than me, that could be doing this moronic job," he groaned. "And, I'm missing out on a million sales."

I raised an eyebrow. "What 'moronic' job is it that you're supposed to be doing?"

"Confirming that everyone who wants to see Frances has a ticket," he said with the usual pouty face.

"Okay, then why are you standing here and not checking?"

"Girl, like who would be brave enough to sneak in line to see Frances? I *know* everyone has a ticket. I don't have to check."

I snatched the clipboard. "Go get Jean-Luc."

"He's making sure Tommy doesn't rearrange his fragrance display. I can see where he's coming from, Toy. Tommy isn't very gifted when it comes to the visual arts."

I smacked my forehead. "Chance, this isn't about where Jean-Luc *thinks* he should be. It's where he's needed and I need him here. So go get him

— now! You can keep an eye on Tommy until I get over there since it's so important to you. I'd think that assisting the freelancers in closing sales would be more important, but that's just me."

"Fine!" Chance threw his nose in the air and stormed away, theatrical as always.

I handed a ticket back to a Cesonne groupie and had just grabbed another when I felt a tap on my shoulder. I turned around to see Sharee.

"You do realize I was managing counters while you were in junior high," she grinned.

"I know you've got it under control, but I just can't miss this, Sharee. I can't."

"Your job is safe and so is your promotion. Go home and get some rest. No one should have to work after being trapped in a room with *those* two for God knows how long," she grimaced.

I clasped my hands together and pleaded, "Please? I'd rather be here with my team."

She looked at me skeptically, then, "Okay, fine. But, if you need a break, take one. I'm not kidding."

"I promise."

She headed over to a cluster of freelancers who were chattering as though they were at a social gathering. This was the reason I needed to be here. It was more like a free-for-all than a cosmetics event; Jean-Luc trying to boss Tommy, Chance not bothering to check people's tickets, and freelancers in the middle of the floor gossiping while potential customers strolled right past them. What was everyone thinking? God only knew what the rest of my team was doing. I was exhausted and pissed off. I started to panic.

I took a deep breath in and blew it out. It didn't help.

"Baby, what is it?"

I turned around. "Jean-Luc," I shoved the clipboard into his chest, "I need you to confirm that each of these people have a ticket to see Frances, and get them into some sort of line. I've got to get this event under control before she comes out," I said, my voice trembling a little.

He grabbed my shoulders and gave them a little pinch. "No problem, honey. I understand completely."

His eyes conveyed to me that he had this under control.

I'd barely taken two steps when I heard Jean-Luc clap his hands like thunder.

I spun around.

"Attention!" Jean-Luc shouted in French. Then, sliding easily into his American pronunciation, he said again, "Attention, please. If you wish to meet the crème de la crème of cosmetics, Frances of Cesonne, I will need all of you to show me your tickets as I come by. This will be much more efficient if I could have everyone in two lines," he roared. "If you do not have a ticket, you may go now."

I squeezed my eyes shut. *Oh my God. Why hadn't I known Jean-Luc would do something like this?* I peeked through one of them and to my surprise, there were two lines forming, just as Jean-Luc had demanded!

"This is how you have to speak to the peasants, baby," he said, lowering his voice, only slightly. He stepped up to the first customer in line.

I blew him a kiss and walked away. Yes, he was an arrogant son-of-a-bitch, but an arrogant son-of-a-bitch who got things done.

On the way to my counter I noticed Chance assisting a freelancer with a sale. I smiled. *Maybe there is some hope left for today.*

Less than fifteen minutes later I was in the Green Room with Sharee and Frances, preparing for the grand entrance.

When I first learned we had a Green Room, I couldn't understand why a department store would need one. Sharee had smiled at my naivety and explained, "Toy, if Christian Louboutin came here to launch his latest shoe, how happy do you think he'd be lounging in a department manager's office?"

I pictured Mr. Louboutin and his entourage sitting on creaky folding chairs while Sharee, or one of her colleagues tried to conduct business over the phone.

"Got it," I replied.

My reverie was interrupted when Frances took a sip of her cucumber water and stood up. I knew she had to know what happened with Debbie earlier, but she hadn't said a word about it, and I was glad. She had her make-up artist reapply her lipstick, then turned to face Sharee and me.

"Toy, you are going to present me to the crowd," Frances said, casually. "I will make a short speech, then take my seat. Sharee will sit next to me and assist." She turned her head from Sharee to me. "Sound good?"

"Yes," Sharee and I said in unison.

My heart picked up its pace I'd never been nervous in front of crowds, but for some reason, I was feeling the anxiety.

The three of us exited the room and made our way to the beautiful marble desk where Frances would be doing her book signing. The crowd was buzzing with excitement. I glanced at the never-ending line of people and felt shaky as I picked up the microphone from the desk and clicked it on.

Pull it together! I poked my chest out and stood up straight. *I can do this.*

There was a brief squeal of feedback that served to silence the crowd. I smiled self-consciously and began. "Hello. I'd like to thank everyone for joining us for this special event. Today we have with us a beauty icon who not only created one of the most successful cosmetics lines in the world, but recently published her first book — a *New York Times* bestseller, I might add — *With Love and Red Lipstick, Frances*. It is with great pleasure that I introduce, Frances of Cesonne Cosmetics."

The crowd roared and applauded when I stepped back and let Frances take the mic.

I watched Frances and the way she mesmerized the audience. She was fierce. Her posture was powerful and her voice was still strong and sexy.

This is the type of woman I want to be.

The next few hours flew by. Frances had just left the floor and was headed to the Green Room. The event had been a total success. We'd sold out of every single one of Frances's books and all of her #11 lipsticks, a little over halfway through her scheduled signing! I had just wrapped up a sale when Sharee approached.

"Toy, Frances would like to see you now before she leaves. I'll stay on the floor and watch the counter."

Her expression was unreadable. I didn't know what to expect from Frances. My heart pounded in my throat, but I managed to keep my cool.

"Okay. Should I just go back and knock?" I felt sweat prickle my upper lip.

"Yes, and don't worry. She doesn't bite, most of the time, anyway," laughed Sharee, before she pulled me into a hug.

"Oh, Sharee! That was just mean," I said, wilting.

"You'll be fine!" She gave me another squeeze, then turned to ring up the next sale.

I plucked a tissue from a box, dabbed at the moisture on my lip and picked up a hand mirror to check my makeup. Not bad, all things considered. I looked tired, but there was no time to do anything about it now.

I pushed my way through the still packed floor and finally reached the Green Room. I smoothed a hand over my hair, took a breath and knocked on the door.

"Come in."

I opened the door and stood awkwardly with my hands folded. "Hi, Frances."

"Toy darling, come sit down," she said, patting the sofa seat next to her.

I sat down, and she deftly slid a cigarette from a pack and lit it. She took a long pull and exhaled slowly, blowing the smoke toward the ceiling. I knew she was aware there was no smoking in here, but she wasn't exactly known to be a conformist.

"So, I hear you had quite the morning," she said, and took another drag.

"It was — memorable," I said, carefully.

Smoke puffed from her lips in rhythm to her laughter. "Oh Toy, how funny you are. You and I both know that it was more than memorable. You were trapped in a small space with two *pigs*. You are a saint, my girl."

She has the pig part right.

"Enough about Debbie. She is gone, and you do not have to worry about ever dealing with that garbage again. The end. So, did Sharee mention you and your team have already surpassed your goal?" she asked, her words drenched in a German accent.

"No, she didn't, but that's fantastic news," I said, trying to keep my cool. *We still have three hours to go and we've already made it! Thank you God!*

"I am going to be frank with you. I do not think you should take a national artist position," she said, ominously.

I felt my heart sink. Apparently, my face betrayed my feelings because she quickly added, "Not so fast. One thing necessary for success is not showing others your emotions. Save that for your personal life. I only tell you that because I think you are special."

"Thank you," I said, careful to keep my voice even.

"I do not want you to take the national artist position because in one month I am opening a Cesonne boutique on Oak Street. I would like you to be the store manager. Would you be interested?"

There's going to be a Cesonne boutique? Would I be interested? Was that really a question? My excitement ignited and I completely forgot what she'd told me about hiding my emotions just moments before. "Frances, of course I am!"

"Wonderful. I think you will be happy to know that Sharee will be taking Debbie's position, and your boutique will be part of her cosmetics territory."

Yes! Sharee finally got what she'd worked so hard for. Then, I froze. *What about my team?*

"You really do wear your heart on your sleeve, Toy. We will need to work on that," she said, smoke swirling from her mouth. "What is bothering you now? Is this not enough?"

"It's my team, I really care about them. They work so hard and I feel bad leaving them." *Well, at least some of them...*

"You continue to surprise me, Toy. Most in your current position would not risk losing this kind of opportunity for others." She took a long drag of her cigarette. "Besides, who said you will be leaving them? Obviously, you cannot bring them all with you, but I am sure you and Sharee can work something out," she said, a twinkle in her eye.

"This boutique is going to be fabulous, darling. You will put together a core team from here, then add to it to create an even stronger one. I will also be launching my new handbag line at the same time we open! It will be huge, and you will be at the center of it all."

I was at a loss for words. I hadn't even dreamed of anything like this happening to me. At that moment, I heard Nikola's voice: *"Carpe diem, Toy. No matter how much we plan and worry, things work out a certain way. By living in the moment and appreciating what you have, you show gratitude for life, and only with gratitude can you receive all the good things to come."*

He'd told me this not even two weeks ago. And he was so right.

"Okay, I must prepare to go. I have a flight to catch," she said, standing up. "I will send Sharee paperwork for you to fill out. She told me you are going on vacation, but if you can get it to my office first thing when you return, that would be helpful. Then, I can have the official offer drawn up."

I stood as well on her cue and extended my hand. "Thank you again, Frances." This all felt so surreal.

Frances playfully slapped it away. "Do not be so American, my dear," then pulled me in for a peck on both cheeks.

I flashed a smile and stepped toward the door.

"Toy, I meant it when I said you are special, but I also meant it when I said to control your emotions. Do not give them away so freely. I could have launched this boutique anywhere in the world, but I am doing it in Chicago. Do you know why?"

I wasn't about to be presumptuous as to the reason she'd made such a huge business decision. "No, why?"

"I have watched your results for a few years now. I saw how you interact with your team, the relationships you have built. And the fact that your counter is beating all my others does not hurt either," she smirked.

"You don't know how much this means to me. You won't be disappointed. Thank you again." I didn't know what else to say. How was I supposed to react to all of this flattery, especially coming from someone like Frances, who had a reputation of being overly critical of everyone and everything?

I opened the door to leave and said good-bye. She nodded her head and took a long drag of her cigarette. I guess that was my cue to leave. I shut the door and practically floated back to my counter. I wanted to tell everyone, to blast it over the PA, but experience told me to keep my mouth shut. I'd talk to Sharee first.

I think what I hated most about events was the fact that we had to wait until all the reports printed before we could leave. This was so Sharee could announce our final results. That could sometimes take upwards of two hours, and tonight was no exception. I thought it was a waste of payroll but I didn't write the rules. Neither did Sharee. Of course, in those two hours, we were told to break down the tables and chairs from the event. Physical labor went hand-in-hand with cosmetics events.

It was almost 10:30 PM when the team and I gathered around Sharee at my counter. Most of us plopped down in chairs. My feet hurt worse sitting down than they had standing up all day. Sharee remained positioned in front of us.

"Okay, thanks for being so patient, guys. You know I don't like waiting any more than you do, but I've got incredible news tonight," she said, waving a handful of papers.

"First of all, congratulations to each and every one of you. You made history today! $165,000! Unreal!"

Though we were exhausted, the sound of that number created a wave of excitement. We applauded, hugged and high-fived one another.

"Great job, team!" I yelled.

"On a different note, I want to announce that Fiona just handed in her resignation. Today will be her last day. However, I'd still like everyone to give her a hand for the commendable job she did today."

I clapped my hands half-heartedly and focused hard on Sharee to keep my eyes from rolling into the back of my head. Fiona must've realized that with Debbie gone, she no longer had any allies. *Poor little kiss-ass Fiona got her own bit.*

Jean-Luc spoke up. "Sharee, Fiona and commendable do not belong in the same sentence." Before Sharee could respond, he went on. "Although on second thought, I do commend her decision to leave."

Fiona glared at him. I bit down on my lip to stifle a laugh. Yvonne, on the other hand, slapped her thigh and cackled like a hyena.

"I can think of a few more peasants who should be sent back to the village," continued Jean-Luc. He eyeballed Yvonne whose laughter came to an abrupt halt. His gaze then settled on Tommy.

"Enough, Jean-Luc, and I mean it," snapped Sharee. The flash of anger lasted only a second, and then suddenly turned into a glow. "Anyway, my commendable news is that I've been promoted to National Director of Sales for Cesonne, and Toy got the green light for Store Manager at the new Cesonne boutique, which will be opening very soon!"

A murmur rippled through the group. Fiona's face went white.

It took Fiona a second to find her voice, but when she did, she raised it above the din. "What kind of boutique is this going to be? Who's going to be taking Toy's place here?"

"It's going to be a Frances first. All of her cosmetics, fragrances, scarves and a new handbag line will be sold there. As far as Toy's replacement, Fiona, that will be up to the new department manager."

Fiona stood up, mad as hell, oblivious to the fact that she was making an fool of herself. "Why wasn't I informed about this managerial opening? I'm the assistant manager. I should've been told!"

"*Were* the assistant," Sharee corrected her. "You tendered your resignation of your own volition, and it's been filed with HR. But to answer your question, Toy's promotion was announced only a couple of hours ago. And unfortunately, because you're now officially no longer a store employee, you'd have to reapply before we could consider you for the position — or really, any position."

"This is total bullshit!" screeched Fiona. "Toy always ends up the golden child, no matter how hard anyone else works. It's so unfair!"

"I think perhaps it's time you collect your things or would you rather I call LP?" asked Sharee, calmly.

"Fuck you, Sharee," Fiona shrieked, and stormed off.

Jean-Luc stretched his arms high above his head. "Well, that was —"

"Put a lid on it, Jean-Luc," shot Sharee.

"What? I was only going to say that this was my cue to congratulate my Blonde Ambition!" said Jean-Luc, innocently blinking his eyes.

When the room settled down, Chance was pouting, though I wasn't sure why. Yvonne was gazing into a compact mirror trying to remove some red lipstick on her teeth with her tongue. Tatyana, Ed, Biljana, and Tommy circled Sharee, no doubt kissing up to her in hopes of nabbing the assistant manager vacancy.

In one fell swoop, Debbie, "Sheriff", and Fiona were out of my life, I had a terrific job offer, and my team had made Cesonne history. The day hadn't ended badly at all. In fact, as bad as the beginning of the day had been — and it could hardly have been worse — I'd not only survived it, but came out on top. *Does life get any better than this?*

"So," beamed Sharee, "is there anything else?"

A few shrugs, back and forth looks and headshakes passed through the group.

"Good. Well, I just wanted to tell you the good news and thank you for all you did to make it happen. Now, get out of here and go celebrate!" To our surprise, the usually serious and professional Sharee actually did a fist pump!

After some cheers and a last resounding applause, everyone cleared out. I stayed behind to gab with Sharee for a few minutes. Before I left the sales floor, I paused to glance back at my counter. It was a little bittersweet. This was the last Norniesakmans event I'd ever do with my team. Granted, they were a wacky bunch, but they were *my* bunch. I swallowed hard at the lump in my throat and headed to the locker room.

I shut the door to my locker and reached down to pick up my Gucci bag. When I stood up, Chance was standing practically nose-to-nose with me.

"You're leaving me? I am devastated, totally devastated! I thought we were best friends," he whimpered, with a hand to his forehead.

"Whoa! This was just announced like fifteen minutes ago," I said, wrapping my scarf tightly around my neck. "I've had quite a challenging day. I was going to call you."

"Oh, so you were going to *call* me and tell me you were leaving me? You weren't even going to tell me face to face?"

"Stop jumping to silly conclusions. You're not exactly the best at keeping secrets, and what I'm about to tell you better not be repeated." I narrowed my eyes at him.

"Okay, so what is it?" Chance backed off of his accusatory tone. "You can trust me."

I raised an eyebrow.

"No, I'm serious this time."

I heaved a big sigh. "It's against my better judgment, but to preserve our B-F-F status, I'll tell you. So help me, Chance, if you —"

"I won't," he moaned, shaking his fists like a infant.

"I can pick my own staff. You're coming with me! That is, if you want to come," I smiled.

"Are you fucking serious? Me and you running Oak Street together?" he bellowed.

"Chance!"

He put his hand over his mouth. "Oops, sorry.

I opened my arms and he threw his around me.

"This is like a dream come true!" He squealed.

"I don't know if it's going to be 'running Oak Street', but it's going to be a lot of fun," I laughed.

"No girl, we'll be running shit! Trust me." He took a step back, put his hands on his hips and looked me up and down.

Leave it to Chance to make it seem like we'd be the next Al Capone and Frank Nitti — running the avenue!

A silence fell as he stared at me expectantly.

"What?" I asked.

"Um, I hope you brought something to change into."

"You've got to be kidding," I groaned. "You still expect me to go tonight after everything that's happened today?"

"You promised!"

I did that pinkie-thumb thing, simulating a phone. "The party you've reached is not available right now. Please leave your number after the beep," I said and sidestepped him.

He followed. "But, you promised!"

This little shit! I should've known better than to promise Chance anything. Damn it!

I spun around. "Are you not aware of the day I've had?"

His voice began to shake. "You never do anything with me anymore, but when you need me, oh, well that's a different story. I'm expected to be there with bells on, and all I ask is for you to come to one stinking party!"

I thought it through for a moment. Okay. I'd go to the party with Chance. In no time, he'd be preoccupied with whomever, and then I'd be able to duck out and most likely, not be missed.

"Fine. Give me the address. I'll run home and throw on some clothes. But Chance, I'm not dressing up and I'm not staying long!" I leveled a finger at him. "I don't want to hear a peep out of your mouth when I'm ready to leave!"

"Okay, okay. Meet me and Jean-Luc in the lobby of the Trump at midnight, and we'll go up together."

"Okay!" I fired back and marched off, muttering under my breath, "The never-ending day."

Chapter 21

From the back of a taxi, I pulled out my phone and composed a text to Ben.

> Me: *Hi babe. Longest day of my life. Way too much to text. I'm headed for this STUPID party I promised Chance I'd go to!*
> Him: *Do you want me to meet you there?*
> Me: *No, don't bother. I'm only making an appearance for Chance, then heading home. I'm so tired...if I could get out of this, I would. I just wanna be in my bed!*
> Him: *I wanna be in your bed too...xoxo.*
> Me: *Ha-ha. Well, I'm here... I'll call you when I leave.*
> Him: *I love you.*

I stared at the screen for a second, then: *Love u too.*

Why had I hesitated? Before I could think about it, I realized we were parked in front of The Trump.

I whipped out my credit card.

"You have no cash? Machine broke," the cabbie said in some sort of Middle East accent.

"No, I don't have cash," I lashed out at him. "Can you please figure out some way to make this work?"

He mumbled something unintelligible, most likely an insult, and then said, "Give me card, I figure something out."

Thought so! I handed him the card. He pulled out a cell phone that had a credit card swiper attached.

"You sign here with finger." He pointed to the signature line on the screen of his phone.

Under normal circumstances, I'd think this was fishy, but I didn't have the energy to argue. I tipped him 15%, signed my name and handed him back the machine.

"Thank you," I said, opening the door to get out of the cab. He didn't respond. *Jerk!* I whipped the door shut.

The cabby stuck his head out the window and yelled, "Do not slam door!"

I resisted the urge to give him the middle finger salute, walked into the lobby, right on time, and searched for Chance and Jean-Luc. They were nowhere to be found. After checking the lounge, I came back to the lobby and dialed them both. Neither answered. I checked the time on my phone. *Hmm. It's been ten minutes. I wonder if the two of them are "romantically indisposed". They better not have gone up without me.*

I waited a couple more minutes, hoping one of them would call me back. Finally, I went to the front desk and told the doorman I was here for Henry Bearling's party. Good thing Chance had told me Henry's last name or I'd have been screwed. The doorman found my name on the list and had an attendant escort me to the elevator. The stocky Hispanic man was around my age, slightly taller than me, with a mop of curly black hair on his head. He gestured for me to step into the elevator, then joined me. He inserted a keycard and pressed the PH button. When we reached the penthouse he said, "Enjoy your night, miss."

"Thank you," I said as the bronze-tinted, mirrored doors closed behind me.

What I saw before me nearly stole my breath away. The exquisite decor was Greek and Roman inspired; marble floors with exposed columns, couches covered in silk and leather, accented by mosaic-topped tripod tables. In the center of it all was a Grecian pool.

I scanned the crowded room and noticed the servers were all young and gorgeous Asian and African-American guys, wearing nothing but loincloths. An Asian DJ was spinning house music on a stage in the center of the room. Henry obviously had a type.

"Do you want me to take you to the spa to choose a swimsuit?" a reed-thin Asian boy asked.

I resisted a sardonic laugh. "Thank you, but I think I'll stay dressed. I won't be here very long."

He offered his champagne tray. I took one of the crystal flutes, most likely Swarovski, and admired the clear faceted base. I tasted it.

"Mmm...divine," I smiled.

He left and returned after a few minutes.

"Maybe you can help me. Would you happen to know where Chance is?"

His smile dissolved. "No," he said, and walked away.

Guess he isn't a member of Chance's fan club. Another waiter walked by.

I got his attention. "Excuse me. Have you seen Henry?" This one looked half African-American, half-Asian.

"Of course. Henry's in his room and will be joining us shortly," he said.

Just then, I spotted Tatyana and Tommy standing at the bar; and to their left were Biljana and Nikola. I felt sick seeing him — especially next to her, and resisted the urge to turn around and leave. I swallowed the lump in my throat. *Will this feeling ever go away?*

"Thank you," I replied, downing the glass of champagne and nabbing another before he got away. *Could this situation be any more uncomfortable?* I knew I had to acknowledge them but I didn't want to. I was stuck.

I grudgingly walked over. When he saw me, Tommy grabbed my arm and pulled me close. He was already hammered. "Let's get a round of shots for my girl, here," he slurred to the bartender.

"Thanks Tommy, but considering my day, I think I'll stick with this." I held up my champagne glass.

It made me sad to see Tommy so trashed. It was plain to see jail had done nothing toward correcting his problem. Would he ever know what a creative, talented, wonderful person he was?

I looked around the room. Nikola tried to catch my attention, but I glanced away. I couldn't allow myself to be taken in by those beautiful, penetrating eyes of his.

I was getting more irritated by the second. I'd only come for Chance and he was MIA. *I should be ensconced in my bed! Oh, and where in the hell is Jean-Luc?*

"Come on, live a little," Tatyana goaded, handing me a vodka shot.

Peer pressure never goes away no matter how old you are.

"I'm already feeling buzzed from the champagne. I can't," I said, and placed both glasses down on the bar.

"Whatever you say. More for me." She downed her shot, then chased it with mine.

I had to hand it to her. The girl could drink.

"Hey, have any of you seen Chance or Jean-Luc?" I scanned the room one last time.

Before anyone could answer, my eyes landed on Yvonne who'd just stepped into the pool and seated herself between two hotties who couldn't have been a day over twenty-one, flirting and laughing hysterically in both the loudest and skimpiest bikini that left zippo to the imagination.

"Is that Yvonne in the red?" I asked, not sure if my eyes were deceiving me.

"Holy shit, that *is* Yvonne!" said Tommy, laughing so hard he nearly choked on his drink.

Tatyana chimed in, "Hey, you cannot say she is afraid of living her life to the fullest." She twirled her fingers in the air at the bartender, then pointed to a corner in the bar area where a low, marble table was placed between two Roman inspired couches. "Come on guys, I have a round of drinks coming. We will sit down."

Everyone followed her. I took a seat in between Tatyana and Tommy on the couch directly across from Nikola and Biljana. Nikola finally managed to attract my gaze. I felt my pulse quicken and immediately broke eye contact.

"I think we are going to leave. I am tired," said Biljana, glaring at Nikola.

"So soon?" he asked. "Not up to another late night, Biljana?"

"*Ne*," she hissed through clenched teeth.

"*Znam deka lazese*," he retorted.

"*Sto*?" she spat.

The two of them continued to argue in their native tongue. I quickly tired of their foreign war, hopped to my feet, and set out to hunt down Chance and Jean-Luc.

Ten minutes of fruitless searching, and I was fuming. *Where are those two jerks?*

"You do not seem like you are having good time."

I turned to my right and found myself looking into a set of hazel eyes that belonged to a tall, handsome, dark haired guy with a slightly crooked smile. He was dressed in a black suit that appeared to be Armani.

"Yeah, well, I'm not. I want to get out of here," I said, looking away.

"I am Adin." He walked around to face me. "I'm working security tonight."

"That's nice," I said, uninterested.

"I'm sorry if I'm bothering you," Adin said, sarcastically.

He had a faint accent. *Sounds similar to Nikola's...*

I turned my attention to him. He had a thin waist and long torso and from the size of his arms, I could tell he worked out. He wore a shadow of stubble on his chin and looked to be twenty-seven or so.

"No, *I'm* sorry. I'm being rude. My two friends stood me up, I've had a very long day, and I really want to go home."

He was listening attentively to my complaint. His gaze was so intense it made me feel self-conscious.

"You have pretty eyes," he said, brushing a few strands of hair from my face.

"Thanks," I said, nervously. "It was nice meeting you, Adin, but I really have to find my friends."

Before he could say anything more, I turned and walked away.

"I work security at Cuvee, Saturday nights. You should come. I'll get you in free. No waiting in line," he called after me.

I ignored him. The last think I needed in my life was another sexy, foreign guy. I was headed back toward the bar when Chance appeared out of nowhere, beaming.

"Toy, before you say anything, I'm *so* sorry. I *just* checked my phone, but I've got the most amazing news!"

I didn't even try to hide my ire. "What's so amazing that you couldn't answer any of my phone calls after you threw a full-blown tantrum for me to come tonight?"

"Wait a minute!" He squinted at something over my shoulder. "Is that Yvonne in the pool?"

I looked behind me and before I could answer, Yvonne spotted us.

She stood up in the water, waving madly, and called out, "Hey, Captain! Come meet my new friends!"

"I'll pass, Yvonne. I've got to go," I said, moving closer to the pool, so we didn't have to yell.

She was rocking her body back and forth to the music, a drink in each hand. At any moment, I expected her boobs to pop out of a top that was essentially dental floss and two pasties.

"Woo-hoo! Is this one hell of a fuckin' pad, or what, man?" she cried. Her boy toys joined her, one on either side; an Yvonne sandwich.

"What is she *wearing*? This image before me is an atrocity and one that will unfortunately, stick with me far too long," said a familiar voice.

I snapped my head in Jean-Luc's direction and gave him the evil eye. "Don't worry about what she's wearing — or barely wearing," I conceded. "She's having a good time, so leave her alone."

"What is wrong, my Blonde Ambition?" He looked wounded.

"What's wrong? Maybe it's the fact that I've been up almost twenty-four hours and I'm exhausted. Or, it could be I was coerced into coming to this party and you two had me waiting around in the lobby, then didn't answer your phones. Pick one."

"Baby, easy, easy," he said, gesturing palms down. "I am sorry we didn't answer our phones, but let us explain."

I crossed my arms and glared at the two of them. "I'm listening."

Chance refused to make eye contact with me while Jean-Luc went on. "We arrived a little earlier than you so we decided to come check out the party for a few minutes. We ended up on the balcony and, well we lost track of time." He looked at Chance. "We have something to tell you."

I crossed my arms. "This better be good."

"We're moving in together," squealed Chance, taking Jean-Luc's hand in his.

Jean-Luc tensed a little, but allowed it.

I looked first at Chance, then at Jean-Luc. "No way!"

"Yes, honey. It is true," Jean-Luc confessed. "We have been seeing each other in secret. I just did not want to announce anything until I was sure. You see, Chance understands me. We read the same fashion magazines, he is an impeccable dresser, and he loves the ballet and opera. We just, how do you say? Click." He smiled down at Chance adoringly.

The ballet? The Opera? Since when? I widened my eyes at him and he winked.

"Well, I'm glad you two are so happy," I said, my anger gone now. They were together and in high spirits. Who was I to dampen them?

"So, you're not mad anymore?" Chance asked, uncertainly.

"No. I'm too happy for you two!" I pulled them both into an embrace and kissed their cheeks. "But I'm going home now, and I don't want to hear a peep out of either one of you." Then, "Wait, where's Henry?"

"He's hanging out in his room with a couple of friends. I just told him I'm in a committed relationship. He didn't seem very happy for me. He almost cancelled the party. Some nerve, huh?" Chance huffed. "I told him if he did, I'd never speak to him again."

The look on my face prompted him to add, "Okay, I did have to cry to get my way, but whatever. He's rich. It's not like this is putting him out or anything. I told him I'd watch over the party until he gets out here."

It was hard to believe Chance hadn't done anything sexual with Henry to get his way, but that none of my business. Jean-Luc had seen firsthand how promiscuous Chance could be. I loved Chance, but I hoped Jean-Luc understood what he was getting into.

I bid them both goodnight and went to say good-bye to the others. I noticed Nikola and Biljana were gone when I approached Tommy and Tatyana. I was stunned to see they were both snorting lines of cocaine from the top of the marble table.

"Are you two kidding me right now?"

"Come on, Toy. It's free and it's a party. Relax," said Tommy, avoiding my eyes as he wiped the excess powder from his nose.

"Yeah, keep thinking like that and see where it gets you." I shifted my gaze to Tatyana, "And, you know he just got out of jail for this same shit."

"Not quite the same thing," she laughed, and snorted another line. "We are clearly using right now, not selling."

"Unbelievable," I said, and headed for the coatroom.

I turned around when I heard Yvonne bellow my name.

"Captain, you leaving already, man? This party's just gettin' fuckin' started." She was now in the hot tub with the same two guys from the pool.

"Sure am. Enjoy, Yvonne. I gotta get some rest." And once again I was on my way.

I grabbed my coat from the attendant and stepped into the elevator. Once we reached the lobby, I practically sprinted outside and jumped into the first cab I saw. I just wanted to sleep.

I called Ben and let him know I was on my way home. He told me he'd made dinner reservations for us at Maple and Ash tomorrow and that he wanted me to have the entire day to sleep and relax. When we ended the conversation, I smiled to myself. It felt so good to have him back in my life. *He really loves me.*

I didn't feel like dealing with another asshole driver who didn't want to accept a credit card, so I dug through my purse, knowing I did had some cash in my wallet. I handed him a crumpled ten-dollar bill, told him to keep the change, and let myself out — just in time to see Nikola step out of the cab behind us.

I hastened to my building without acknowledging him.

He fell in behind me. "Toy!"

"Nikola, no."

"Toy, please. I need to talk to you."

"I'm sorry. I really, really am," I called over my shoulder, "I just can't deal with this anymore."

"I need to tell you something. Please," he pleaded.

"Tell it to Biljana," I said and kept walking.

He followed me into the building, then the elevator. Before I knew it, he'd pressed the button for my floor.

"What do you think you're doing?"

"I just need five minutes. That is all. I *beg* you."

I knew for a man like him to use the word "beg", he must really be desperate. *This is so hard!*

The elevator stopped, the doors opened, and I headed for my apartment with Nikola hot on my heels. We arrived at my door, and now I was pleading, "Nikola, I'm tired from today's event, and I'm tired of whatever game we've been playing."

"Never has it been a game," he protested.

"Nikola..." I hung my head.

"Just five minutes?" he pleaded.

I turned around wanting to shove him away, but when our eyes met the memories came rushing back to me; the first time I'd laid eyes on him in the men's department; running into him at the sushi restaurant, the first snow, the first time we'd made love, the last time we'd made love...

I felt my resolve weaken. Without answering, I turned back around and slipped the key into the lock. I walked inside and he followed.

"Okay. Five minutes and not a second more." I kicked off my heels, hung my coat on the doorknob, and made my way into the living room.

Without removing his shoes or coat, he followed me. "I know you had a long day," he said, softly. "You can go change into something more comfortable if you want. I will pour you a glass of wine."

"No, I'm fine." I grabbed a blanket from the chair next to me and plopped myself on the couch. I rolled my neck from side to side, failing to ease the day's stress.

He sat down on the cushion next to me and at first, I thought he was staring at my watch, and then I realized it was the ring. I saw a flash of something in his eyes. Hurt? Anger? Both? I couldn't tell. He regained his composure and gazed into my eyes.

He ran both hands through his hair, inhaling, then exhaling deeply. "I cannot stop thinking about you. I know we did not meet by accident, Toy."

"Maybe so, but you have a huge complication. Biljana's pregnant, or did you forget?"

"No, I didn't forget. She is pregnant," he said, evenly.

"So why are you here, Mister I-can't-leave-her-what-kind-of-man-would-I-be?"

"It is not mine," he shrugged.

"What?" *Had I heard him correctly?*

"Biljana broke down and came clean. She said she felt so rejected by me, she started seeing her neighbor, Daniel. She confessed that she is sure the baby is his."

After a moment, "What brought her to confess?"

"Well, she knew the truth would come out when the baby was born."

Although that was a good reason, something else had to have made her spill the beans. "Is that all?"

Nikola let out a heavy sigh. "Biljana knew about us, Toy. I do not know how, but she knew. And when she saw you become engaged to Ben, I guess she felt safe to tell me."

"I'm sorry," I said, quietly.

"I am not. It made me realize that you and I are meant to be together." He leaned over and brushed my cheek with his fingertips.

I pulled my head back, out of his reach. "Nikola, this past month with you was incredible, but it can't go on. I'm marrying Ben."

"He is not right for you. He will not make you happy," he declared. "He does not know you like I do."

"How can you say that? You've known me one month! Ben has known me for years."

"Time is irrelevant. You know what we have is real. We both knew it since the first moment we looked into each other's eyes." The look on his face was as resolute as I'd ever seen.

I knew he was right. We did have something, but it wasn't enough to erase the years I'd shared with Ben.

"I can't do this," I said, and put my head in my hands.

He touched my knee. "Yes, you can. Let me take you away from all of this."

My head jerked up. "What?"

"Come to Europe with me." He reached out and took my hand in both of his. "I want you kiss you on the tour Eiffel. I want to walk with you along the beaches of Zlatni Rat. Most of all, I want to wake up with you in Hallstatt to the most magnificent view you will ever see in your life."

I looked into his eyes for a long second. "This is exactly what I mean. What you just described is a fantasy. It's not realistic. You and I can't just leave everything to go travel the world. It's not practical. Who'd pay our bills? Who'd finance the trip? Why dream of things that can't possibly happen? It's time we both live in the real world."

He looked up for a moment, and then began again. "What if everything you ever wanted was at your fingertips and all you had to do was reach out and touch it?"

"What do you mean?"

"I told you I came here to work and send money back to my family. That was only partially true. I did come here to work, but not because my family needs the money," he said, cryptically.

My patience, tried the entire day, was waning fast. "Then why did you come to America?" *Please don't tell me you're an international fugitive or something crazy like that.*

"Because my bullheaded father and I could not get along. He wanted me to go into the family business, but I refused to work and started gambling. It created more problems between my father and me. We finally reached a compromise: I go to Chicago and work with his brother, who I always liked very much. If I had not agreed, my father would have cut me off."

"Cut you off from what?" I rapidly blinked my eyes in confusion.

"Suffice to say that my uncle's trucking company is just one of many businesses he and my father share. My family is quite wealthy, but even without their money, I have done very well here in the US for myself. When I told you I want to take you to Europe, I meant it. It is not some fantasy. It could be our reality if you let it happen," he said, his eyes imploring.

"So, now you're this super-wealthy guy with a gambling problem who came to the U.S. to get away from his *wicked* father," I exhaled, heavily. "I don't know what to believe anymore, Nikola. I'm so tired I can't process any more information." I laid my head back against the back of the couch.

"Believe that I am in love with you! And you cannot marry another man simply because it is comfortable. Believe in *us*, Toy!" he cried.

My eyes welled up. "Each time I start to believe in us something bad happens. I can't keep doing this to myself." I stood up and wiped away a tear that spilled down my face.

He pulled me into his arms. "Let me spend the night. I just want to hold you while you sleep."

"That's not a good idea." I shook my head definitively, even though in my heart I wanted him so badly I could hardly stand it.

He leaned in and kissed me and for a minute I forgot everything; Ben, work — everything.

"Thinking I might never kiss these lips again has been agony," he whispered, and brushed his lips over mine again.

I broke the embrace. "I can't, Nikola. This isn't right." I looked down at the engagement ring Ben had given me this morning and was awash in guilt.

He cupped my face in his hands. "You do not, *cannot* understand how in love with you I am."

The tears returned. "I don't know what to say."

His hands dropped to his sides and his eyes seemed to glaze over. "I cannot lose you."

"I made a promise to a man this morning. A man who loves me very much, flaws and all and I know him, Nikola. I can't say the same about you. I can't break off our engagement on a whim," I sobbed, my heart aching.

"You are my true love," he whispered in my ear and kissed my forehead.

I opened my mouth to speak, but he put a finger to my lips.

"Say nothing. Just remember this moment," he said, his eyes boring deep into my soul.

We stood there a short moment as if trying to memorize each other, and then he left. A part of me wanted to run after him, but I didn't. The minute the door shut I lost all self-control. I cried until every last tear was spent, my lungs aching from the sobs.

I made my way to the bedroom, fell into bed fully clothed and broke my cardinal rule of going to bed with makeup on. I stared at the ceiling and remembered how my dear Grandmother Genny had always admonished: "Want to feel like a princess? Marry a man who loves you more than you love him." *That would be Ben. I made the right decision.*

Exhausted, I turned onto my side with Nikola's words ringing in my head, "You are my true love..."

Chapter 22

I woke up around 11:00 AM unable to move. I stared at the ceiling trying to process everything that had happened the day before. The engagement, the stockroom incident, my promotion, Nikola asking me to go to Europe with him — it all felt surreal.

I held up my left hand and examined the ring on my finger. I was suddenly overwhelmed with fear. Was I making the right decision marrying Ben when I still had such strong feelings for Nikola? I knew what Ben and I had was real. I knew who he was. We'd been through ups and downs and still loved each another. No matter how much passion I felt for Nikola; what if it was like an intense flame that burned out quickly, then left you cold? I couldn't be sure it was love. But if it was, was it possible to love two people at the same time? And if so, what do you do with that? How do you decide? *Arrgghh!*

I tossed the blanket off and with effort, slung my feet over the side of the bed. I was still in last night's clothes and sleeping in my makeup had left half my foundation smeared on the pillow. I walked into the bathroom and looked in the mirror.

"Yuck," I said to my reflection. My hair was in tangles and my eyes were muddied with clotted mascara. I felt as disgusting as I looked.

I undressed, stepped into the shower and turned on the hot water.

I scrubbed my hair and my body wishing the tribulations of yesterday would disappear down the drain with the suds. I wrapped myself in a towel and was brushing my teeth when the phone rang.

I dropped the toothbrush, spat without rinsing, wiped my mouth with the towel I was wearing and rushed to grab the phone. *Damn it, Nikola! I can't talk to you!* My heart pounded in my throat as I set it back down.

I'd made a commitment to Ben. I had to break all contact with Nikola, even though the thought of never seeing or talking to him again caused an ache in my stomach I feared might never go away.

I went to the kitchen and grabbed a Coke from the fridge, then traipsed back to the bedroom. I sat down on the edge of the bed, picked up my phone and scrolled through my messages. I'd deleted Nikola's contact information from my phone but I still had texts from him in my message history. I scrolled through them until I came to a number starting with a 312 area code. Sure enough, it was the same number that had just called me. I opened our message thread, stared at it for several painful seconds, then hit Delete.

I smoothed away a tear that had spilled down my cheek. Before I could put down the phone, it rang. I let it ring a few times, then cleared my throat and answered.

With as much cheer as I could muster: "Hi there, handsome!"

"Someone's in a good mood today," piped Ben. "How's it going?"

"Oh, I'm exhausted," I sighed. "You know how I am after these events."

"I know I said I'd give you the day to sleep, but then I thought about it. In all the years I've known you, I can only recall two times you've ever slept past noon, even when we stayed out all night."

I laughed. "What if I told you I've changed in the past year?"

"Not you, Toy. One of the things I love most about you is I know what to expect."

You mean I'm predictable.

"I know you. You're like clockwork. I'm the same way. See? A match made in Heaven. Anyway..."

I zoned out and in the back of my mind I could hear Nikola saying, *You never let go, Toy...*

"Toy?" Ben prompted.

"Yes?"

"Does that work for you?"

"I'm sorry, can you repeat what you were saying. I must've spaced out. I need a little more sleep."

"Sure, babe. I said I'd send a car to pick you up at seven. Is that time good for you?"

"Yes, seven is good. Wait a minute. Why are you sending a car? I can just take a taxi."

"Can't I take care of my girl?"

"Of course, you can," I said, loving the way he called me his girl.

"Can't wait for tonight."

"Neither can I," I said, genuinely excited to spend time with him. "I'd better get some more sleep or there's no way I'll make it out tonight."

"Alright, I'll let you get some rest. Love you."

"Me too. See you later."

I hung up the phone, set it beside me, then slid into the bed and pulled the covers up over me. I tossed and turned for the next hour. Each time I closed my eyes, I saw Nikola's face. I turned on my side and hugged the pillow, trying to quiet my mind. I was almost asleep when my phone rang.

After fumbling around, I found it and untangled it from the bedclothes. The front desk of my building was calling.

"Hello?"

"Hi Toy, this is Mike. I have a Ms. Tatyana here to see you. Can I send her up?"

Tatyana? What the hell is she doing here? Who gave her my address?

"Toy? Can I send her up?" he repeated.

"I'm sorry. Yes, go ahead." I recouped. "And, thank you for calling to let me know."

"No problem. Have a nice day," Mike said, politely, and then hung up.

I got out of bed, threw on a pair of Victoria's Secret yoga pants and a White Sox T-shirt, and walked into the living room.

A couple of minutes later I heard the knocking. I yanked open the door and said, "Okay Tatyana, what's the —"

I froze. There stood Nikola!

"What are you doing here?" I exclaimed. Confused, I looked around him for Tatyana.

"Tatyana is not here. I paid the doorman handsomely to call and say it was her. I told Mike I wanted to surprise you. He and I have become friends over my past few visits," he said, sheepishly.

I'd never seen him so on edge. His hair was disheveled and he looked like he hadn't slept. Still, I felt the electricity between us. I took a step back.

"Why'd you have the doorman lie to me?" I asked, shocked at his audacity.

"Because I knew you would not see me otherwise."

I didn't know what to do. We stood there awkwardly for a long moment. His look of desperation melted my determination to keep him out, and I gave in.

"Okaaay," I sighed, waving him in. "Don't worry about your shoes. Let's just go into the kitchen."

"Yes, thank you."

I'd hurt him by not inviting him to get comfortable. I could see it on his face. God, if only he knew how much this was killing me too. Still, I had to be realistic. Nikola was tempting, but I held on to a warning I'd once heard, not to end a good relationship for something new and exciting, because before you know it, the new love grows old and your former love is gone.

I opened the fridge and pulled out two bottles of water. I put one in front of him and he grabbed my hand.

"You are not over me," he said.

I gently pulled my hand away and looked up at him.

"No. How could I be?" I moved to the other side of the island and took a seat. "Why does life have to be so complicated? Not very long ago I felt like I was finally getting myself together. I'd accepted that Ben and I were done and I was determined to focus on myself, my career and not get involved with anyone. Then the moment I saw you it was like..."

"It was like everything and everyone around us disappeared and only you and I existed." He rounded the island toward me.

I looked up at him and thought my heart would break in two. "Yes." I choked out before I dissolved into tears.

"Do not cry, *moja ljubov*. You are making this hard. Just let go. Come with me to Europe," he insisted, wrapping his arms around me.

"Then what?" I looked up at him with my tear-streaked face. "We'd get past the honeymoon phase and you'd tire of me."

"What I would give just to have the *chance* to tire of you," he said, and kissed away a tear.

"So, you agree with me?" I said, as I pulled away from him.

"No! I disagree. I meant I would give anything to even have the opportunity. I will never stop loving you." He cupped his hand under my chin and lifted my face. *"Never."*

I tore my eyes from his and focused on the ring on my finger. "I don't know what to do anymore. I don't even know what the right decision is!"

"What is in your heart, Toy? If marrying Ben and living some safe life is what your heart tells you, then do it. But I don't think that is what you want and I know it is not what you need," he said, and backed away from me.

"What if you're both in my heart? What then? I can't just cut him out of my life now that you tell me Biljana's baby isn't yours. Just like you had loyalty to her, I have loyalty to him."

He knew I had him there. The anguish on his face confirmed it. "Only one of us is in your heart." He let out a heavy sigh and made his way to the door. "I hope for your sake Ben is that person since you plan on spending the rest of your life with him."

Nikola was almost to the door when I leaped up and ran, stopping just short of him.

"Don't leave without kissing me goodbye," I begged, afraid I would never feel his lips against mine again.

He turned around and drew me into his arms. He kissed my tear-streaked face, my neck, then found his way to my lips, kissing me longingly, lovingly. We clung to each other in silence. There were no words left to speak. All that needed to be said was said with that last kiss.

He wiped his face with both hands, took a breath, and just like that, he was gone.

It was almost 7:00 PM. My eyes were swollen from crying and my body exhausted. I replayed our kiss over and over for the rest of the day. Finally, I'd forced myself to get up and had thrown on a comfy DVF dress, tights and Chanel ballet flats. Like a zombie, I packed my suitcase, and after bundling up like a dog-sled-driver, waited in my living room for Ben's car to pick me up.

A couple of minutes after the driver called to announce his arrival, the phone rang again.

"Hi, baby," said Ben.

I forced myself to sound lively. "Hi!"

"I'm so ready to see you. Is the car there?"

"It just arrived."

"Great. Just wanted to make sure. I'll see you shortly. And Toy, I love you."

"I love you, too."

If only the words I'd just spoken were true. I was beginning to hate myself. *What kind of liar have I become? No. I do love Ben, I really do. I'm just confused. I have to get Nikola out of my mind once and for all. I need to focus on the man I've chosen to spend the rest of my life with.* A knot had formed in my stomach.

I tossed the phone in my purse before slinging it over my shoulder, grabbed my suitcase and exited my apartment. Once I stepped into the elevator, I struggled with all I had to put on a happy face. Mike, the doorman was at his post and called a "Hello, Miss." I walked right past without looking at him, and out of the building.

The driver must have had a description of me, because the minute I set foot outside, he was out of the car. He held the door for me as I stepped into the car and popped my suitcase into the trunk. The ring on my finger caught the streetlight and it glistened. I stared at it thoughtfully. A year ago, an engagement ring from Ben would have cinched my dreams and sent me soaring. Now, it just felt heavy.

"We all set?" asked the driver, gazing at me through the rearview mirror.

"Yes, thank you," I replied.

We pulled away from my building, and I felt the knot in my stomach tighten. Telling Nikola I was loyal to Ben had been an irrevocable step. *This is the right decision,* I reassured myself. *Now, I have to be strong and stick with it.*

We sat at a red light on Michigan Avenue waiting for a never-ending stream of pedestrians to cross. The weather, dark and threatening, didn't help my mood any. Snow would start any minute now.

Just as I was about to shoot a text to Ben to tell him I was running a little behind, I received one. It was the 312 number I'd been trying to forget. *Nikola.* I sat for a minute. I debated on whether or not to open it, totally aware that I could be opening a Pandora's Box. Unable to resist, I clicked on it.

"To burn with desire and keep quiet about it is the greatest punishment we can bring on ourselves." Federico Garcia Lorca.

"Pull over!" I cried.

"What?" The driver glared at me in the rearview mirror. "If we pull over, we might not make it to the airport on time and this weather isn't getting any better."

I pounded the back of his seat with my palms. "Please, just pull over."

The second he stopped the car, I leapt from it, my heart slamming against my ribcage.

How could Nikola have known? I racked my brain trying to remember if I'd told Nikola about Mrs. Ibenski and how the love of her life had sent her the exact same quote all those years ago. No! I hadn't. I was sure.

The driver rolled down the passenger side window. "Lady, what are we doing?"

"I don't know!" I shouted. "Please, just give me a minute!"

In spite of my panic, I was lucid enough to know that moments like this defined people's entire lives.

The driver tossed his hands in the air, then returned them to the wheel, irritably drumming his fingers. "Miss, it's starting to snow. You better make up your mind."

I looked up through the falling snowflakes; images of Ben and Nikola flashing through my mind.

I thought about the emotional roller-coaster ride both of them had put me through, and that's when I had my epiphany.

I walked in my front door and plopped down on the couch. I didn't even bother taking off my shoes and coat.

I scrolled through my Contacts list, found the number I was looking for, crossed my fingers for luck, and hit call.

"Hello?"

"Lizzie? It's Toy. I hope I didn't wake you," I said, doubting I had, even though it was 2 AM in Madrid.

"Not at all. I met this Spanish God the night before last and I've been at his villa ever since."

"Of course, you have," I laughed.

"You know me so well," she giggled. "Anyway, what's up with you?"

"I need to get away from here," I sighed, trying not to become weepy.

"Toy, what's wrong? I haven't heard you sound like this since your parents divorced."

"I have so much to tell you, so much but, I want to tell you in person."

"Well that's going to be challenging considering we're an ocean apart. What's going on?"

"Remember when you told me I was always welcome to stay with you in Paris? Does that offer still stand?"

"Totally. When were you thinking?" she said, without hesitation.

"As soon as I can find a flight under $2000," I moaned.

"Then I guess you should pack your bags now," she said, matter-of-factly. "I'll get you on the next flight in. My best friend isn't waiting around because she can't afford it, and she's sure as hell not flying coach when is her best friend is Elizabeth Mitchell!"

I giggled. Under normal circumstances I'd never let her spend such so much money on me. But, in light of my current situation, I was willing to accept her generosity.

"Thank you so much, Lizzie," I said, my voice finally cracking.

"Get the hell out of here!" she yelled, playfully. "Now go pack your bag and I'll tell you when to get your ass to O'Hare. I'll call my travel agent now."

"But it's after midnight."

"*And*?" she asked in true Lizzie fashion.

"Okay, I'm already packed. I'll wait to hear back from you."

"Pack lightly! I'm going to take you on one hell of a shopping spree and I don't want to hear any objections. Got it?"

"Got it," I said, suddenly feeling lighter, less weighed down. Lizzie always had that effect on me.

"I'll be in touch shortly. Love you."

"I love you too, Liz —" but she'd hung up. I rose from the couch and went into the kitchen. I sat down on a bar stool with my phone in hand, preparing to send one of the most difficult messages of my life. I scrolled down to Ben's name in my phone and began typing.

> Me: *Ben, I want you to know I realize after you read this text we may never speak again, but it's a risk I have to take. I can't marry you. My feelings have changed. Deep inside I've known this since you came back into my life, but I wanted it to work so badly I ignored my instincts. I love you, but after you left me this last time, I realized something. I don't need a man to complete me, I need a man to grow with as a person. I need a man to love me even when he has doubts, and to work through those doubts instead of leaving me. Love isn't a fairytale, Ben. It's not always going to be easy or exciting, but making it through the difficult times it what defines real love. I apologize for doing this via text. I know it is cowardly, but I didn't want this to be up for discussion. I will leave your ring with the doorman. Take care of yourself and please know that I did love you and will always have a special place for you in my heart. Good-bye.*

I took a deep breath and hit the send button. There was no going back now. I placed the phone face down on the counter and braced myself for the calls I knew would come. Even as Ben rang over and over and tears blinded my eyes, I knew I'd done the right thing.

He finally stopped calling and a few minutes passed by. The text alert went off on my phone. I hesitated to pick it up, sure it was Ben. I finally flipped it over and was relieved to see it was Lizzie.

> Lizzie: *Done and done. Be at O'Hare by 11 PM. Your flight is at 1:10 AM. I'll meet you at the airport in Paris. Love you!!!*

Me: *Thank you! Call you when I land. xoxo*
Lizzie: *xoxo*

I placed my phone back down on the counter but picked it right back up. I knew by the knot in my stomach I still had unfinished business. *Nikola.* By now I'd memorized his number. I typed it into the phone and began composing my message.

Me: *Nikola, I thought you should know I'm not marrying Ben. You were right. I was settling for comfort. Still, I can't be with you. From the beginning, I never knew what was real and what wasn't when it came to us. Knowing your love of poetry, I thought this would be more fitting than any words I could write:*

"When you fall in love, it is a temporary madness. It erupts like an earthquake, and then it subsides. And when it subsides, you have to make a decision. You have to work out whether your roots are to become so entwined together that it is inconceivable that you should ever part. Because that is what love is. Love is not breathlessness, it is not excitement, it is not the desire to mate every second of the day. It is not lying awake at night imagining that he is kissing every part of your body. No...don't blush. I am telling you some truths. For that is just being in love; which any of us can convince ourselves we are. Love itself is what is left over, when being in love has burned away. Doesn't sound very exciting, does it? But it is!"
Louis de Bernieres
Good bye, Nikola.

I knew I couldn't bear to read what he might reply, so I turned off my phone. I was sure I'd done the right thing when it came to both Ben and Nikola, however badly it hurt, and it hurt like hell. I allowed myself one last cry.

Then, I pulled myself together and prepared for the trip I hoped might help piece my life back together.

A few hours later, I flagged down a taxi passing by my building. The driver was a tall, broad-shouldered black man who practically jumped out of the cab to help me with my bags.

"Let me get these for you."

"Thank you," I said, softly.

I stood there as he put the bags in the trunk, then we both got into the cab. I slipped into the seat behind his and he made eye contact with me through the rear-view mirror.

"Where are we off to?" he asked.

"O'Hare, please."

"You got it," he said in an accent I couldn't quite place. *Arabic? French?*

I stared out of the window as we rode in silence. About thirty minutes had passed when he finally broke it.

"You are too young to have such a sad face," he cajoled.

I smiled a little. "It's been a long day."

"It is always the long days which make us appreciate the short ones," he sighed, knowingly.

"Yeah, I guess it's just life."

"Still, life is good. It is always teaching us something. Whatever made your day difficult today will make you stronger tomorrow."

He's right. When I step out of this taxi I'm going to leave all of this sadness and depression behind.

Before I knew it, we were pulling up to the Air France terminal. A couple of minutes later I was standing next to him behind the car. He pulled my bags out of the trunk and set them on the sidewalk.

"Apres la pluie, le beau temps." The French words rolled smoothly off his tongue.

I tilted my head.

"After rain comes sunshine," he said.

"Right," I smiled. "*Au revoir, monsieur.*"

He waved goodbye and got back into the cab. I watched him drive away.

Then, I looked up at the sky and out loud, repeated his words, "After rain comes sunshine," knowing I was finally ready to start my new beginning.

I walked into the airport and didn't look back.

The End

Made in the USA
Lexington, KY
15 January 2018